T0281944

THE
SILENT
EMPEROR

BOOK TWO OF THE HIDDEN LEGION TRILOGY

ALSO BY
SNORRI KRISTJANSSON

The Hidden Legion
The Silent Emperor

Swords of Good Men
Blood Will Follow
Path of Gods

Kin
Council

THE SILENT EMPEROR

BOOK TWO OF THE HIDDEN LEGION TRILOGY

SNORRI KRISTJANSSON

SOLARIS

First published 2024 by Solaris
an imprint of Rebellion Publishing Ltd,
Riverside House, Osney Mead,
Oxford, OX2 0ES, UK

www.solarisbooks.com

ISBN: 978-1-83786-222-1

Copyright © 2024 Rebellion Publishing IP Ltd

The right of the author to be identified as the author
of this work has been asserted in accordance with the
Copyright, Designs and Patents Act 1988.

All rights reserved. No part of this publication may be
reproduced, stored in a retrieval system, or transmitted,
in any form or by any means, electronic, mechanical,
photocopying, recording or otherwise, without the
prior permission of the copyright owners.

This book is a work of fiction. Names, characters,
places and incidents are products of the author's
imagination or are used fictitiously.

10 9 8 7 6 5 4 3 2 1

A CIP catalogue record for this book is available from
the British Library.

Designed & typeset by Rebellion Publishing.

Printed in Denmark

MIX
Paper | Supporting
responsible forestry
FSC® C104608

To Morag,
Who has the patience of several Saints.

I

SICILIA

'REPEAT IT!'

The silence in the taverna was charged with gleeful anticipation of violence, and sunburned and wine-reddened faces stared at the man in the middle. Standing well over six foot two and broad as a doorway, he looked to be chiselled out of rock and fury.

'No,' came the unhurried reply, followed by a very slow, gravelly hock of spit all the way from the back of the throat. The ball of phlegm landed exactly between the two, forming a point of no return. 'You heard me the first time.'

A chorus of oohs and in-drawn breaths. Blood would be spilled tonight.

'I said—repeat it!'

'Why?'

'So your family can be told of your last words when someone hands them your remains in a bag,' the big man growled. There was a scrape of stools being pushed back as those closest to him moved away.

'See—I don't think that's why you want me to repeat it.' An artful pause. 'I think it's because you've forgotten what the problem was.'

'What? No! You—'

'—*and* I can tell you,' came the interruption, razor sharp, 'that the problem is that you are thick as two planks, ugly as your pig-faced mother and furious that you could comfortably fit your cock in a keyhole.' An eruption of laughter and shouting. Three large men immediately appeared at the big man's side, fighting hard to hold him back and slowly losing.

Three tables back, Aemilius leaned in so Taurio could hear him. 'Should we, uh, intervene?'

'Are you mad?' the big Gaul replied. 'Best seat in the house!'

'But—'

'Don't worry, boy. She is just rinsing her feelings out. Probably won't hurt him too bad.'

Standing like a skinny torch in the middle of a hastily cleared floor and at least a head and a half shorter than her opponent, Rivkah lapped up the attention. 'See, I think your friends might know, too, judging by how hard they are trying to stop you,' she barked at the big man. 'And judging by the way you grabbed my arse just now, you like them nice and young, too. Maybe you're hoping they won't know any better. Maybe you think they'll be obedient. Or *flattered*.'

'Shut up, whore!' the man bellowed, working a muscular arm free. 'I'll shut your mouth!'

'Not with your cock, you won't.' Rivkah smirked to bellowed laughter.

The big man broke away and charged towards her—and it was almost as if she'd waved a hand and disappeared, folding herself into a space considerably smaller than a human should fit in and dancing underneath his elbow, skimming past his hip, twisting and delivering a vicious and fiercely precise kick up his arse.

Staggering from his own momentum and trying not to show the blossoming pain in his tailbone, the big man still managed to turn back towards her. 'I'll gut you like a fish, you little slut,' he growled. The knife trembled in his hand and the sounds of the crowd changed. They'd been up for a nice bit of slapping, a little blood and maybe a scream or two. Nobody had signed up to see a poor, defenceless child slaughtered, and they all respectfully waited for someone else to intervene. The few spectators who had not washed away all of their conscience with bad wine found it in themselves to shout slurred warnings.

Somehow, the young girl seemed unconcerned. Instead, she just smiled calmly. 'Now, you will note,' she said to her audience at large, 'that he pulled a knife first. Do we all agree on that?' Her absolute lack of panic confused her opponent, who blinked and shook his head like an angry bull. 'Do we?' she insisted, reaping a few nods. 'Good.' The daggers were not there—and then they were, like her hands had just suddenly grown them. 'That means this… is self-defence.'

The big man with the knife seemed suddenly somewhat less certain of himself.

Rivkah floated down, agonisingly slowly, into a relaxed combat stance. 'Well then, *Hercules*,' she purred. 'Is this what it was like with your last *little slut*?' She shifted her weight to the left and took a delicate step. The mass of bodies shifted with her, as if a taverna full of fighting men had suddenly realised that someone had left a bag of snakes in its midst. 'Was this what you expected?' Her voice rose, and cut, and sliced its way through the crowd. '*Was this what you wanted?*' She lunged, uncomfortably fast, and a thin jet of blood sprayed from the big man's forearm. He yowled, clumsily switching his knife to the left hand and clutching his right arm to his side. She smiled. '...No?' The anger had been pushed out of the big man's face and replaced entirely with fear. Opposite him, the girl who had only moments ago presented herself as easy prey looked barely human, and mostly like an avenging demon from the netherworld.

'*Now* can we intervene?' Aemilius whispered to Taurio.

'Hmm,' the big Gaul replied thoughtfully. 'You know what? I may be wrong. I reckon the big boy might lose one or two bits tonight if we don't.' He pushed his stool back and scouted about, stealthily necking the contents of an unattended jug. 'Ah. There.' He snatched a big wooden plate off a nearby table and started pushing his way towards the circle of combatants, forcing Aemilius to move fast to follow him. Rivkah was hidden from sight, but another pair of *oohs* and an *aah* from the crowd told the story clear enough. The burly frame of Taurio suddenly stopped, and Aemilius felt the big Gaul fill his lungs, throw his arms wide—

'*Thank you, thank you, thank you, that* is *all* for *tonight*,' he bellowed at an incredible and uncomfortable volume. 'The *show* is *over*.' Easily louder than any five men in the cramped space, the sheer force of his voice made those near to him wince and back off as he marched into the circle, completely ignoring the brute with the knife. Judging by the state of him, the man posed little threat to anyone anymore—blood was running freely from a nasty gash on his cheek, and his right arm was now clutched firmly to his side, fingers hanging limply.

'We'll take the murder-kitten home with us, and feed her, and scratch her behind the ear—Ow!'

The stool clattered off his leg and Rivkah snarled at him. '*Piss* off!'

Behind the big Gaul, the bleeding man was being swiftly and none-too-gently helped to a seat by his friends. A bucket with rags to dress his wounds had appeared from somewhere, and Aemilius found himself wondering whether this was the kind of establishment that had one of those at the ready, just in case.

'A new challenger!' someone hollered.

'Well padded, too!'

'Come on then, lardy! Give her a fight!'

Taurio bowed graciously, ignoring the apparent threat of Rivkah. 'I will do no such thing. This is my stepdaughter, adopted by my dear departed wife, and I love her even though she has the temper of a bitch in a rosebush.'

Rivkah glowered at him. 'Where were you when the bastard was grabbing my arse?'

'Having a moment's respite from your charming company,' Taurio shot back to chuckles from the audience. 'I figured someone else could deal with you for a bit. I didn't expect you to gather so much *attention*.'

There was just the lightest emphasis on the word, but enough that Rivkah got the message. The look that passed between them was so quick that only Aemilius caught it. Then—fast, but slow enough that everyone could see what was happening—the knife was airborne. In a flash the plate was up in front of Taurio's face, and the *thwack* when the point slammed into it was like a slap across the audience, followed by a collective gasp. Everyone could see that the knife had gone clean through, and the point had stopped about a fingernail's width away from the big Gaul's nose.

He lowered the plate, slowly enough to drag the audience's attention to his face, and waited for a masterful beat—

'*That*,' he huffed, and pulled out a small purse, jingling with coin, 'was rude. We've talked about this. Don't throw knives at Daddy.'

Rivkah grimaced at him. 'You're not my real father, anyway. Because I don't look like the arse-end of an old pig.' More laughter from the audience, and even though he knew them both, Aemilius still had to manually lift his jaw for it to be anywhere close to his upper lip. They'd wanted a show—and now they were getting a show.

'That's enough! No spending coin for you this week.' With that, Taurio lobbed the purse to the group gathered around the bleeding man on the chair, somehow managing to hit a gap in the bodies and land it straight in the brute's face with a satisfying crunch of metal on cartilage. He advanced on Rivkah with fatherly authority, shoved a meaty arm under the young girl's armpit and around her back and hauled her, struggling and squirming, out of the circle and towards the door. Aemilius watched her twisting this way and that, admiring how convincing it looked. If she wanted to, he felt pretty sure she could have slipped Taurio's grasp in an instant and left him holding a selection of body parts, but she was playing the troublesome child to perfection. Instinctively, the crowd parted and Aemilius only just managed to follow in their wake. Rivkah's stream of curses in Hebrew had them sufficiently amused, and they all craned their necks to see if there would be a further twist in the tale before the night's entertainment disappeared into the darkness.

Well, almost all.

Aemilius did not notice the leather-faced man with the neatly trimmed band of grey hair, tucked away in a darkened corner. He did not see Grey-hair snap his fingers and summon a youth, whisper a short command in his ear and send him sprinting out of the taverna.

DUSTED WITH GLITTERING stars, the night sky stretched above them. The rhythmic thud of hooves on hard earth made the silence almost comfortable. Aemilius leaned forward, gently touching his horse's neck. The trader at the dock had been a tad too keen to sell her and she'd done some reasonably convincing stomps and tosses of protest, but it had really not taken him long to get along with her. A murmured word or two in her ear had brought about an understanding quickly enough that he fancied he'd seen a suspicious glance from the trader, who had not tried to palm off an old nag on any of his other companions. As it happened, once they agreed on how to go, his mare kept pace with her younger and stronger companions perfectly well. There was a lot to be said for experience. 'Good girl,' he mumbled absent-mindedly, and the horse snorted once, as if in agreement that she was indeed a good girl.

'Why'd you stop me?'

'Didn't like the look of 'em,' Taurio replied. 'Remember Durocortorum?'

'Yes,' Rivkah replied tersely.

'And how did that go?'

'Perfectly fine. We're still alive, aren't we?'

Taurio sighed. 'Yes. But I am old now, hell-spawn, and I simply cannot be bothered to hide in the bushes for a week.'

'Can someone tell me what happened in Durocortorum? Or is that too much to ask?' Neither of them replied. 'Fine,' Aemilius sighed. 'I'll guess. Rivkah picked a fight—'

'Correct.'

'Didn't. He came at me.'

'You called his mother a whore and said he came out of her arse.'

'Men who can't handle facts shouldn't drink.'

'Okay. I'll go again. Rivkah picked a fight, and took it too far—'

'Again—correct. He is getting better, isn't he?'

'Shut up. He started it. Pissy little bitch.' Even in the darkness, Aemilius could hear the scowl.

'And then all of a sudden, we had a dead body that unfortunately turned out to have seven cousins, all of which were related to seemingly everyone in a village of about three hundred people who very suddenly really wanted to nail our little angel here to a wall. And they were woodsmen, too, so we had to use all manner of tricks to avoid having to kill them all.'

'And I still don't understand,' Rivkah snapped. 'Why always with the holding back? Don't you sometimes just want to let rip?'

Taurio sighed. 'We've been through this a couple of times before. The Legion relies on—'

'Yah yah yah, goodwill and secret benefactors and looking out for people and all that. And when you hunt the monster, you must not become the monster. Blah blah. And I say—people are shit.' Beneath them, the horses continued at a steady pace and did nothing to disagree with the statement.

'Anger is sometimes... useful,' Taurio said, his deep

voice soothing. 'Just like a campfire is warm. But would you sit on a campfire?'

'I'd sit you on a campfire,' Rivkah muttered, in a tone that Aemilius now recognised as something that might, from another mouth, be *you're right and I know it and I like you, but I will rather eat scorpions than admit it*. Silence settled, and they rode on. The air felt sweet, and he thought he could smell a faint aroma of lemons. Something about Sicilia was just... right, somehow. Familiar. He couldn't quite place it. The gentle wind on his face, the sensation of salt on his tongue, the cawing of the gulls in the morning, the crunch of sun-baked soil just after mid-day. With no conversation and little riding to do, he allowed his thoughts to wander.

A Sardinian.

Interesting.

He could see them in his mind's eye, the Lord and Lady, eyes twinkling as they sized him up. Was this like Sardinia? He vaguely remembered his mother's tales of where he grew up, but it was getting harder remarkably quickly to recall his family. It was almost as if every single thing that happened to him pushed something else out—and there had been a *lot* happening in his life since that fateful day when the winged monster landed on the path in front of him and his cousins. Why, if we're so Sardinian and that's so interesting, did I have to grow up in the middle of nowhere in Hispania?

He had no answers to this.

Neither did the crickets, or the lemons, or the night sky.

The hooves beat out a rhythm.

On-the-run, on-the-run, on-the-run.

* * *

THE HORSES SLOWED down to a canter and then a walk as the ground rose gently beneath their feet. Idly, Aemilius wondered whether Sicilian horses smelled more strongly, or whether he was simply better at recognising it after he became—he still couldn't quite bring himself to say it, and wasn't sure whether he was scared, amused or both—a legionnaire.

The fire, banked and shielded from prying eyes, danced across familiar shapes resting around a wagon. 'Well met, travellers. Did you get what you wanted?'

Taurio dismounted, landing lightly. 'I got a bag full of whatever passes for vegetables on this godforsaken rock and two hens, chopped and plucked. Rivkah got her arse grabbed, and Aemilius got a scare.'

'Oh dear,' Prasta tutted. 'So, are we packing up, then?'

'No, no,' Taurio said expansively. 'Not at all. I rescued her before—'

'Rescued,' Rivkah spat. 'The only thing you rescued was your face.'

'Excellent.' Abrax did not move a muscle, but the flames grew a fraction brighter, lighting his face. There was the hint of a smile on it. 'We wouldn't want another incident like Durocortorum.'

'Will you shut up about Durocortorum already? That was a year and a half ago!'

'The Gaul has still got burrs up his arse.' Prasta grinned.

'The only burr I've got up my arse is a certain Celtic caterwauler,' Taurio rumbled.

'Be that as it may,' Livia interrupted. 'We move on tomorrow. Two days ago, in Syracusae I found us a merchant willing to take us from Panormus to about three days' ride south of Neapolis at noon. We have people there.' This was met by an appreciative murmur from the group, and Taurio and Rivkah sat down by the campfire. Aemilius listened to them from a couple of yards away. Like so many other places, Aemilius had heard of Neapolis, but it was only a word that he knew. He idly pondered what it meant to "have people" but consigned himself to finding out eventually. Maybe it'd be another retired gladiator with a pet hydra running a hole-in-the-wall taverna. That was a lot of his life now, it seemed. Gradual discovery of what might or might not kill him in the next three heartbeats. Without thinking he had taken the reins of the horses and realised he was midway through brushing them down, listening to the banter going back and forth as Taurio relayed the heavily dramatized story of Rivkah's epic battle with a Sicilian hill troll and how he, the humble Gaul, was actually somehow both the real hero and the actual victim, complete with expertly judged commentary by the angry girl with the knives. This was where they were happiest—sparring with words, insulting each other in inventive ways, at ease in each other's company.

The struggle under the Temple of Serapis had felt so final. After a chase across half the Empire they'd thought they had the Magus Donato cornered, only to be foiled by the emergence of a creature that had made him never want to see another snake ever again. He had been so exhausted when he'd slumped down on the deck of the merchant ship in the shadow of the great lighthouse that he'd just wanted to sleep forever. Granted, after their encounter with the nightmare from the deep, the sea hadn't felt exactly safe, but even in his feeble state Hanno had still provided a security that other travellers were not afforded. It had been easy to get lulled into gentle rest, aching muscles pressed up against wooden boards in a way that was, while not exactly comfortable, then at least predictable—and after the week he had just had, he'd settle for knowing where the next bit of pain came from. He had almost missed out on the quick transactions between Livia and a friendly merchant with sharp eyes. Robes had been passed out, bags procured and almost like a change of season—subtle and gradual—they had turned from battered monster fighters to tired travellers that could disappear in a crowd. By the time they stepped off the boat they were... unremarkable.

Perhaps they were a group of travellers assisting an African with his elderly grandfather.

Perhaps they were a Roman family travelling with a slave, a scholar and a cook.

They definitely did not look like a battle-hardened group of monster hunters who could stare down any sort of abomination, in the midst of fighting an invisible war against an elusive enemy to save an empire that did not acknowledge their existence. And even though the memory of their journey across the water was comforting, for reasons he could not name Aemilius felt suddenly uneasy.

And then, he realised.

The talk around the campfire had died.

The horses, he also realised, were groomed now, and had been for some time. Slowly and silently, he stepped towards the legionnaires, tucking away his horse-brush. 'How many?' he heard Taurio mutter.

'Too many,' came Hanno's feeble voice. 'There is not much water in the ground, so it is hard to tell... but it trembles. Twenty horses. Maybe more.'

'It wasn't me!' Rivkah protested, before anyone else had had the chance to blame her. 'I didn't even kill him!'

Abrax rose. 'If you had, he'd have deserved it,' he said with warm finality. 'Now, we see what the winds bring us.' Silently, the Legion fanned out behind him. One of the horses whinnied softly, snorted, then fell quiet.

They can feel it, Aemilius thought. *Hooves on the ground. Something's coming.*

'There,' Livia said calmly. 'South.'

A line of torches inched into sight. Riders, moving at a canter.

After a while, Prasta spoke. 'Are you *sure* she didn't kill anyone?'

'Yes,' Taurio said. 'This… this is not Durocortorum.'

'They are taking their time, for one thing,' Livia remarked.

'And they've brought their friends,' Prasta said. 'Down the hill. East, a touch to the north. They've figured out where we'd bolt.'

'Well,' Abrax said. 'We have—unusually—done nothing to cause any offence. Have we?' he added.

'Why is everybody looking at me?' Rivkah said. 'And I don't care if it's dark. I can *smell* you looking at me.'

'We have done nothing wrong,' Taurio replied. 'Except not be from here.'

'Which is sometimes enough,' Livia added.

'We will wait.' The tall magus smiled in the darkness. 'We will wait, and we will talk.'

A tense silence followed as to the south the line of torches inched forward. To the east another group of riders spread out, forming a barrier just about visible by torchlight.

'Where is he?' *It doesn't matter whether it is day or night*, Aemilius thought. *A commander always sounds the same*. The speaker, clearly a man who was used to being obeyed, had not raised his voice. He had not added a touch of threat. He had simply nudged his horse at a walk out in front of the torch-line, coming to a stop about twenty yards across from Abrax. Then he had asked, politely, and now he was expecting to get.

And for all of his commanding, what he got was mild confusion.

'Welcome, traveller,' Abrax said in his most honeyed voice. 'I would invite you to break bread with us, but I am afraid we don't really have enough for... twenty?'

'Thirty-five,' Livia replied in the dark. 'Fifty if you count the ones down the hill.'

'...fifty unexpected guests.'

The man on the horse smiled. It was not a pleasant smile. He sat in the saddle like one who had spent most of his life there, and even though he wore no armour, he was every inch a soldier. 'I have not come for your bread,' he said, with a poorly hidden note of disdain. 'I just require the boy.'

There was a silence then, and in the dark Aemilius felt Taurio shift towards and in front of him.

'I am *terribly* sorry,' Abrax said, still smiling. 'I had heard the rumours about Sicilians, but I am afraid we don't have enough boys to share with fifty men either.' Behind him, Aemilius heard Rivkah cackling.

The mounted soldier's face was stony, but his horse snorted and tossed its head. 'The boy,' he snapped.

'And which *boy* might that be?'

'The son of Marcus Livius Sculla, traitor to the Empire.' The words came down like the blows of a sword. 'By order of the Governor of Sicilia.'

'Well,' Abrax said slowly. 'I'm afraid I can't help you there.'

'Listen, you moor bast—'

'*Because*,' Abrax boomed, loud enough to startle the soldier's horse, 'we have no *boy*. And if you refer to our travelling companion Aemilius of Hispania, he stays with me and my friends, most of whom you cannot see and none of whom are the least bit worried about you and your assembled rabble of farmhands and white-hairs. Now,' he said, all traces of honey vanished from his voice. 'You have your line of cavalry, and it is a fine line. How about if I draw a line of my own—and if you think it still seems like a good idea, then *come and get him*,' the magus growled. A quick flick of the wrist and a leg-thick, waist-high wall of flame burst into being between the two, snarling and snapping and feasting on anything it could touch, and chaos erupted.

Horses whinnying, crying and bolting. Panicked shouts from the men. At least one scream of pain. A shout from somewhere behind them, far away in the dark. Across the dancing flames, the soldier on the horse stared daggers at Abrax. Without looking away, the magus's arm shot to the side—and moments later, three dead trees burst into flame a hundred yards down the hill in *just* the right places, panicking riders and horses alike and throwing the charge of the rear guard into disarray. Yanking on the reins far harder than necessary, the soldier turned his horse around and barked a command. There was pure relief in the thundering of hooves away from their flame-guarded camp.

Silently, the Legion listened to the sound of the retreat, which blended beautifully with the crackling of the fire.

'Wine?' Taurio offered casually. 'I find that after growing up within the Roman Empire, the smell of burnt wood and panic always makes me thirsty.'

'Please.' Aemilius reached for the shadowy shape of Taurio's arm, which was suddenly holding a wineskin where he could have sworn that but a blink ago there had been a well-worn club getting ready to be wielded. *Get the taste out.*

'Could you keep the fire on for a moment longer? It's nice and warm.' There was a grin in Rivkah's voice. 'Or maybe that's just the joy of smelling fifty Sicilians shitting themselves all at once.'

'He was a smart one.'

'He was,' Abrax agreed. 'They'll be back, with more of their friends.'

'In daylight, I wager.' Livia had joined Prasta by the fire, which now resembled less of a raging lion and more of a contented house cat. 'With slings, bows and javelins, and whatever else they can find that will bring some pain from a safe distance.'

'You are wise as always, your exalted eminence,' Taurio rumbled. 'And also to take a better look at us. Not sure it would do us good to be seen for the common criminals we are.' He busied himself refreshing the troops with his never-ending wineskin. 'Might make travelling even more annoying. And no,' he said, interrupting Rivkah. 'We can*not* just kill them all.'

There was a scoff, a hock and a spit in the dark.

Aemilius reached for the wine again. The taste was still there—it was fainter now, like a half-heard sound, but he could still feel it. Nothing like the immediate and overwhelming first wave of raw, powerful fear. It had been like a creature within him, seeking access to muscles that weren't in the right places. There was something else there, as well—some kind of knowledge—but he couldn't see it, couldn't understand it. Like smoke in the night, it drifted away from him just as another, persistent and annoying thought intruded.

Why did he want me?

Who was the man? And who was the governor? And why had they wanted *him?* His father was many things— boring, harsh, silent—but Aemilius imagined it might have been mentioned over dinner at some point if he was a wanted traitor to the Empire.

'Hey! Aemilius *of Hispania!*' Rivkah somehow managed to make a location sound like a Hebrew swearword. 'Find a thick stick and smack yourself with it to save me the trouble!'

Aemilius shook his head and snorted, casting off the last strands of fear. Around him the Legion had nearly finished quietly and efficiently packing up their camp. The fire was already dying down, and when darkness settled back on the plateau the Legion was gone.

A SLOW PURPLE heralded the coming of dawn in the distance, but darkness still lay over them like a veil. The horses picked their way calmly down a gentle slope in single file, with Rivkah as the outrider and Prasta guarding the rear. Beneath their feet the ground had changed, and the sound of the hooves was less of a crunch and more of a soft thump.

'Aemilius of Hispania, though.' Taurio sat in the saddle, eyes more than half-closed. 'Not a bad name, that.'

'I guess,' Aemilius muttered. *But is that me?*

'Any idea why hook-face wanted you? He sounded pretty... definite about your father.'

'I don't know.'

'I see. Now—the problem we have here is a serious one.'

'What? Why?'

'Because I would normally leave it at that, but I'm afraid I can't.'

'Why?'

'Because,' Taurio said heavily, 'I'm *bored*. And it is early in the morning, and I have not had even a hint of breakfast, and I'm bored. Did I mention I'm bored? So, tell me the tale of your family, Aemilius of Hispania. You say you don't know—but you might, really.'

'I—'

'Still half a day's ride,' the big Gaul interrupted. 'And in not too long, eighty or so mad Sicilians are going to arrive at our camp with a collection of their grandfathers' siege tools, and then they'll find us gone and think about whether to follow us, and odds are they'll either do that or send one of their short and light ones on a fast horse to every town on the way, and just the chance of all of this means that we'll have to pick up the pace as soon as we have the light, but until that happens I am *bored* and I hate being bored. So, indulge an old man, and tell me the story.'

By rote, the words started marching up and out of him. 'My father is Marcus Livius Sculla, Governor of Caesaraugusta. We trace our lineage to the Aemilii of old, and our family's history is proud. My father always said we should live by the motto "ama familiam, servi imperium."'

'Thrilling. What is your family vegetable?'

'Uh, I—'

'I'm pulling your toe, kid. It's clearly the parsnip.'

'What?' Aemilius near-squealed. 'Why would you say that?'

'Scrawny and pale. Useless on its own, but'—the broad arm gestured to the slowly shuffling Legion—'essential in a stew. Get to the good bits! I don't know one poncy bedsheet from another, but even I understand that the Aemilii probably didn't wipe their own arses.'

'One of the twelve mighty families of Rome.' Livia was balanced perfectly in the saddle and did not turn to look at them. The words rained from her like truth. 'Their fortunes have gone up and down, but they are generally considered respectable and noble. I've known a couple of Aemilii, and they are less likely than some of the others to stab you in the back.'

'Great,' Taurio said. 'Thank you. This has put my mind—and back—at ease. Proceed, lord parsnip.'

'I don't know too much about my father's career. I was born in Sardinia, where we lived on my grandfather's estate. Father managed it well, and it grew prosperous, but when I was only three something happened, I think, and then we left the estate to my uncle and moved to Rome, and then he was made Governor of Caesaraugusta a bit after that.'

'The horse-fucker was pretty certain, though. What could your father have done to betray the great Roman Empire?'

'I reckon he fornicated with the Emperor's favourite goose,' Rivkah offered helpfully.

'Sounds unlikely,' Prasta opined from the back. 'Much more likely to be dealing in illicit goods—I reckon he stole and sold virgins' undergarments.'

'Fair enough,' Taurio offered. 'But while, looking at our boy here, that sounds highly likely—'

'Hey!'

'—my simple peasant mind fails to understand how either of those things betrays the Empire.'

'Maybe burdening us with Aemilius *of Hispania* is enough.'

'I'm telling you—I don't know! I'm trying to think, but no one ever told me that my father had done anything wrong. When my uncle died, he became the heir of—'

'You say something happened.' Aemilius marvelled at how Livia could make a simple four-word sentence conjure up a court where he was on trial. 'How many uncles do you have?'

'One.'

There was a thoughtful pause. 'Are you sure?'

Aemilius shook his head and squeezed his eyes shut. The Hidden Legion had taken him away from everything—were they now planning to take everything away from him? 'Uh—yes? Yes! I have one uncle. I know how many uncles I have!' He felt his pitch rising with the colour of his cheeks.

'The only way you can tell your arse from your elbow is by the smell, and even that is a half-chance, so I'd say it is well within your capabilities to forget a couple of relatives,' Rivkah dead-panned, but the others seemed to accept Aemilius's lack of knowledge and stopped both the interrogation and the insults. They rode on in silence as the purple veil above them drew back to reveal a blue sky. The change in pace was almost imperceptible, but once it was comfortably light enough to go a little faster Aemilius felt the pull as Abrax urged his horse into a gentle trot. They couldn't go too fast because of the cart where Hanno sat slumped, looking like someone had tossed a sack carelessly into the back. He had not spoken since the night-time encounter, and Aemilius felt his stomach tighten with worry.

Just how much had the battle with the sea-monster taken out of their friend?

II

VIA POPILIA

'Hanno!'

  'What's the matter?'

  'He's not waking up.'

  'Water. Quick. Get him water.'

  'He won't drink. He's just…'

Aemilius stood back and watched the Legion cluster around the diminutive form in the back of the cart. With confidence they had no right to exhibit they had rolled into Panormus, rumbled straight onto a boat bound for the mainland and been long gone before hook-nose and his friends had had any chance of showing up. They'd alighted at midday and immediately set off towards the north on the Via Popilia at a pace that was slightly faster than urgent but slower than suspicious. They'd encountered people, sure—some had stepped in their path, others had been wise enough not to—but for two days they had simply been on the road. No monsters, no armies of angry people, no hard-faced commanders. Just travelling.

And just when he had started to feel at ease, Aemilius had realised that Hanno wasn't moving. He had been watching the water-magus at the back of the cart— partly because he wanted to seek out a moment alone with him to talk more about magic, and partly because there was absolutely nothing else to do—and on occasion he'd toss, or twitch, or shift himself… and then suddenly he realised that Hanno hadn't moved for the entire day. He'd nudged his horse closer, and tried calling to him gently, and then, with his heart beating faster and faster, startled an elegant string of swearwords out of Prasta on the driver's plank by coming all the way up to the back of the cart and jumping onto the back of it. The little magus had been cold to the touch—too cold, and up close his skin had a grey pallor to it that was very much like he imagined the colour of the dead to be. Moments later the cart was stopped and Prasta was crouching beside them, quickly checking Hanno's vital signs and rummaging in her pouches for something, anything, muttering under her breath in a language Aemilius didn't understand but did not sound good. And now he found himself here, having been shouldered out of the way by the older legionnaires, watching from a distance. He felt a growing lump in his throat, and a heat in his chest, and he squeezed his eyes shut to stop the tears—

A gentle touch on his arm. 'Don't,' Rivkah whispered. He looked at her, and she was just there, close enough that he could feel the warmth and solidity of her horse up against his calf, and he examined her face, but there was none of the familiar fury. 'Don't,' she said again, quietly, through clenched teeth. 'Because if you start crying there's a reason for crying and if there's a reason for crying, I'll start crying and that will be your fault and then I'd have to smash your face in with a rock.'

He blinked. '…why would you need to smash *my* face in?'

'Because your face is the most annoying thing I've ever seen, and that's reason enough. But the skinny little toad is as tough as they come, and I refuse to believe that he's gone, and if he is then someone will have to pay, and you are the closest.'

'He's not gone,' Prasta said over her shoulder, not taking her eyes off the diminutive form in the cart. 'But he is absolutely going. We have to get back. We need to get—'

'Rider,' Taurio snapped.

As one, they looked up from where Hanno was slumped, and much to Aemilius's dismay the big Gaul was right. *If he comes close enough to say a single word to us, he is fantastically dead,* was the first thought that popped into his head.

But there was no threat to this particular rider. For a start, even from a distance his horse looked like it had been fed once, two years ago, and whoever did it had not been generous. The rider didn't look much better, and Aemilius almost thought he could hear the rattle of bones as the two scrawny creatures hurtled towards them with no regard for their own or anyone else's safety.

'What in the name of Diana—' Livia muttered.

Taurio pushed his horse forward, in front of the cart. Anyone coming close would have to go through the big Gaul, and by the set of his shoulders it looked like attempting that would be a spectacularly bad idea. Despite the shambolic nature of his horsemanship, the rider seemed to come to the same conclusion. He pulled on the reins hard enough to make Aemilius wince, and half-jumped, half-fell off the horse and to his knees. 'Help,' he wheezed. 'Help us.'

For a moment, no one spoke. Abrax's face seemed carved out of stone. 'Who needs help, traveller?'

It was as if the magus had pulled the pin out of a log pile. Looking on the verge of tears, the man's mouth could hardly keep up with the words tumbling out. 'It's been taking our children and it stalks the woods and there's more of them now and we are just so afraid and hungry and our goats are dead and we tried to fight it, tried to fight them but even Gino couldn't do anything and then it ripped his arm off—' Kneeling in front of the legionnaires, the scrawny man dissolved into great, racking sobs, and Aemilius realised with shock that he wasn't looking at a man at all. He was looking at a boy no older than himself.

'*What* attacked you?' Abrax snapped.

But there was no more sense to be had out of the boy. He had fallen into a rocking rhythm, back and forth on his knees on the road, clutching himself and muttering the same three lines of a prayer to Ceres over and over and over, asking her to bless his family and his farm. Not knowing what to do with himself but feeling he should do something, Aemilius dismounted and walked over to the boy's horse, murmuring soothing sounds and clicking gently with his tongue. He realised that he was holding a horse-brush and couldn't quite remember when he'd reached for it. The animal whickered gently at him and tossed its head once but allowed him to approach.

'Abrax—tell me—*tell me* that you are not thinking—' Livia's voice had an edge that could have cut through a rock from a hundred yards.

'We have to go. There is no question, only duty.'

'But he's *dying!*' Prasta wailed.

'And what if we ignore this—' Abrax gestured to the boy.

'Scrawny little dirtbag,' Rivkah spat.

'—what then? What if this is the point where we could contain whatever it is? What if we leave it for a week and it multiplies and grows? And what if we come back and we lose three of us, rather than one? Five? All of us? What then?' Abrax snapped. 'There will always be difficult choices.'

'How do we know that it isn't just bandits? Or whatever?' Rivkah said.

'They don't tend to rip people's arms off,' Taurio remarked. 'At least, not in this part of the world. Although once in Persia—'

'It's not bandits.' Aemilius was surprised at the strength and conviction in his voice. 'It's something with teeth. Something… wrong.' He became suddenly aware that the other legionnaires had all fallen watchfully silent.

'How do you know this?' Abrax's words came out slowly, but with crushing weight. This was a question that was going to need to be answered.

Shit. The truth—that he had no idea—sounded like the wrong thing to say at this moment. *Make something up. Please. Right now.* 'Something—something the boy muttered. I heard him say teeth. And something about howling in the night. And then he started doing'—he pointed to the rocking shape of the boy—'*that* again.' The lie flew out of his mouth and landed, fully formed, in front of him.

There was a moment of silence that seemed to stretch forever. Then Abrax spoke. 'If this is another of Donato's traps, we will give him all we have—but he will not surprise us again. As legionnaires, we have no choice. We must do both. We must rush Hanno back home, and we must investigate. So here is what I propose.'

'We split up,' said Livia.

Abrax looked annoyed. 'Yes. That is what we should do.'

'I'll take the cart. Taurio, Prasta?'

'She's the muscle and I'm the charm, as usual?'

'If we put the boar up front, his smell alone will clear the roads for us,' Prasta replied.

Rivkah looked at Abrax and Aemilius. 'And—what? I get to babysit an old man and a useless parsnip? *Great*. Try not to get yourselves killed. I'll try not to kill them.'

Aemilius turned back to the boy's horse and focused on brushing it down, using the chance to look away so the others wouldn't see his relief.

Teeth.

Howls in the night.

He *knew* it, and he knew that it was true. He could almost sense some kind of outline of a thing—strong, fast and merciless, and far bigger than it should be. It walked in the night, and behind it were more and more of its kind, and the *smell* of it was danger and death and yet again he felt the sickening surge of adrenaline, like he wanted to run away—to *bolt*...

...but *how* did he know this? The boy had said absolutely nothing, and Aemilius felt a surge of irritation. 'Get up,' he snapped. 'And take us to your village.'

The boy did not react in the slightest.

Aemilius knelt down, and murmured very quietly, 'Take us to your village or I will put you on your horse, find the way there myself, tie you to a stake and feed you to the beast. And he will rip your innards out and feast upon your guts, and he will howl at the moon, like this.' He whispered a soft *awoooo*. The boy stiffened, and his eyes flew open. He looked around in a panic, scouting for the danger, and Aemilius felt a little embarrassed, like he'd been caught bullying a child. 'You are safe,' he murmured to the sitting shape. 'You will get our help. Now take us to your village.' The boy latched onto the last word and practically melted into Aemilius's arms. 'All right, yes, fine,' he muttered awkwardly, lifting the boy to his feet and feeling a soft horror at how little he weighed.

'Is he back among the living?' Rivkah said, mounted on her horse.

'Just about,' Aemilius said, helping the boy up into the saddle. The horse nudged him gently as thanks for the rub-down, and he muttered a couple of soothing words to the effect of *look after your rider, he needs you to go home*. 'He's going to take us to his village.' Turning to the boy, he used a voice most often reserved for the dim, the elderly and the hard of hearing. '*Aren't you?*'

The boy nodded, wide-eyed, and kept his eyes on Aemilius as he mounted.

When he was in the saddle, Aemilius found that Rivkah was giving him an unusual look. 'What did you say to him? He looks terrified.'

'And what of it? Am I not Aemilius of Hispania, snake-charmer, monster-slayer, creepy witchy skull-smasher?' he replied, with confidence that he did not feel. 'Perhaps my reputation precedes me.'

Rivkah snorted. 'Ah. Yes. I forget. Many pardons, your malevolence.'

Aemilius put on the least convincing tough-guy scowl he could manage, and Rivkah smirked. When she looked away, he felt a surge of relief. *But why?* Thoughts kept intruding on him, only to slink back into the shadows in the recesses and alcoves of his mind when he tried to catch them and pin them down. The decision having been made, they swiftly said their goodbyes to Livia, Taurio and Prasta, and were on their way soon enough and Aemilius found himself, through some unspoken agreement after a discussion that he had somehow missed, in charge of the village boy. The scrawny rider still seemed terrified of him but had recovered enough to be able to answer simple questions.

Had he seen the creature? No.

Had anyone else? Yes, but they were all dead.

How long had it been going? Two weeks.

How many people were left in the village? Not sure.

Many? No. Lots were dead.

How did it kill? Rip the throat out. Claw at the eyes. Bite at the groin.

Were there others like it? Maybe.

During this cheerful conversation they made their way north along the Via Popilia until the boy veered off onto a well-used dirt track. Looking ahead, Aemilius watched it wind towards forested hills and disappear. *There could be anything in there. Anything at all.* Visions of the horrors he had faced in the past week came back to him—flying abominations, scaled nightmares and that thing beneath the waves—and he shuddered despite the late-morning sunshine. Casting a glance back over his shoulder at his travelling companions went some way towards calming him again. Abrax looked like he had aged by at least a decade in the time since he saw him first, but the fire-magus still sat ramrod-straight in the saddle, imposing and commanding in equal measure, like something riding out of a legend. Next to him Rivkah looked diminutive, like a child with her father, but Aemilius was starting to learn the signs of danger. A snake basking on a rock was still a snake.

Their guide… was another matter. The boy's age was less clear again—he'd looked like a man while riding, a child while begging, but every step that moved him back towards his part of the world seemed to give him back a little bit of strength. He had not said anything since they turned off the main road, so Aemilius was startled when the boy spoke. 'It's smart, you know.'

'Mm,' he mumbled. In his mind, he conjured up an image of a fisherman, slowly giving out more line.

'It used to wait. And hide.'

'I see.'

'At first.'

'When did it come?'

'Two weeks,' the boy answered instantly. 'Since the killings started. First signs were three weeks and two days. Took some sheep a couple of days later. And then it got bolder. Took little Pietro two nights after. Ten summers, he was. Ripped him to shreds.' *What would Livia do here?* Thinking about it for about three blinks, Aemilius held his peace and watched the boy, lost in a hazy recollection. 'His belly was torn open, and his throat was gone.'

'Throat and belly… could it be some kind of wild animal?' Aemilius suggested gently. 'A wolf, maybe?'

The boy scoffed. 'I don't know where you come from, but it was like nothing any of us have ever seen. And the worst of it is—it leaves no tracks.'

'Everything leaves tracks,' Rivkah said curtly.

'Not this one, oh no,' the boy replied, warming up. 'We think it might be a spirit.'

'Spirits don't rip out throats,' Abrax said, a fair shade more gently than Rivkah. 'If it can open up a human, it is of this world—and if it is, it can be killed.'

The boy laughed nervously. 'I hope so. I hope so.' He fell back into muttering. Aemilius half-closed his eyes, feigning rest and straining his ears to pick out information. He had come to terms with the fact that he could not burn a monster to a crisp or slice it into ribbons, so his duty was to learn anything he could to give the others any sort of an advantage.

'…and then he says "Go, Seppius. Get help, Seppius." And what do I find? No soldiers, no governor, just a bunch of old—oh, they're going to be so angry— they'll feed me to Lupa—oh, Seppius, what have you done—O Ceres, benedic familiam meam, benedic villam meam—'

Despite his misery, though, Seppius led them onwards and upwards. As they crested a hill Aemilius looked over his shoulder. The Via Popilia stretched out below, a straight line carving through the land and hopefully taking Livia and his friends north at speed, bringing their little water magus to safety and health.

But where was this path taking him? They were already high enough that he thought he could see the sea on the horizon when he looked over his shoulder, and up ahead was more of a climb. In the distance ahead of them, mountains towered.

Where was Seppius's village?

They led their horses on at a gentle walk, and Aemilius thought about the boy riding with Cerberus snapping at his heels. *In my life, right now, that is not just a fanciful notion.* It was a sobering thought, and he spent some time trying to combine in his head some kind of nightmare offspring of the hydras he had seen and his father's hound. Seppius's path led them up then down, curved around and snaked through the hills, but always higher and higher. Each crested hill brought another to be climbed.

'How much further, bone-bag?'

'Back off,' Aemilius snapped, rather more fiercely than he thought he would. 'His name is Seppius.' Outwardly, he ignored the stunned look on the boy's face. *If he wants to think me a mystic, let him. Could be useful.* He turned to their guide. 'But do answer the question. How much further?'

'Not far,' the boy said, voice trembling. 'Over that hill and through the forest.'

Rivkah harrumphed, and Aemilius thought about how utterly terrifying she must be to people who didn't know her. *But do I?* The question hung above his head, and he concluded that no, he did not. Not really. He understood that she'd had a hard life, and the fierceness of her loyalty to the Legion suggested that she hadn't had many friends or allies before.

Before.

It occurred to Aemilius that all of them had had a "before." All of them had been something else, accepted what they thought was reality—and then, the veil had been pulled from their eyes and they had seen the things that no one else should see. Things that no one wanted to see. For a moment, he imagined how wonderful it would be to just *not* know about sea monsters the size of a fleet, and blood-sucking child-snatchers, and caves full of snakes...

'Through there, is it?' Rivkah's voice snapped him out of his thoughts. The pitch suggested that whatever it was, she was unimpressed.

'Yes,' Seppius replied nervously.

They had crested so many hills that Aemilius had stopped looking. However, what lay beyond this one was not another gentle dip and a slope upwards. The downward path eased its way towards a forbidding wall of trees, stretching to both sides as far as the eye could see. They stood before a vast valley covered in a sea of green, with wave-tops of the oldest and nastiest trees fighting for the sunlight.

'Shame the twig isn't with us,' Rivkah muttered. 'She'd have had a thing or two to say about this one.'

'What do your people call this wood, boy?' Abrax rumbled.

Seppius swallowed. 'Blackhowl,' he stuttered.

'Great,' Rivkah spat. 'Was Murder Woods taken?'

'Uh...'

'It's not an actual question,' Aemilius sighed. 'I can translate. She is saying that she is very excited to see the sights of your charming region and wishes to immediately immerse herself in this new experience.'

'I'll immerse you, *Aemilius of Hispania*,' she muttered as she nudged her horse onwards. 'Right. Let's get this done.'

Above their heads, the sun started a slow slide towards the horizon.

THEY DIDN'T NEED Prasta and Taurio to track it.

The severed leg was a hint.

The palm-wide trail of blood was another.

And if they'd missed those two, the cloud of flies buzzing happily over what they established eventually were the remains of one, rather than two deer would have been the final clue. Looking like she was glad of the distraction, Rivkah was off her horse and kneeling by the sprawled carcass. After a while she rose. 'Is this it? Is this the work of your monster?' She didn't even look towards Seppius.

'Yes.'

'Hard to say.' Rivkah swung up into the saddle. 'But it is a messy eater. Sure it wasn't just a boar? Or someone bringing over a big cat from Africa? We had that last year.'

I have never seen anyone demonstrate contempt by mounting a horse before, Aemilius thought. He waited for the inevitable response from the villager—tears, outrage, something—but there was simply silence from the boy.

'Well?' Rivkah snapped, annoyed.

'I saw my first corpse when I was three,' Seppius said, and Aemilius felt the hairs on his forearms rise. 'Seven times in my first five years we fought off raiders, other villages, barbarians. And how many times did the *empire* help us? Never.'

'She didn't mean—'

'Yes, I did.' Rivkah glared at Abrax.

The boy looked at her, and suddenly he didn't look so helpless anymore. 'Our hills love us, but they are neither soft nor gentle. I have seen death, many times—and this is different.' He dismounted and knelt by the deer, deftly teasing out of the mess a section that looked like it could be the neck. 'Look here.' He lifted the meat up towards Rivkah, seeming entirely unconcerned about her horse snorting and stamping in protest.

'Back off,' she hissed. 'And tell me what I'm supposed to see.'

'Teeth.'

'So? Everything has teeth.'

'Yes,' the boy said. 'But where?' He gently placed one finger, then another, easily eight inches apart.

Rivkah looked again at the slab of meat in the boy's hands, sneered and huffed. 'Let's go,' she snarled, spurring her horse onwards. The boy mounted slowly and quietly, wiping the blood off his hands on his tunic once he was in the saddle, and followed Rivkah at a walk. Out of the corner of his eye, Aemilius caught a glimpse of Abrax. It was hard to tell if the fire magus was bemused or worried. He turned to follow the others, and—

Like pulled wool, the distance to Seppius stretched

And then the boy was small, and low, and the trees fell away from him

And Aemilius watched himself, and Abrax, and Rivkah, and Seppius from above

And he could see a… faint trail of something, a heat, a scent

Leading to the deer

One large shape, several smaller shapes

A group

And then he was falling towards the ground again, faster and faster and

He gasped for breath as he felt himself crash into the back of his own skull and jolt in the saddle. The horse tossed its head once beneath him but kept on walking.

'Are you ill?' There was concern in Abrax's voice.

'What? No,' Aemilius mumbled. 'Just tired. Think I fell asleep a little bit there.' A nervous giggle escaped, and he groaned inwardly. *I am not cut out for secrets.* Why couldn't he just tell Abrax the truth? *Because then I'd have to say more, and I might get it wrong or sound like a child, and that would be embarrassing.* The heat of shame coursed through him and drove away the chills. He looked up to the skies above, wondering.

What... just happened?

RIVKAH RODE UP front, communicating with every angle, twitch and turn of her back, shoulders and neck that the first person to so much as say a word to her would get a knife up their nose for their troubles. In contrast, Seppius seemed to draw life from the forest around him. He was sitting straight and easy in the saddle now, gently nudging his horse forward seemingly without thinking.

'If Prasta was here,' the big magus mused next to Aemilius, 'she'd say how all forests have a soul, a character, like people. You just need to stop staring at each tree on its own.' Aemilius made a non-committal noise. He had only been riding with the Legion for two weeks, but he'd learned enough to know that there was wisdom coming, and there was nothing he could do to stop it. 'She'd say that forests can be like a gleeful young maiden, a surly old man, or anything in between.'

'And what would she say of this one?'

To Aemilius's surprise, Abrax fell silent for a moment. 'I... am not sure. But I don't think it would be particularly nice.'

Aemilius roused himself from his saddle-daze and looked around, trying to *see*.

And he saw trees. Old trees with the sturdy trunks of survivors. Spreading his gaze and looking at the trees as not individual things but part of a whole, bones of a skeleton, he thought of the forest as a beast, a mighty beast, buried just underground. He saw a faint light, only just making it to the forest floor through a thick, protective layer of green, soft with decay, largely untroubled by humans. He felt a gentle shiver, a twitch in his spine—*danger*—but it was a fleeting feeling, the echo of a bell from another village rather than a full-fledged scream. There was something there, something that he knew, something that he felt. 'I...' he began, but the words caught in his throat and the picture of the forest disappeared. What was he about to say? Was he about to correct Abrax, the wise fire-magus? Was he about to use all of his two weeks of experience as a legionnaire to, what? Set him straight? Offer some of his peerless forest ranger wisdom? '...mm,' he muttered, hoping that this would end the conversation and stop his cheeks from burning. The big magus seemed content to have his own observation accepted without comment and rode on in silence.

Aemilius rode on next to him, trying to remember to breathe. He felt *stretched*, like an over-full wineskin. Tears welled up from somewhere within, and he slowed down his breathing to fight them back. The smell of mulch and bark filled his nostrils, and an idea came with them, like a soft-pawed ghost, but he pushed it out before it could make itself known.

Less, not more.

Balance.

He created in his mind a simple seesaw. No, a scale. And he tried to place things on the scale, calmly, on either side, balancing them. His experiences thus far, the kind words and the sharp barbs (from Rivkah, mostly), the wins and the losses and the mortal danger (again, a reasonable amount from Rivkah)—his cousins, shredded—his parents... deep breath... Hanno, lifeless on the cart... another deep breath...

And even though the balance was precarious, the scales stayed even.

Slowly, ever so slowly, Aemilius opened eyes that he hadn't realised were closed, and allowed the forest to come to him.

'It is not evil,' he said, and felt calmly and quietly panicked about it, because the voice was his and not his. There was a strength there, a knowing, and the words wanted out. 'It is merciless.' The quiet coming from Abrax was nothing short of deafening. 'But there is evil within it,' Aemilius continued. 'We did right to come here.' He hazarded a glance at Abrax, who was looking at him with the intense focus of a seasoned horse trader. '...I think.' Aemilius smiled nervously.

Excruciatingly slowly, Abrax's left eyebrow rose by a fraction, and then he ended the conversation with, '... mm.' A very thorough assessment had just been made.

But of what? Aemilius wondered.

IT SEEMED THAT the woods of the Blackhowl did not view them as intruders, so nothing of note happened as their horses sauntered through. At some point Seppius had, without asking, inched his horse ahead of Rivkah and taken the lead, guiding them past a couple of forks in the path, but the fading day was spent weaving through the trees. Aemilius only noticed that they might be drawing close because his horse picked up its speed ever so slightly in response to Seppius's mount. He blinked, and realised he was staring at a log pile. After a day's riding and feeling like he was getting further and further away from all humans and sinking into the ancient woods, the sign of industry was almost uncomfortable. The path was more worn, too, and Aemilius realised he might encounter people soon. As he dragged himself up from his stupor, he wondered idly at the freedom that surely had to come with Rivkah's attitude of not giving a single fistful of horse shit about what anyone else thought. The first cabin they encountered was deserted. The door hung off one hinge, and a large chunk of it was missing. Glancing ahead to where Seppius rode, Aemilius braced for a quip from Rivkah, but none was forthcoming. Instead, they rode on as the trees thinned around them and green lines started appearing. The Blackhowl had pressed itself so upon Aemilius that it took him another moment to recognise that he was looking down at tilled soil. *How...*

There was no hiding the pride in Seppius's voice. 'You dig down—far down—until you can saw through the roots. Then you fell the tree, and return the soil, and sow. And then, when you feel strong enough, you move on to the next tree. And slowly, through generations, you get enough light and space to feed more and more people.' As the boy talked, the path twisted them from side to side, and they were out of the wall of trees and into a big, natural clearing. 'Welcome to Iaspura,' he added.

As they came out of the forest, they were stood on the edge of a rough circle wide enough to make the trees at the far end look as big as Aemilius's thumb. A line of water snaked through the middle, and around it, like mushrooms, a collection of houses had sprouted. Set a good distance apart, they still presented a front, a huddled mass against the oppressive forest on all sides. The path led to the outskirts of the village, and across a bridge, but did not continue out.

'What's on the other side?'

Seppius looked almost startled that Rivkah had spoken without threat. 'The mountains,' he replied. 'And those who go there often don't come back.'

'Right,' she snarled, having spent her good mood for the day. 'Let's go get this done, shall we?' Urging her horse onward, she overtook Seppius and headed towards the village.

'Abrax, my friend. I appeal to you, for you are wise beyond even your advanced years—'

'Behave yourself, Aemilius of Hispania, lest you want a singed eyebrow,' Abrax said with entirely insincere outrage.

'—are you sure that our work here will be most successful and easy if we let her be our spokesperson?'

'I will have no cheek from—oh. Yes. No, that would not be wise.' Spurring his horse on, the fire-magus chased after Rivkah at a gallop, robes flapping in a most un-dignified way.

'After you?' Aemilius said, only just hiding a smirk. Looking mildly confused, Seppius set off towards his home. Behind and far above the sun continued its descent, sending claw-like shadows towards the centre of the clearing.

As far as Aemilius had been able to ascertain, the Legion was not used to entering villages as conquerors or long-awaited rescuers. To be greeted as barely tolerated family members seemed to be wishful thinking. But the entry into Iaspura seemed to make even Rivkah and Abrax uneasy.

'Whatever it is has really shat on their doorstep, hasn't it?'

'It has, Daughter of Abraham,' Abrax rumbled. 'The fear is thick and unpleasant.' His demeanour had changed since riding into the clearing, and his shoulders had slumped ever so slightly.

'I know Taurio said no one wants to know about monsters,' Aemilius said, mostly to himself. 'But the people here...'

'They know.' Abrax's mount whinnied in agreement.

Seppius had disappeared into what was easily the biggest building in the village—a squat, rectangular lump of a thing with thoroughly and recently reinforced doors and barred windows. There was still a bit of sunlight in the sky overhead, but it was fading fast. The shadows from the trees on the western edge had crept up to within a hundred yards of the bridge they had crossed—much like the rest of Iaspura, a sturdy construction with no material wasted.

'Did you see the claw marks?'

'I did. Looked like someone had mixed some cement to fill in the gaps.'

Confronted with the reality of the situation, all of Rivkah's bluster and foul mood had disappeared. *They sound like builders. Or carpenters,* Aemilius thought. *Just about to go do a job.*

'Here we go,' Rivkah muttered.

Even through the thick stone and layered doors, raised voices could be heard. The door swung open, spilling out light and arguments, and Seppius stormed out, slamming it behind him. He roared in frustration and beat his chest with a clenched fist, looking out at the tree line as if daring whatever was there to come at him personally.

Abrax coughed discreetly, and Seppius's head snapped towards them. Some mix of anger and embarrassment fought for control within his face, with apology winning out.

'My people are idiots.'

'They often are,' Rivkah said, with a smile.

'Let me guess,' Abrax said. 'They said they would not leave the safety of their imperial palace'—he swept his hand regally over the stone cube—'for anything less than two legions and a Praetorian guard?'

'And they called you an idiot for not fetching Tiberius himself?'

Seppius stared at them, open-mouthed.

'This is just what happens,' Aemilius said kindly, mostly to make sure a moth didn't fly down the boy's throat. 'And your people aren't idiots. They are just…'

'Afraid,' Abrax said.

And at that moment, just as the shadow of the setting sun reached the village brook, an unearthly howl tore the sky apart.

III

IASPURA

THE SILENCE AFTER the howl was absolute.

All around them, nature held its breath.

Aemilius looked at his hands and watched them trembling ever so slightly.

And then—

An answer. A howl, softer, from the other side of the clearing.

A third, from the north.

And soon, the evening sky was alive with the calls of the pack in the dark. *It is time for the final hunt. Time to kill.* Aemilius looked around, searching for a voice, but the thought that had just appeared in his head was gone again, like a shadow.

Rivkah dismounted and touched the side of her mare's head with more affection than he'd ever seen her show a human. 'I háte my job,' she muttered. 'Told you it was wolves.'

'A fair amount of them, too,' Abrax said. He stood in his saddle, looking intently into the crawling shadows, and wincing.

Aemilius tried to ignore the presence and the pressure of the Blackhowl in his head. 'They're coming,' he managed.

'Are they? Are you sure?' Rivkah laced every word with maximum contempt. 'Because I thought maybe there was a festival or something. You know, one of the ones that starts at night, in the middle of a forest called I'm going to murder your family.'

'Turn your anger to the enemy,' Abrax admonished. 'Aemilius, Seppius. Find me anything that burns. Straw, preferably. Spread it thick on the ground in a wide circle around the bridge.'

Pushing himself away from the pull of the forest, Aemilius grabbed the petrified Seppius by the arm. 'Come on, warrior,' he said with spirit he certainly didn't possess. 'Let's make ourselves useful before whatever hounds that Hades has loosened upon us actually get here.' With movements that Aemilius recognised all too well, Seppius's legs decided to work long before his heart or head did, moving the young man faster and faster. Soon they were sprinting together towards a big farmhouse on the north side, and it was not just the running that made Aemilius's heart thump. The cries of a herd of horses, tied up and screaming, made his back teeth ache. *Quiet*, he whispered, almost to himself. *There is no danger. The teeth are for us.*

'There! The cart!' Seppius yanked at his arm. 'Fork up as much as you can! I'll go get a horse.' He was gesturing at an empty cart that had definitely seen better days, parked next to a pile of hay that reached almost to chest-height. Wasting no time, Aemilius grabbed a pitchfork and started swinging, enjoying having something simple to do. Three quick swings in, the noise of the horses had receded to an almost-quiet. He had managed about five forkfuls when Seppius led a horse out of the stables and proceeded to put it before the cart with swift, assured movements. The terror that had gripped the boy seemed to have given way to muscle memory, for now there were jobs that needed to get done. The moment he was finished he turned to Aemilius and nearly shouldered him out of the way. 'Here—give me that,' he said, grabbing the fork and proceeding to send the hay flying. Moments later the cart was more than half-full.

A pressure—no, an *ache*—made Aemilius look up and to the black pool of night spreading from the woods. Something in the shadows twisted and shifted. Far away, but not nearly far enough.

'We need to move,' he said.

Seppius made to protest about orders, but something about the urgency in Aemilius's voice changed his mind. 'Get in, then!' he snapped, vaulting up onto the horse and leaving Aemilius to scramble head-first into the cart, only to be rewarded with a mouthful of hay as the old box lurched into movement.

In the gloom behind them, the wolves broke into a run.

'Go, go, go!' Aemilius shouted, to Seppius and possibly the horse. It didn't matter, as neither of them needed any encouragement. The series of creaks and cracks from the cart gave no assurance that it would make it in one piece—at this stage, if they got the cart to the square where Abrax was waiting in no more than five pieces it would be quite the accomplishment. They thundered back down the lane they'd run, watching the silent shadows effortlessly keeping pace behind them.

Another pack loped along in silence on the other side of the riverbank.

A softly glowing orb had appeared above the central square, lighting the way to their target. Seppius urged the horse onward, turning as sharply as the cart would allow, and within what felt like moments they were at the bridge. Slowing down, but not entirely fast enough for Aemilius's liking, they rattled over and stopped only inches away from Abrax and Rivkah.

'Took your time,' the short girl quipped, grinning at Aemilius's attempts to stand up and get out of the cart. Seppius had already started forking the hay onto the ground.

'That's right,' Abrax rumbled. 'We'll take a stand on the bridge. Give a man's length of distance from the houses— we don't want to burn the village. Leave half for the other side,' he instructed Seppius. Not needing to be told twice, the boy led the horse and cart back across the bridge and resumed his frenetic forking. Gritting his teeth to ward off a throbbing headache, Aemilius worked alongside him, spreading out the dry, crisp hay in a large area in front of the bridge. Through a haze, he could sort of imagine what Abrax might be planning, but inside his head it was harder and harder to keep thoughts apart and tell which ones were his own. He kept feeling like he could see and smell himself, that he was everywhere at once, one and part of a whole, but one that kept twisting and changing shape, that he was spinning and spiralling—and most of all he felt fear. Real, raw fear. Just when he felt he could have a chance at reining in his overwhelmed senses the howls rang out again. They were closer. Much closer.

'Bridge,' came Abrax's clipped command, and Aemilius watched, half-dazed, as Seppius walked towards them with his back turned, spreading the hay out as he went. *Some farmer is going to be furious,* Aemilius thought and barely suppressed a nervous giggle. Their enemies were closer now—felt, but not yet seen. They were shadows, shapes in the falling dark. Abrax's orb fought back against the creeping night and occasionally caught on flashes of yellow eyes, but it was not enough to see everywhere.

Four of them
On the bridge

Aemilius shuddered as the thought passed through him, followed by the ghost of an image of himself seen from a distance. He peered into the darkness. *Was someone attacking them with sorcery?* Abrax would know. Would he? Wouldn't he? The magus had not been forthcoming about just how much magic he had left in him, and he had looked decidedly less healthy and strong after they'd entered the clearing. Rivkah had also been in a foul mood—even worse than usual—for most of the ride. Did she know or understand something he didn't? *Probably. They all did.*

'Why aren't they attacking?' Rivkah snarled. 'This isn't the right way to go about it. *We* stalk the prey.' She glared into the night. '*Hey! Flea-bags!* We're *here! Plenty* of meat on the old one!' The orb of light above them flickered briefly, but the outrageous insult wasn't quite enough to break Abrax's concentration. 'I can *smell* them. You! Bag o' bones! How many do you think there are?' Seppius paused for a while before answering. *Gathering up courage, no doubt,* Aemilius thought.

'I don't know,' he said calmly. 'But they have been growing in number. More than thirty. There is one who leads them, and he is Death.'

'Yeah, yeah. Big wolf, we know,' Rivkah said. 'And just how big is this…' The rest of the sentence trailed off and was ended by a whispered string of swears in Hebrew. Beside her, Seppius muttered a hasty prayer. Aemilius blinked. Abrax's orb had created a circle of light around the bridge. It was enough to see by, but no more. And what had just padded into the ring, demonstrating an air of absolute command and disdain that the four of them had the audacity to place themselves between him and his interesting food box, was…

…no. He couldn't call it a wolf.

It was wolf-*shaped*.

But it was close enough to the size of a horse. Its fur was grey in patches and black in others, caked in matted clumps of blood. Above a black collar with steel loops and glints of purple, bone-crunching jaws lined with sharp teeth curved upwards into a malformed, demonic smile, but the worst thing was the eyes. They gleamed with hate, and they were trained on the four on the bridge.

And behind it came an army.

The wolves padded out, silently, from everywhere. Every alley, every corner. They filed in at a respectful distance behind the monster, all eyes trained on the bridge. On the north bank the pack flowed to meet them, stopping short of rushing the bridge, and then the animals all stood still.

'What is this?' Rivkah whispered. 'Why aren't they attacking? Can you burn them?' She turned to look at Abrax and hissed.

Aemilius's head snapped back. The magus looked like he was about to throw up.

'It's the bastarding rune again,' he wheezed. 'It's not as bad as Xeno's, but… there is no way I can get all of them.'

'You *knew*,' Aemilius whispered. 'You've felt it since we entered the forest. You *knew* you would struggle. Is that why...?' He gestured at the hay strewn all around them, but the question faded into nothing.

'I hoped,' Abrax whispered. 'And we'll see how it goes. The wolves are protected, but...' He drew himself up to his full height and snapped out three terse words in an old language, flicking his hands to both sides. There was a whoosh of air heading downwards, and—

All around the bridge, straw burst into flame.

The reaction was instant. As one, the wolves leapt back, scrabbling over each other to get out of the way. The flames, knee-high, licked at their fur. Yelps and howls erupted but died down quickly as the beasts, nimble-footed, retreated to safety. Only the hiss and the crackle of the flames remained in the cold night air, as they danced around the monstrous wolf.

Which didn't even flinch.

Smoke billowed from its fur where the fire touched it, and still the beast did not move. Abrax shuddered, raised an arm to the sky, closed his fist slowly and flung it towards the animal. A ball of fire erupted from him, growing in size as it hurtled towards the baleful eyes of the creature, and exploded all around its head.

'Stop!' Aemilius felt the big magus's knees buckling next to him. 'This is what he wants!'

'Wh—what?' Abrax sighed, leaning against the bridge railing.

'It's some sort of rune of protection, isn't it? The flames aren't hurting him at all. Donato wants you to spend yourself on the beast, give him everything you've got until you are easy and exhausted prey. Look!' The wolf still sat there, just eyeing them, in the middle of their burning circle. A feeling drifted on the smoke into his mind, and suddenly he knew. He didn't know how he knew, and wasn't entirely sure about what he knew, but there was no time to lose. 'Rivkah.'

'Yes?'

'Kill him. And kill him fast, because when the fire dies down the pack will return.' Aemilius looked at her, ethereal and terrifying in the firelight. 'Unless you are scared of a little puppy?' She looked at him and grinned, and looked more wolf than the wolves, and walked off the bridge, towards the beast.

'No!' Seppius shouted. 'Don't! He'll rip—'

Aemilius elbowed him hard in the sternum. 'Shut up for a moment. This is our only chance.'

'But the other wolves will fall on her!'

Ignoring the growing terror in the boy, Aemilius swallowed his words and his fears and his thoughts, and he watched. Picking out the patches where the fire had died down, Rivkah slow-danced her way towards the beast, who watched her with detached, superior interest. Her daggers were out, and she was crouched down, sidling to the right. Slowly, the dire wolf started moving to match her pattern. He saw it the moment before it happened. The tensing, the quick bend in the knees—and then the massive wolf leapt, flying through the air towards Rivkah, jaws agape and paws out wide, spanning a sickening distance. And Rivkah was down, rolling low under the animal and through a patch of burning straw without flinching, disappearing from its field of vision. The wolf's head snapped round, and it twisted, impossibly, in mid-air, powerful back legs landing and crouching, preparing for another leap. It exploded towards Rivkah again, but this time she didn't roll. She crouched down again, just ducking a swiping claw, and jabbed both arms up into the wolf's underbelly, digging her heels in to not be bowled over by the beast's momentum.

The noise was too loud, too deep and too wrong. It sounded like the howl of a hundred voices, a gust of wind through a crack in a rock in the underworld. The big wolf landed, but this time there was no elegant twist. Black blood streamed out of the gashes created by the blades, and something thick was spilling out along with it, but the beast was not defeated. It turned slowly, head dropped down towards Rivkah's eye level, and growled, jaws crunching. It advanced, pushing her to retreat towards a wall of flame, dragging a line of its own guts on the ground.

She glanced over her shoulder at the fire, at the gaping crowd on the bridge. *Did she just... wink?* But her eyes were back on the wolf. Snarling and staring up at him, she bared her teeth, looking like nothing more than an upstart puppy. Then she took her eyes off the monster again, stared straight up at the sky—and howled. A shrill, sharp howl.

Answer. The thought came to Aemilius, and drifted out into the night. *She is your sister, and she will set you free.* For three heartbeats he was certain the bottom of his stomach had dropped out and his veins had turned to lead, and he grasped a handful of cloth at his side and hoped he wouldn't fall over.

Out in the darkness, a howl went up to match—and then another—and then another—

The beast sat back, lifted up its massive head to howl at the moon, and Rivkah leapt forward and sliced its throat open from left to right and right to left, spinning away before the fearsome jaws snapped her head off. The movement took the beast's body off balance, and it fell to the side with a thud. Scrabbling to stand up, it almost reached its feet, and then Aemilius, Seppius and Abrax watched from the bridge as Rivkah took four steps forward and rammed a dagger up under its jaw, so far in that her fist disappeared into the underside of the monster's head.

And just like that, what had been a vision of evil on four legs was just a carcass, dropping lifelessly where Rivkah had been standing a moment earlier. She looked back over at Aemilius as if to say '…and?' Around her, the flames from the burning straw were dying down, caressing her slight frame with flickering light—

Aemilius just about managed to register a surge of anger as a human figure charged from a pool of shadow around the corner of a hut, sprinting towards Rivkah's back. Staring at the fire had made him half-blind so he only saw the outline of it, but he couldn't help but see the thick staff that was swung at the girl in a wide arc at hip-height. He yelped and watched as she caught what must have been the gust of the quarterstaff, scissor-kicked and somehow twisted herself horizontally in mid-air, but the vicious swing still caught the side of her outstretched leg and sent her spinning with a blood-curdling scream.

Everything happened at once.

He started towards Rivkah's prone form, only to realise that Seppius was already ahead of him, pitchfork in hand, screaming at the top of his lungs. Their enemy—a slim but strong-looking man, clad head to toe in thick leather—looked up to judge the new risk, and shouted something in a harsh, guttural language.

Another four men emerged from the shadows, all dressed in the same thick leather armour, wielding wrist-thick staves topped with vicious-looking hooks. Aemilius had just enough time to think about how this was the end, and how they would now be beaten to death over the corpse of a monstrous horse-sized wolf, when a wave of feeling hit him so hard he staggered backwards. 'Seppius—' he managed, as the first of their assailants moved towards Rivkah.

The young man had somehow managed to interpose himself between the fallen girl and the new enemy. 'What?' he growled.

'Put down the pitchfork,' Aemilius said with a detached calm.

'What?' Seppius snapped.

The blood in his veins had turned to ice. 'Put. It. Down.'

Their opponents did not seem to understand the words, but they understood the tone. Surrender. A vicious smirk spread amongst them. On the ground, Rivkah cursed in Hebrew, tried to rise but fell and screamed.

'Step back,' Aemilius said with the same, calm authority. 'And get down on the ground next to her.' Ignoring Seppius's incredulous stare, Aemilius held his hands up, showed his palms to the men, and walked over to Rivkah where he sat down. Very reluctantly, Seppius followed.

'What are you doing?' Rivkah hissed. 'Stand and fight!'

Aemilius closed his eyes. He didn't know what he was doing, or why—but he knew that it was right. Or hoped it was, at any rate. *Well—if it isn't, we are all dead*. He lay down on his stomach and curled into a protective ball. 'Keep your head down, and stay very, very still.'

'What the—' Injured and angry as she was, Rivkah was still quick—so she didn't finish the sentence. Instead, she dropped flat to the ground and curled up just before the first wolf came charging out of the darkness, leapt over her and cannoned into the man in the leather armour. Within moments, the square was thick with snarling animal bodies, fighting with each other to get to the men with the staves, ignoring the three on the ground completely. In an instant, the triumphant grins of their enemies were replaced with terror, as it did not matter how they flailed with their hook-staffs. There were teeth and claws everywhere, and the fury of the pack doubled whenever one of their targets went down. Screams were quickly drowned and cut off as the men were ripped to pieces—and then, suddenly, there was quiet.

'Keep very, very still,' Aemilius whispered. They waited for what seemed like an age, and then he opened his eyes. On the bridge, Abrax was leaned against the railing, looking much closer to dead than alive. The orb shone above them, but faintly. Below… was carnage. The corpses of the five attackers were mangled almost beyond recognition. The wolves had launched themselves at their targets with an urge to destroy, and the men's faces were shredded to a bloody pulp.

Of the wolves themselves there was no trace.

'Serves them right,' Rivkah growled. She had managed to scrabble up onto one knee. 'Fucker would have broken my leg.' She spat in the general direction of a leather-clad corpse.

Seppius blinked as he tried to comprehend what he was seeing. 'They look like—'

'Dog trainers,' Aemilius finished. 'The old man who

trained my father's hounds would wear armour like that. It's not for fighting. It's for protecting against bites.'

'Didn't quite work, did it?' Rivkah's voice was dripping with satisfaction. 'Guess the big one kept the others in check. Looks like the children of the forest did *not* appreciate how they had been treated.'

Aemilius glanced towards the sealed-up stone house, and suddenly felt like he would rather not be here to explain what had just happened. While the big magus was still alive, Abrax did not look like he would be taking charge of anything any time soon, and Rivkah was injured. *Which leaves… me?* 'Seppius—I need your help.'

'Anything.' The look in the young man's eyes suggested that this was not an exaggeration.

FOR ALL ITS size, the monster had been surprisingly light. In death, it looked almost… deflated. Seppius had quickly and almost gleefully requisitioned a big, strong hay cart for them, and helped lump the carcass in the back. Abrax still looked like he was fighting to keep his insides in, and Aemilius felt sorry for him. They had not wanted to get too close, but it was clear that there were inscriptions on the collar of the beast that had a very strong effect on the magus. Rivkah could still not put any weight on her leg and rode her horse awkwardly, wincing with every jolt. It was left to Aemilius to put his horse before the cart, and just before they rode off Seppius had given him a bone-crunching hug to say goodbye. As the cart rattled slowly through the forest in the dark, Aemilius thought about the satchel at his feet.

Before he set off, while Rivkah was busy swearing at the stirrups and Abrax was very reluctantly helping to drape a thick blanket over the oversized wolf, hiding it completely from sight, he had gone to the mangled corpses of the dog-trainers, armed with his sturdy knife and a suspicion.

He'd cut open their armour.

And he'd seen, making the decision to switch off any and all feelings; instead, he had thought like Prasta, worked methodically and just *collected*. And what he found sat between his feet like hot rocks, and he very much wanted someone clever to say that it was absolutely fine, but in his heart he knew that it very much wasn't.

IV

VIA POPILIA

THE THREE LEGIONNAIRES rode in silence, as they had done for most of the day, until finally Livia spoke, sitting in the back next to the still form of Hanno.

'Go on.'

'What?' Taurio rumbled, shifting uncomfortably on the drivers' bench.

'Say it.'

'I haven't even—'

'But you're *thinking* it,' Prasta interrupted. 'I can *smell* it on you.'

'See? I told you my musk was irresistible. She can't help—'

'No, you need to admit it.'

Taurio turned up his nose. 'No. I will not *admit* to anything. I admitted to stealing apples once, when I was a boy, and that did not turn out well for me. So, no. No admitting.'

'Oh,' Prasta said. 'Shame.'

'Why? So you could enjoy—'

'I wouldn't particularly enjoy it,' she interrupted. 'I just thought—'

'Oh dear—are you well? Would you like to go have a lie down? Thinking is very hard for some people.'

'I just thought you were more of a man than this.'

'Agreed,' Livia added, voice drenched in melancholy. 'I mean—I've seen you do remarkable things, my burly friend.'

'The riots in Autricum—'

'The tracking and slaying of the five-headed Macedonian snake, through water—'

'Oh, and the bamboozling of an entire Praetorian guard!'

'The drunken monk! I'd forgotten!'

Both women launched into a remarkably accurate impression of Taurio's voice singing bawdy songs about a nun, a donkey and a candle, rising in volume until the horse was tossing its head in irritation.

'Fine, fine,' Taurio mumbled. 'I will humour you, but *only*'—he held up his hands, palms out—'because the hell-cat isn't here. I trust that you are women of maturity and sense, and that you will be able to hear this and allow it to exist between friends, and then allow it to leave on the wind and never be spoken of again.' He looked at each of them in turn, sternly.

'On the black eyes of Morrigan,' Prasta said solemnly.

'May Romulus himself come down and bite my arm off,' Livia added.

Taurio looked suspiciously at her for a moment. 'All right.' He sighed and looked away from them, towards the horse, and over its head. Bracing himself, he drew a deep breath and pursed his lips.

'This road… is incredible,' the big man sighed.

The Via Popilia stretched out before them, an almost obscenely straight line through a winding, curving landscape. Every stone was in its place, and the crisp edges were not touched by encroaching nature.

'Yes,' Livia said with pride. 'Yes, it is.'

'Never thought I'd put my life on the line for roads,' Prasta mused, 'but after arse-rattling back and forth over my beautiful isle on tracks whose only distinction is in the different levels of squelch, I have come to deeply appreciate the Empire's engineers.'

'Who obviously deserve a bash on the head for being Romans... but late in life.'

'Is that the most kindness you'd extend to a Roman, my friend? You'd kill us when we're old?'

'In your case, Your Highness, I'd wait until you're well past eighty.' Taurio paused. 'So, another seven years...?'

Livia rapped him smartly on the back of the head over Prasta's cackling. 'Lard-bucket,' she shot back, but there was no retort from Taurio.

Instead, he had resumed his staring at the road. 'Are there... any garrisons nearby?' he asked slowly.

'No.'

'...interesting,' he mumbled. 'Because that is a very particular shade of red.'

Up ahead in the distance, a tiny blot of colour on the road was growing slowly bigger. Livia very carefully maintained her speed exactly as it was, but all three of them kept their eyes trained on whatever they were heading towards. They had passed Capua without trouble—Livia's cunning quarter-mastery had provided them with traveller garb that was just invisible enough, their cart attracted no attention, and the horses were nothing to write home about. Almost all the people on their way had been dismissed with a curt traveller's nod, no one had tried to sell them anything and it had been enough for aspiring cut-throats and strong-arms to take one glance at Taurio and another at Prasta to convince themselves that their work would be easier elsewhere. It had been steady going, and Campania had felt safe. It was an unfamiliar and almost uncomfortable feeling at first, but they had gotten used to it quickly. So why was there a collection of what looked a lot like uniforms standing on the road ahead? All banter instantly set aside, the legionnaires slid into an alert silence as they rolled smoothly towards the growing red spot on the horizon.

'IN THE NAME of Tiberius Caesar—*halt!*'

'Great,' Taurio muttered under his breath. 'A sparrow who thinks he's an eagle.'

The speaker was tall, broad about the shoulders and thick-armed, with close-cropped hair and the look of someone who hadn't had to fight his own fights for a long time. The fact that he was standing in front of thirty-two javelin-armed soldiers, neatly arranged in rows that firmly blocked the road added an extra bit of authority. He looked at them suspiciously. 'Names, occupations, destination!'

Accidentally placing a hand on Taurio's forearm, Livia looked demurely down to the road. 'My name is Diana of Tarsus, and I am travelling to the Aedes Vesta to deliver these two eminent healers, Grimmor and Skeela, to Vestalis Maxima. We have with us an old African, who they'—she gestured to Taurio and Prasta—'will be performing rituals on.'

The centurion glared at her and snorted. 'Do you have any proof of that?'

'Proof?' She paused. 'I, uh… I can show you this…?' She reached into the folds of her tunic.

'*Stop!*' the centurion bellowed. Behind him, thirty-two javelins all rose in chorus and pointed at the cart.

Livia froze. 'I have a medallion,' she said nervously. 'I can show you.'

'What did you think she was going to do?' Taurio snapped. 'Pull out a dagger and charge?'

'*Silence!*' the centurion bellowed. 'All of you! Out!' Prasta hissed angrily as she descended next to Taurio, but kept her mouth shut. 'And the old man you say you have in the back!'

'Please,' Livia pleaded. 'He is very weak and cannot be moved.'

'Leave him alone,' Taurio growled.

'*You do not give commands!*' For a moment the centurion seemed like he was going to abandon all protocol in favour of a scrap, but the glint of silver caught his eye.

'Here,' Livia all but whispered. 'I am Diana of Tarsus, and I am with the temple. Please. Forgive the impetuousness of my fellow travellers. They are not brought up in civilisation, and as such do not understand the might and terror of the Roman army.' Prasta's hand had landed on Taurio's lower back and grabbed a fistful of material, which was being very firmly and painfully twisted to hold the big Gaul back. 'And how it relies on its officers to be able to meet every challenge with the immovable conviction that protocol will win the day.'

There was the shadow of disappointment in the burly centurion's face. 'Go in peace, Diana of Tarsus,' he snapped. 'And on the way to Rome you should talk with your companions about the correct way to respond to an officer in the army.' He smirked as Taurio seemed to limp back onto the cart, followed by Prasta.

'Thank you,' Livia said, all silk and honey as the soldiers behind the big man parted to make way for them. The centurion huffed once, then looked right through her and to the south.

THEY DIDN'T SPEAK again until the soldiers were no bigger than a thumb behind them, at which point Prasta turned to Taurio and smiled a steel-wire smile. 'Are you *trying* to get us killed, you trotter-faced arse?'

'That man was an officious little bully,' Taurio snarled, 'and he deserved to have his face staved in.'

'He wasn't *little*,' Prasta growled back. 'And he had thirty-two soldiers standing behind him. Stave their faces in, too, would you? I'd say they'd have turned you into a hedgehog, but I won't do that.'

'Oh yeah? Why?'

'Because I *like* hedgehogs,' Prasta snapped.

'So do I, if they're cooked correctly.'

'You—'

'Shut up, both of you.' Livia's voice was calm. 'Did anything about that strike you as odd?'

'Romans,' Taurio snapped. 'All of them.'

Prasta took longer to think. 'Four conturbia, for a roadblock, in the middle of the heart of the Empire?'

'Yes,' Livia answered slowly. 'Now, granted, we have not had our ear to the ground for a couple of days—'

'—or weeks.'

'—or weeks,' Livia allowed. 'But... if it's monsters, we'd know. Wouldn't we?'

'We would,' Taurio huffed.

'So, if it's not monsters, and it's nothing we know about... then what is it?' Livia mused. Snapping the reins gently but firmly, she looked ahead, up the Via Popilia. 'What are they afraid of?'

ON THE SAME road but much further south, Aemilius listened to the sound of cart wheels on cobbles, Abrax groaning occasionally and Rivkah swearing constantly, working on her leg, rubbing and massaging. After slow progress in the moonlight and steady pace up the road in daylight, they had stopped for food and rest as the sun set. He had slept until he was woken up by Rivkah throwing a pebble at the side of his head, and they had set off again in the middle of the night. By now he had gotten used to the leaden feeling of exhaustion and was not entirely sure his legs would support him if he was to leap from the cart. After her slumber-breaking marksmanship, Rivkah had gone to sleep in the cart and he cast an eye back to where they lay, her and Abrax, sleeping next to each other and looking for a moment like two normal humans rather than two different physical manifestations of death, next to a pile of rugs.

And for a beautiful moment Aemilius just saw it as such.

Rather than, say, a couple of rugs draped across two highly competent killers and an obscenely large carcass of an evil, necrotic wolf-king. The reality of his situation sank back in, and he sighed, allowing time to pass. In the still of the night, with the cart rattling along at a pace that suggested the horses were awake but only just, Aemilius thought back.

His recollection of the fire-night in the village was blurry, but it was still there.

And now, with time, he remembered more.

Watching himself on the bridge from a low vantage point.

Scenting the night air, and the pack.

The fear—and the rage.

He stared at the realisation, and it was too big, and it could neither be accepted nor ignored.

These were wolf senses and wolf thoughts.

He rolled his eyes and muttered, 'Great,' under his breath. *I've lost my mind. Hanging out with this unhinged crew means I'm imagining things.* And exactly *what* was he imagining? That he could commune with the animals? Speak to the birds? The memory of being high above himself tingled in his spine. Up ahead, the horses whinnied softly. 'Calm,' he whispered absentmindedly, and they settled back into their placid walk.

Aemilius paused and thought.

But everyone speaks to the animals, he argued back to himself. *Farmers do it. Quintus did it.* And he held his breath for a moment as his heart broke again for the gruff horseman, then he sighed and the horses snorted their sympathy.

But the animals don't speak back.

That was the unthinkable idea. That night in the village he had felt the wolves telling him... something. He'd *known* that they would come for the handlers when the pack leader was dead. He'd known... because they'd told him they would.

Well, maybe not *told* him. Or told *him*.

But they'd thought it, and he'd heard.

Casting his eye back over his shoulder, he thought about telling Abrax and Rivkah about his discovery.

And then he laughed contemptuously at himself for a good sixteen hoof-beats. He could just imagine the first ten or so jokes Rivkah would throw at him, and Abrax's raised eyebrow and silent judgment. And worse... *what would happen if they'd ask him to prove it?*

A light touch on his forearm made him jump almost out of his skin. He stifled a yelp. In the dusk he could make out the shape of Rivkah. 'Sleep,' she said, not unkindly. 'You've done a lot. And if you stay awake too long your head goes funny.' Clambering up from the cart, she hissed in pain when she sat down in the teamster's seat. 'Providing there is anything in there already,' she mused.

You'd be surprised, Aemilius thought as he climbed into the hold and pressed himself into a corner, folding a rug under his buttocks and closing his eyes. *You'd be surprised.*

NIGHT BECAME DAY and day became night, and around them the landscape changed. The rolling hills of Lucania became the peaks and valleys of Campania, and once they crossed the Val Orcia and the bridge over the Arno the colours of nature softly changed, too, turning darker and richer.

And then, on midday of their second day on the Via Julia Augusta, Aemilius saw a cart in the distance and somehow he didn't need to ask or be told. He *knew*. A snap of the reins and the horses grudgingly moved from a walk to a trot. In the cart, Abrax groaned in the manner of a young drunkard deeply regretting the fourth amphora of the previous night.

'What's the rush?' Rivkah slurred, not yet awake enough to be outraged at being woken by the increase in pace.

'It's them.'

A brief silence, and then movement. He could feel the cart responding as she clambered up behind him and lowered herself into the seat. 'How's the leg?'

'Fucking should have jumped in amongst the wolves and bit his face off myself.'

'So. Better, then.'

'Yeah. Not by much, but it'll take weight.'

'As long as nothing's broken—'

'It's not. And I know the difference.' She paused, stretching her leg and kneading at the muscle, hissing. 'But it was close.' She glanced at him. 'You're looking mighty comfortable driving a cart loaded with a sick magus and the corpse of a monster.'

He thought about this. His bones ached with weariness, and every muscle in his body felt like it had given up on screaming at him a while ago, but she wasn't wrong. *I… am.* 'Aemilius of Hispania is not bothered by a trifling wolf-giant, and will happily rescue the occasional lord of fire,' he said airily. Beside him, Rivkah smirked. 'What are you smirking at?'

'Just amused.' She paused, winced and stretched again. 'Never thought I'd be happy to lose a bet.'

'Let me guess—you bet Livia that I'd die within the week?'

'What? No!' Hand on her chest, the girl looked outraged. 'How could you think that of me?'

Aemilius looked at her levelly. 'I may have only joined the Hidden Legion a little over a week ago, but I am long past believing whatever *that* is.'

The lithe girl grinned in the manner of something that kills things. 'Oh, please forgive me, your exalted eminence… but you were wrong, though. Taurio, two days.'

He shrugged. 'Fair enough, I suppose.'

The soothing rhythm of hooves on stone and the steady roll of the wheels gently overtook the conversation, and they sat in companionable silence for a while, watching the cart up ahead. Aemilius found himself getting a warm feeling in his chest at the thought of seeing the others again, and a thought snuck into his head.

Friends.

There was something to be said for battling monsters and facing death together.

Beside him, Rivkah stretched again, but more softly this time and without wincing. 'What's in the bag?' she asked lazily.

Her question had the immediate effect of making the bottom of his ribcage disappear and his heart fall down to roughly where his knees were. He had forgotten about the bag between his ankles, and now he wished he'd thrown it away while the others slept. He took a deep breath. 'I... don't know.' He could feel her looking at the side of his head now, the predator in her awakened, and his heart started racing. 'I went back to the corpses and I looted them,' he fumbled.

'Ooooh!' she purred. 'Aren't *you* the little battleground filcher?' She paused for a moment. 'But that makes no sense.' She frowned. 'How can you not know what's in the bag, then? You should be coming away with purses, and rings, and the occasional bit of jewellery. What did you actually get?'

Aemilius winced. 'I don't *know*,' he said, hating how reedy his voice sounded, 'but I think they might be...'—*please don't mock me*—'magic things. Do you want to see them?'

Rather than poke fun, Rivkah looked away and swore

in Hebrew. After a moment, she turned back to him. 'No. What are you going to do with them?'

'I was planning to hand them over to Abrax, but he hasn't looked like doing more than just surviving.'

'And Hanno is…'

'Yeah.' Aemilius stopped a sentence that neither of them wanted to finish. There was a pause. 'So… any ideas?'

'Nah. If it's got an edge or a point, I'm in. But magic? I will never, ever, be able to do it, or understand it, and I am hoping I can remain at least civil with the people who do, so they don't use it against me.' Without thinking, she stroked her forearms and Aemilius had a horrible memory of vines shooting out, entwining her in a crushing embrace.

Magic… is terrifying.

'I am sure someone will know what to do,' he muttered. *Because I certainly don't.* Suddenly, he felt a little less at ease. Driving a cart along a straight-arrow road was, in the grand scheme of things, easier than dealing with mysterious black magic wielded by unexplained enemies. There was some reassurance to be had in the fact that they were, however, inarguably making ground on the cart up ahead. He could make out Taurio's bulk next to what could only be Livia in the driver's seat and felt like he could see Prasta's head in the back of the cart.

'*Oi! What's that smell?*'

Rivkah's near-scream made his heart skip at least three beats and very nearly startled the horses.

'*They'll let anyone on the road these days,*' Taurio bellowed back as their cart slowed to a halt. '*Also, aren't you too young to drive?*'

'Caught up to you, though, didn't we?' Rivkah hollered.

Snorri Kristjansson

Livia and Taurio had now turned around in their seats. Feeling suddenly awkward, Aemilius waved and immediately hated it. *Why can't I be confident all the time?* However, he didn't have time to berate himself more, because the horses needed to be slowed down and soothed, and then they had pulled up next to the lead cart. He watched as Livia's features clouded, and saw her jump gracefully off the driver's seat and race to the back of their cart, leaping in.

'How long has he been like this?' she barked.

'Easy,' Rivkah snapped back. 'We didn't make him sick.'

'He is too close to the runes,' Aemilius blurted out.

'What runes?' Livia snapped.

He mutely sort of nod-glanced at the blanket pile. Turning, Livia glared at it with the fury of a bear-mother, reached for a blade and got ready to dispense justice. 'No—maybe don't—' Aemilius managed, but he was too slow. She grabbed the edge and pulled hard.

A couple of things happened at once.

The corpse of the wolf-king was exposed, in a cloud of flying fur. Death had not been kind to it, and rotting had set in quickly. Where exposed, the flesh was sunken, putrid and of far too many colours, and rather disturbingly there were no flies whatsoever. Livia's face instantly went a pale green, and she managed a retching '…hurrgh' before throwing the blanket back over the mess.

And then Abrax threw up all over her legs.

'…do that,' Aemilius finished meekly.

A silence descended. No one knew quite what to do, and even Rivkah had the good and common sense to not crack a joke. *Perhaps she's not quite sure about her leg yet,* Aemilius thought.

75

'Well,' Livia said after a few breaths that felt, on balance, pretty much like an eternity. 'It looks like you've been busy.' She knelt down by Abrax's side and touched his forehead before glancing at Rivkah. 'Do you have any water?' she asked, calmly and kindly. Moving with much more swiftness and grace than he'd seen from her since the start of their journey, Rivkah dismounted from the cart in an instant and found her waterskin. The older woman looked at her with concern. 'And what happened to you?'

'Long story. Bastard caught my leg with a quarterstaff.'

Livia winced. 'Looks like he wasn't messing around. What happened to him?'

'He had his face eaten by fifty wolves.' Rivkah grinned.

'Good.' The set of Livia's jaw suggested that if the wolves hadn't gotten there first, she would have done the exact same thing herself. Aemilius marvelled at the fact that her legs were liberally covered with the insides of Abrax's guts, and she had made the vomit almost invisible by being able to simply not care about it.

'How is Hanno?'

Another silence, and not a good one. Not waiting for any explanation, Rivkah turned and made her way to the lead cart, peeking in.

The slump in her shoulders made Aemilius's blood go cold. He turned to Livia. 'Is he…?'

'No,' she said. 'He is hanging on by the thinnest of threads, and I think Prasta is there with him tying it together every time it snaps. We have very little time.'

'Right—hell-beast, get in the back,' Taurio shouted. Not really waiting for a response, he snapped the reins and the horses lurched back into a walk.

Aemilius glanced at Livia who nodded, and he followed suit.

* * *

ON THEY WENT, picking up speed, watching the farmland stretch out around them and then, in the distance, watching the forests rise out of the horizon, and the land rise with them. Up ahead and above, clouds caressed mountain peaks, and the road led the Legion straight on towards them. After a while Livia had satisfied herself that there was nothing more she could do for Abrax, and had climbed into the driver's seat next to Aemilius. He offered her the reins, but she kindly refused. He'd felt a little buzz of pride then, which the sheer tedium of the road had left behind fairly quickly.

'So,' he said, out of boredom. 'Tell me, where exactly are we going?'

'Follow Taurio.'

'I was planning to... but where?' When no response was forthcoming, he added, 'Are we going to the home garrison of the Legion?'

'Yes. Val Camonica. The Fort.'

'What's *The Fort* like?'

'You'll see soon enough.'

'Is there anything I need to know?'

'Not really. We'll do the talking, present you as the chosen one and target of our mission, and then we'll go from there.'

And just like that they were back to the silence of the road, the clop-clop of the hooves and the rattle of the cart.

Up ahead, Taurio turned off onto what looked like an almost disused track. Aemilius glanced at Livia.

'Follow him. He knows the way.'

Doesn't suggest a vibrant and healthy movement of troops, Aemilius thought. It didn't look like the Legion had sent out a, well, legion any time recently. His arse quickly put paid to further speculation, as the old track was a lot less forgiving than the pristine Roman road they had just left. Without a word Livia climbed back into the cart bed to see to Abrax, and Aemilius was left trying to mirror Taurio's path along the track. Up ahead a still green wave of pine trees rose. It looked impenetrable—but they soon came upon a small gap, invisible before you were almost stood at the tree line. The forest swallowed them, oppressive, damp and dim. The path they travelled could only very kindly be called a track and was more like the memory of one, but eventually the trees thinned out almost imperceptibly, and then opened up into a clearing in a deep, forest-clad valley that headed sharply upwards into the mountains.

'There,' Livia said.

Startled by the break in the silence, Aemilius almost squawked, 'What? Where?'

'The Fort.'

Shaking his head to dislodge the confusion, Aemilius started scanning. 'I can't see anything,' he confessed after a while.

Livia stood up in the cart bed. 'To your left. See that scar in the hillside, like someone gave it a going-over with an axe?'

'Yes.'

'Now look into the shadows. See the brown ridge?'

'Yes.'

'Keep your eyes trained on it. That's our wall.'

Aemilius frowned and stared—and he realised that rather than a tree line, he was looking at a fortified wall of tree trunks. And just as he was staring... something moved.

'There! Someone on the, uh, wall! We've been spotted!'

Livia smiled. 'Oh, we were spotted a *while* ago.'

Feeling unsettled and suddenly crowded by the valley, the hillsides and the trees, Aemilius had his head on a swivel. 'What? Where? By whom?'

Livia's smile did not fade, but she added the sigh of a patient mother with a dim child. 'When we came out of the forest. And before that, in the forest. And before that, at the edge of the forest. And before that, by the farmhands.'

And I saw nothing. Aemilius sank back into himself and nudged the horses forward. He had been so happy to stare at the back of Taurio's cart rather than the open road, but he couldn't help but wonder. *What am I getting myself into? What kind of magnificent, majestic, clandestine...* His thoughts lost all momentum and collapsed on themselves in the face of what he was seeing. Taurio had turned the cart up a slight incline, past a thicket of trees and suddenly they had a clear approach to what had looked at a distance like a part of the hill.

Upon closer inspection, the ridge was, in fact, a man-made timber wall, easily fifteen foot high. The trees looked old and weather-beaten, and the gate seemed much the same. There was nothing of what he imagined a Roman fort to be—no shows of engineering, no crisp lines, no... empire.

Livia seemed to sense his disbelief. 'This valley leads up into the mountains, and it can be held with a small force. Absolute hell to dislodge. Used to be a garrison here, about two hundred years ago. It had been abandoned for a while when we moved in.'

'And is *this* the base of the Legion?' He couldn't keep the shock out of his voice. 'This is *tiny!* You couldn't keep a hundred men here! Is this *it?*'

'Well…' Livia said. He glanced over at her and caught the ghost of a smirk.

Up ahead, Taurio finished a quick exchange with someone out of sight, and the gate swung open.

V

THE FORT

MUCH LIKE THE rest of the Legion, the Fort was not all that it seemed.

Although it might have looked unconvincing a moment ago, driving through it Aemilius noted that the timber gate was made of lumber as thick as a man's body, strapped together with wrist-thick ropes in deep grooves. The outside bore long-weathered marks of blows by big things, sharp things and hard things. *A long time ago someone really went at this*, Aemilius thought as his mind raced to take in everything he could see. *Several times. And got absolutely nowhere*. Looking around, he was starting to see why.

The cart rolled into a deep, oval courtyard that might be big enough to comfortably fit about a thousand men, mostly shaded by the overhanging cliff that rose high enough to make his neck hurt finding the top of it. At their back the wall stretched for about a hundred yards to each side. As the gates swung shut, he could see massive iron reinforcements at its back and sturdy steps leading up to battlements set so that a man of average height could stand comfortably on them and be almost completely covered. *And here we are. It looks old and battered, but this could take a full-on assault from an actual legion, if not two or three. And the forest would mean getting equipment in place to batter down the walls would be a difficult job at best. A fantastic base of operations. Except...*

...there's nobody here. Suddenly wary, Aemilius tried to look in all directions without moving his head... but there was not really anything happening. There was no bustle of activity. There were no soldiers practicing and going through the motions, no runners and rookies doing menial work, no camp, no fire, no laundry. Three buildings were tucked in far under the overhang, backing onto the sheer cliff at the back of the circle. They were nondescript affairs at two stories high, flanked by what could be the front of a big barn oddly tacked onto the wall. On the far left, a squat hut looked like it had been banished to a corner, like a naughty child. He couldn't help but stare at the cliff, rising and rising above them. *Any invaders would have to lower themselves down a drop of about a hundred and fifty feet to get here.* He noticed what looked like a small cave about midway up the cliff face. *Stick a blade out of that, cut the ropes and send in the dogs to tidy up.*

Whoever had opened the gate had melted away out of sight, but a slim woman of medium height and indeterminable age had just appeared in the doorway to the house in the middle. He watched as Taurio jumped off the driver's perch and bowed his head, looking oddly... *afraid?* Having had time to develop a sense for it, Aemilius didn't need to look. He could *feel* Livia's smirk and remembered her words. *They'll do the talking.* But why was Taurio afraid of a random woman in a hut? She looked about half his size and had none of the obvious threat of Rivkah. He watched a quick exchange between the two, followed by the woman putting two fingers in her mouth and whistling a quick, three-note signal. Almost immediately another two women appeared from the shadows of the doorway. *They must have been waiting,* Aemilius thought. *Or maybe she created them by whistling. Yes. Why not? She is probably a magus as well. Or a witch.* He felt his soul trembling gently with the strangeness of it all and stifled a panicked giggle. Then he saw the quick, assured way in which they approached the back of the cart and unloaded Hanno onto a stretcher that seemed to materialise in the air. They had the unmistakeable air of healers who would brook no nonsense, and Aemilius's spirit soared with hope. He had neither seen nor felt Livia get off the seat next to him, so when she appeared out of the corner of his eye, one shoulder in Abrax's armpit and bearing the load of the big man with surprising ease, he was startled. Out of habit he looked the other way, half expecting to see Rivkah having somehow magically appeared to mock him for looking like a stranded fish... but she was limping behind the healers, supported by Taurio. Prasta was busying herself with something in the cart. He was, for the moment, alone.

Jumping off the driver's plank he set to work unhooking the horse from the harness, but he had hardly lifted the horse brush before Prasta turned to him. 'Don't worry about that,' she said. 'It will be sorted.' Aemilius looked around and saw no place to keep horses or anyone to tend to them. *Will it? By whom? How? And where?*

Those questions, and a fair few besides, were on his

lips when an olive-skinned and dark-haired woman in flowing green robes did not so much step as waft out of the building to the left. 'Prasta!' she called, drifting towards the cart. 'You heaven-spirit!'

In the back of the cart, Prasta's head snapped up. 'Salura!' She leapt off the cart and bounded towards the woman, sweeping her up in an embrace. 'You're here!'

'Wouldn't be anywhere else, my sparkling star,' the woman purred. 'Oh, the things you sent me.'

'Wonderful! Did you find the cart?' Prasta exclaimed with delight, the words tumbling out of her.

'Delivered two days ago. I was very worried about you, but she told me you would be fine.'

Prasta only squeezed harder. 'I am *so* glad you got some of it.'

'Oh, we did. I even got in before him.' She nodded towards the squat hut in the corner. 'And I thought that I could feel your hand in every cut. Fantastic work.'

'As well you know, flattery will get you the best bits, old witch,' Prasta said, grinning.

'Hey!' Salura said, punching Prasta's arm in mock outrage. 'But do tell me—who is the fish-boy?'

They are looking at me they are looking at me

He managed to close his mouth, but only just, before Prasta looked over at him. 'Look sharp, boy. You are in the presence of Salura Silver-Fingers, the greatest potion maker the Empire doesn't know about. She has saved *my* life five times, and countless others. If she set up shop in Rome tomorrow, she would be rich by next week.' The woman rolled her eyes at Prasta and answered her compliments with a grimace. 'And this,' Prasta continued, turning towards her, 'is Aemilius of Hispania, the target of our mission.'

Salura looked to the ground for a moment. 'I heard about...'

Prasta nodded quietly.

When the dark-haired woman looked up again, there was a lot less of the sparkling welcome. 'Let's hope he was worth it, then. Shall we? I am sure they are waiting for us.' With that, she turned and started walking towards the building in the middle. The gangly bard nodded for Aemilius to follow.

THE BUILDINGS WERE simple, flat stone things, with small, sturdy doorways. He did not count himself a big man, but he still had to bend down to avoid fairly serious head injuries. Inside, there was immediately a lot more space. *Easy to defend.* He allowed himself a small smile in recognition of this new legionnaire mindset, before uncertainty leapt back at him from the dark corners of the building. *I am about to be presented. Like what?* Lambs and slaughter came to his mind, and he wanted to slap himself. *Come on, Aemilius of Hispania!* He had cracked open a Mormo's head with a jar full of fire. He had bamboozled a cyclops. He had... *what?* The voice in his head snarked at him. *Commanded the animal kingdom?*

Yes! Aemilius argued with himself *...maybe?* And immediately climbed down. *What am I saying? That I am like Abrax and Hanno? And Graxus?* He shuddered, and almost lost track of Prasta and the woman, who had disappeared around a corner. At the back of his mind something complained about dimensions, and how he should have reached the back of the building by now, but he paid it no heed. He only barely noticed the lack of windows and the change in the quality of the light as he chased after Prasta—who was nowhere to be seen. Around the corner, however, were steps curling up and out of sight. Aemilius looked around for any other way they could have gone, and found none, so he followed slowly. He had not, he realised, spent a lot of time imagining what the headquarters of the Legion might be, but this was not how he had pictured it. He'd thought a palace unlikely, but this? This was, he realised, hewn out of the very mountain. Although, as his feet pounded the steps, he noted it had been done extremely precisely. Two circuits and he was standing in a corridor. Looking to his left and his right, he turned—

He didn't see the blade until it was at his throat.

'And who might you be?'

The voice was calm, and curious, and it belonged to a slim woman of medium height, medium build, and as Aemilius held down the squawk in his throat and forced himself to look better, indeterminable age, who had somehow materialised out of the shadows. He thought she might be older than his mother, but he was not willing to bet his life on it. A life, he noted with ice-cold panic, that was very close to being over. He steeled himself and looked at her face. It was... strikingly ordinary, except for the eyes. Blue-grey steel circles that looked far sharper than the dagger, which he was pretty sure could cut a hole in a thought. He found that he struggled to hold her features in his head even as he was looking at her, and somewhere in the back of his mind a headache took hold. The cold and very sharp point of metal at his throat nudged him back to his present situation.

'I—uh—Aemilius,' he blabbered, trying to speak without making his Adam's apple turn into apple slices. 'Prasta,' he managed. 'Following Prasta.'

The woman lowered the knife slowly and made a mildly annoyed noise. 'The next time that lot tidies up after themselves will be the first. Come with me.' With that she turned sharply on her heel and disappeared down the corridor, leaving Aemilius to scramble after her. In his mind he made a count of the times his life had been threatened by monsters versus the time it had been threatened by short women with blades and found himself rather wishing there was a hydra or three somewhere, just to even out the score.

A brisk walk took them to the end of the corridor, and a door exactly like all the others, which swung open silently as she pushed through and ushered Aemilius into a square chamber, about sixty feet to each side. Light streamed in from thumb-sized holes in the ceiling, and candles burned to illuminate the places where they couldn't reach. The middle was dominated by a big, sturdy wooden table, on which was strewn a variety of parchments and maps, rolled out and weighed down by fist-sized bags. He was momentarily relieved to find Prasta, Taurio and Livia sitting to one side, but the looks on their faces immediately crushed that feeling into a fine powder. *They look like my cousins after smashing Father's amphorae.* The stern woman snapped her fingers and pointed at an empty chair next to Livia, and Aemilius's feet and arse obeyed before his mind had time to catch up.

'Found this,' she said levelly. 'Surprised he's still alive.'

'So are we,' Taurio rumbled, immediately wincing at something. Aemilius thought he could see Prasta's hands and elbows, but not her feet. *Add another shin-bruise to Taurio's tally.* The thought was oddly comforting.

The woman looked Taurio over, from head to toe. 'Indeed.' And with that she was gone again. The door swung silently closed behind her.

Aemilius looked at the Legion, who all seemed to be studiously trying not to look at anything. Finally, he broke the silence. 'Who is that?'

Livia held up a finger. *Silence.* She motioned, counting down from five torturously slowly. When her hand went down, she finally spoke. 'That was Cassia.'

Beside her, Taurio and Prasta looked nervous.

'She put a knife to my throat! I nearly died!'

Taurio's eyes went wide, and he turned to say something to Prasta, but unusually no words came out. By his side, the rangy bard grinned. 'You truly are charmed, Aemilius of Hispania. The list of people who have seen Cassia's knives and lived to tell the tale numbers…'

'…one, as far as I know,' Livia said, looking meaningfully at him.

He felt the cold wave of fear sweep through his insides and wondered idly if it knew in which direction it was travelling. *Maybe I'll just keep it and not let it go*, he thought. *Maybe I'll just be terrified all the time.*

'Imagine if you could combine Livia and Rivkah,' Taurio added helpfully, 'but three times as deadly as both combined and give it the heart of a snake.' He glanced at the door again, nervously, as if saying the words had the power to make the tiny woman appear.

'So what we're saying is that if you are actually *alive*…'

'It must mean that she likes you,' Livia finished with a wink. 'Luck is on your side, young Aemilius.'

And with that, he suddenly remembered. 'Where is Hanno? And Abrax? And Rivkah?'

'With the healers.'

'But—' And his brain finally caught up to the staircase, the height of the buildings, the length of the corridor and the size of the room. '*Where?*'

Some of Taurio's worries seemed to fade a tad, and there was a hint of sympathy in his features. 'Oh, I forget. It's your first time. This place is a warren,' he rumbled. 'Took me a week to learn the bits that I needed, and there's way more besides.'

'We were incredibly lucky to find two brothers—magi who had the ability to turn stone to water. There were always caves in the hillside, but they gave their lives to expanding, fortifying and creating this magnificent— and secure—space.' Livia reclined. 'It took ten years, but it has been worth it. There are stores with enough food for a month's siege. A small branch of an underground river has been diverted for drinking water. There are rooms for study, bed space for five hundred soldiers and healing quarters. There is also Flaxus's tower—'

Taurio butted in. 'It was originally a viewing post, but it got taken over by our very own featherhead.'

'Arrow-straight lines, two fingers wide, let in light and air. They are coated with silver,' Livia said with pride, pointing to the round dots of light. 'For reflection.' She looked pointedly at Taurio. 'Can be shuttered in case of an attack.'

'You can't demand that I praise the Roman Empire for the work of Armenian sorcerers,' the big Gaul protested.

'And this room is…?' *I don't need to ask*, he thought. The table. The maps. He'd expected some sort of big seat for the leader, but there was none. Instead, a practical and meticulously neat desk was tucked away in the corner, with the only concession to luxury being a woven blanket twice folded, placed on the chair next to it as a cushion.

'This is where—' Livia began, but then her mouth snapped shut.

A moment later, the door swung open, and Aemilius felt himself needing to work just a little bit harder to catch his breath. The woman they had called Cassia walked in first, but it seemed to take her just the blink of an eye to step to the side and become almost invisible up against the wall.

Command always looks the same.

And the woman who walked in behind her was a commander. She looked less like she had been born and more like a vein of granite had just been polished into human form. Standing at nearly Aemilius's height, she had every feature of Roman nobility—the aquiline nose, the piercing stare, the strong jaw—all of which had somehow been layered with a kindness and gentility that the Roman upper classes were not necessarily known for. He watched as every bit of lethality leached out of the legionnaires, and they all turned to children in her presence. Aemilius found he could not conceive of anyone raising a hand to hurt this woman, and furthermore that he felt compelled to give his life stopping them if they did.

'...and here we are,' the woman said. A benign smile softened her features, and he felt immediately at ease. 'Welcome home. You have delivered, Livia Claudia—as you always do.'

'Thank you, Mater,' Livia muttered to the tabletop.

'I was dismayed to hear of the death of Quintus Aurelius,' she continued, and somehow when *she* said it, Aemilius felt at peace. 'He lived a hard life, longer than most, and died a brave and heroic Roman. He walks with the Gods.'

There was a moment where no one said anything, and Quintus was there with them, in their memory. Mortified, Aemilius wiped away a tear as surreptitiously as he could, dropping his arm a moment before he felt the woman's attention turn to him, like the sun emerging from cloud cover. He felt heat rising in his cheeks.

'Welcome.'

He was sure he knew, or had at any rate at some point in his life heard, some words. None of them came.

Mater smiled at him before she continued, 'I am Mater Populii. And you… are Aemilius. Son of Marcus Livius Sculla, last in the line of the Aemilii.'

'Thank you. Yes. Yes, I am,' he blurted out.

'Good. You can talk,' she said, smiling. 'I expect you will be wanting food, too.'

Aemilius's mind broke into a full panic gallop. *Did I look hungry? Am I supposed to say no? Or yes? Does she mean now?* 'What? No—I mean, don't bother on our behalf, uh—'

'It was not, you will note, a question.' The woman's voice changed, only ever so slightly, but the effect was that of a full and properly chilled bucket of water straight to the face, complete with bucket. Aemilius stopped as if frozen, only just noticing the silent laughter-shake of Taurio's shoulders two seats down by his side. 'Hunger and worry make for bad decisions, and I need to bring order to'—she swept her hand majestically over the table—'this. We will reconvene once you have had food and seen your friends. Make haste but don't rush.' Mater Populii nodded once at Cassia, who snapped her fingers and pointed out the door.

Within moments they were all lined up behind her, like dogs brought to heel. Without further warning Cassia marched off, and they had to step lively to keep up. Caught between Prasta and Livia, Aemilius thought to whisper a question, but they were moving too quickly for him to gather his thoughts. Through a door, down some steps, to the left, another door, up a bit, down a bit, and suddenly—

They turned a corner and a cavernous room opened up in front of them. Long benches stretched out in neat rows ahead, leading towards the back where three separate cook-fires smouldered under a gaping black hole in the ceiling up above.

Here, finally, were people.

Dotted about the big dining hall were small groups—three here, four there, one or two groups of eight—sitting at tables, conducting quiet conversations. Nobody cast a second glance at them, but Aemilius had the odd and uncomfortable feeling that he had been *noticed*. One look he did not miss, though, was the one that passed between Livia and Prasta.

'Where *is* everyone?' the angular bard hissed.

Livia was tight-lipped. 'I knew it was bad, but this...' The words faded into nothing, and Aemilius had just enough sense to realise that Cassia had also disappeared.

'She's gone again! Where—when—' he stuttered.

'Get used to it,' came Livia's clipped reply. 'She's more than half shadow, that one. Comes and goes as she pleases, and those who know how she does it are all dead. But as we have already established—'

'—she likes you,' Prasta finished with a half-smile as she sat down at a table a reasonable distance away from the other groups.

Aemilius registered movement at the far wall, where the pots and kettles were. 'How do we, uh,' he tried. 'The food...?' Taurio and the women gently ignored him, tension and travel draining from their bodies as they made themselves comfortable.

Home.

Safe.

The thought appeared in his head, and a moment later it felt like someone had up-ended a gigantic cooking-pot of molten lead somewhere inside him. He felt the wave of it—the terror of the sudden and unexpected, the horror of realisation and worst of all the constant pressure of fear—drain away, from his head and his heart through his hips and his knees towards and through his heels and his toes, and he felt giddy with it, like he could float away from the chair and the ground and himself, and had it not been for Prasta's surprisingly strong and quick grip he would have done exactly the opposite and fallen off his chair. He felt his face turn a fetching shade of beetroot instantly—but in her eyes he just saw an understanding.

Once upon a time she felt like this, too.

He looked around, at Taurio, Livia and the various groups of calm and quiet people, all of whom were presumably three different kinds of deadly each, sat in a dining hall in a stone chamber deep in a hill in Umbria.

They've all felt like this.

And just when the strangeness of it all threatened to overwhelm him, a figure appeared at his shoulder—an old woman, slight of build, carrying a plank with four bowls of steaming stew which were distributed onto the table with swift hands. The part of his brain that had learned manners only just caught Prasta and Livia respectfully bowing their heads, and so he did the same, feeling like the appetite he was holding back with sheer force of will would have made the Beast of Iaspura look like a little puppy. The woman acknowledged them, just about, produced a basket of bread from somewhere about her person and a moment later she was just a moving shape weaving between the tables, heading back to the pots.

Unable to resist temptation any longer, he looked at his bowl.

The stew looked like the first prince and heir of polished wood and molten gold. Stirred by the movement of landing on the table, knuckle-thick chunks of meat drifted contentedly on swirls of glorious, liquid thickness. The occasional carrot slice bobbed up to the surface, only to sink back down again. The aroma of it rose to his nostrils and immediately threatened to pull him down into it, and under, and woe betide him if he didn't get all of it into his face immediately. As if controlled by the Gods, his hands seized the bowl and brought it to his lips, tipping and swallowing. The void that had been created by the draining of the fear was immediately filled with warmth and love, and when he came up for air all he could do was grunt.

'Yup,' Prasta said, sipping hers with a spoon. 'She does a mean stew, does old Mina.'

Inside his head he was making several honest attempts at conversation, but all that came out was three heavy breaths, followed by another dive into the bowl. Slowly the urgency faded away, and he became able to savour the taste. *The monsters are a definite downside... but the food makes up for it... almost.* Allowing himself to breathe a couple more times, he found that the stew settled him and settled in him, and a question escaped. 'Why is it so bad that there are few people here?'

'Means that everyone is out somewhere, and that they are out for a reason.'

'We told you, didn't we? It's been a busy year,' Prasta added.

'Yes—but not *this* busy.'

'This is true,' Taurio rumbled.

'And where are Hanno? And Abrax? And Rivkah?' He heard the faint note of panic creeping in at the edge of his own voice, and hoped the others didn't.

Livia's expression softened somewhat, from a frown to something that might almost be a smile. 'The healers. We told you. We'll go see them after we finish—not that you've got much left.'

'These were our orders, were they not?' Prasta sounded serious and looked anything but.

'They were. And on occasion, our orders are not entirely disagreeable.'

A part of Aemilius railed against the mirth. *Our friends were crippled, lame and nearly dead! Why are they so happy?* But the core of his being was full of stew, and somewhere within him he also experienced a new and unfamiliar feeling. He found that he trusted Taurio, and Livia and Prasta, trusted them truly, and his worries eased just a little. Soon enough they were done with their stew, mopping up the remains with chunks of freshly made bread, and Aemilius found himself sending intense feelings of love to the ghostly presence of the woman they had called Old Mina.

'All is well,' Taurio proclaimed, slapping his belly. 'Let's go see how the others are doing, shall we?'

Aemilius was not aware of any more attention being

given to them when they stood up than when they sat down, and still there was a niggling feeling of being *watched*. They had been too far away for him to have a good gawp at any of the other diners, but he got the distinct impression that every single one of them would be pretty hard to sneak up on.

Probably why they are still alive.

He had no time to think further upon this, because the others knew where they were going and he didn't. Taurio picked a different exit door to the one they had entered through, walking down a crisply made set of deep steps easily wide enough for more than two people to pass. It was hard to judge how far down they went, but it felt like descending at least two floors of a tenement house. Soft amber stones wedged up into the corners above cast a golden light onto the steps. *Is this magic as well?* he wondered, and then stopped wondering, as his life mostly seemed to consist of things he would have been entirely unable to imagine three weeks ago. *It is light and light is good*, he concluded, and surprisingly a large part of his brain was content with that.

The stairs levelled out into a corridor with doors that looked to be just a little bit wider than average. A heady mix of herbs seemed to linger in the air here, and out of the corner of his eye Aemilius caught Prasta smiling. *This is her domain.* Salura the potion maker could not be far away. However, none of his compatriots seemed to even slow down or consider any of the options. *They all know exactly where they are going all the time,* he realised with a half-sigh. *Maybe one day I will, too.* He did not have too much time to get annoyed about his ignorance, though, as Taurio stopped by a closed door that looked exactly the same as all the others.

'Here?'

'Yes,' Livia said, pushing past him and into a comfortably lit room with a simple bed in the middle. On it lay Abrax, resting. He had been washed and dressed in grey robes that looked worn but well cared for. He raised his head ever so slightly and glanced at them.

'I take it I did not miss the briefing?'

Aemilius noted the smiles all round.

'No,' Prasta said. 'She has most graciously decided to wait until you are up again.'

An officious, broad-shouldered and swing-hipped woman in blue robes bustled into the room. 'You lot,' she muttered in the instantly recognisable tones of someone who has long since consigned themselves to a lifetime of not ever quite being given the time and space to just get on with it. 'Can you please tell this idiot to look after himself?'

'Oh, come now, Ioana!' Abrax protested. 'I am very careful!'

'So you won't be wanting this, then?' the healer shot back, shaking a small leather pouch that sloshed in her hand. Aemilius stifled a laugh. The mighty commander of fire and magus of legend had been reduced to a naughty boy.

'Sorry, Ioana,' he muttered. 'I will be careful.'

'Good! Now sit up and drink.'

The big black man did as he was told, levering himself up slowly. *He looks...* Aemilius hunted for the word, and then it came to him. *Drained.* He thought of the relief, how he'd seen the others relax, and wondered what it must be like for the magi, constantly holding and controlling the connection with the element they understood, constantly on like a torch that never burned out. And just as he was thinking all of these things Abrax tenderly accepted the waterskin from the healer and sipped.

Aemilius became dimly aware that his mouth was moving, as if it was trying to form words, but his brain was not giving them away. It was fully occupied taking things in. He watched as his friend's skin smoothed before his eyes, the spine straightened, and the big man's frame gently *filled*, as if he was a sail catching a fair wind. The sound that came from the fire magus was somewhere between a rumble and a grunt. He rolled his shoulders, closed his eyes and seemed to flex his entire body like a large cat just waking up after a long sleep. When his eyes opened again, Aemilius had to fight the urge to take a step back. He could have sworn there was actual fire there, a white-hot blaze of fury that threatened to immolate the world.

The man who rose had none of the prone man's road-weariness. Instead, he turned to the healer and bowed gracefully. 'Thank you,' he purred.

The healer looked up at him, comprehensively unimpressed. 'You know the cost,' she snapped. 'Look after yourself, please.' As an after-thought, she added, 'You're one of the good ones.' He bowed his head again, silently, and held it there for a good four heartbeats, a pure show of respect. Ioana the healer gave the lot of them a disapproving once-over. 'I suppose you're going to trail me like a group of idiot ducklings to see the little one?'

'Yes, please, matron,' Livia said, every inch the well-mannered noble.

The healer swished around and marched out, nearly hip-checking Aemilius into the wall. He made a mental note to get out of the way faster next time. 'Well—come on, then,' she snapped. And like a group of idiot ducklings they followed in a straight line. As he half-shuffled, half-ran after the healer, Aemilius came to the conclusion that the next movement Ioana the healer wasted would be the first. Every step and swing of the hips radiated effectiveness, and in some dim corner of his mind he was grateful that she wasn't of the fighting persuasion. He skittered along in her wake into another room, this one populated by two waif-like blue-robed creatures that reached only just past his shoulders. *Children? In here?* But he couldn't quite get a fix on either of them for long enough to determine whether they were young, smooth-skinned or entirely in or of this world. The short sisters were in constant motion, checking this, adjusting that and tending to the wizened form laying on the bed before them.

Maybe it was the time that had passed, or the dangers he had faced, but until now Aemilius had managed to push away the very real threat to Hanno's life. The still, silent helplessness of his friend hit him like a brick to the face, and his knees buckled. He reached out to steady himself, hoping to catch onto something, and somehow, silently, Taurio's thick arm was in the right place at the right time, and he caught his balance just in time to see the healer whirl and face them. 'If you leave it this long again,' Ioana snarled, 'I will personally grab every one of you by the bits that hurt the most, drag you up before Mater and *demand* that your entrails be given over to Egenny for making *weather reports*.' Her glare could have cut a hole in the stone wall behind them. 'And I will give up my own precious knitting time to make sure you stay alive while he does it, and I will ask him to be *very* thorough.' None of the legionnaires moved a muscle. 'Understood?' A low, swamp-reed whisper of a 'yes' passed through the assembled group. 'Good. Now stand still and shut up.' Satisfied that the message had gotten across, she immediately dismissed them with an about-turn and approached Hanno.

At first, the sound just sort of *appeared* to Aemilius, and he couldn't figure out what it was, or where it came from. It took him another moment to realise that it was singing, and yet another to comprehend the source. Moving like silk in the wind, the healer had taken three quick steps towards the old man, and was standing by the side of his bed, singing softly in a language he could not recognise. However, he did not need to know the words to understand the meaning. It was the song of healing, the note of soothing, the sound of life given to those who needed it. Tenderly, she raised a flask to his lips and with utmost precision dripped a single drop onto his lips.

Hanno twitched.

Another drop, and a tremor passed through the body under the sheets.

The sounds of Ioana's song swathed them all, embraced them, held them close and warmed them, and Aemilius felt the tears well in his eyes.

Ioana leaned over Hanno, and whispered something to him, and got a feeble groan in return. Tipping the flask ever so gently onto the old man's cracked lips, she dripped another drop—and Aemilius's heart leapt when he saw a shrivelled tongue snake out and dab at the liquid. Even in the closed room, with an uncomfortable amount of rock sitting above his head, he thought he could feel a draught. *Or maybe it's magic in the air.* He glanced quickly at Abrax and thought he could see something on the magus's face—a recognition? But then Ioana was holding the flask to Hanno's face, and three drops went in his mouth, and it was like watching rain on parched ground. The grey, shrivelled lips seemed to change colour before his eyes, vitality spreading through the old man's face, driving age away before it. The water-magus's mouth was open enough for Aemilius to see that his friend's teeth were gritted. 'Is he—?'

'If you're too far gone it hurts like a scorpion's kiss,' Abrax whispered. 'The whole body—'

Without taking her eyes from Hanno for a second, Ioana's arm shot out, flat palm towards them, and Aemilius resolved to hold off on breathing for a while. Before him, waves of life were flowing through the little magus, his limbs going from being those of an old man to something resembling the late stages of middle age, muscle returning and blood pumping faster, harder, bringing strength and power. *An interesting difference. Abrax grew hotter and stronger, but Hanno seems to be getting… deeper.* Something about the water-magus's face was oddly still, but in a terrifying way, like the sea. There was something else about the process, but it was hard to pinpoint…

Breathe

Breathing is good

Breathe now

The words appeared inside his head like a whisper, and he realised that one of the spectral creatures was standing by his elbow. He felt looked at, and commanded, and he remembered that he had indeed not breathed in for a while. A gasp of air was quickly followed by a rush of blood to the face as he realised that more people were looking at him than he was comfortable with. He didn't dare look the scary healer's way. 'Sorry,' he wheezed. 'Forgot.'

'Push here.' Ioana was moving her hands around Hanno's body methodically, much like a farmer would, muttering commands at him which were immediately followed by the tiny man slowly, and carefully, doing exactly what he was told. 'Now pull.' She glanced at Aemilius. 'Your newest one is… interesting,' she said, in a tone that suggested she was quite surprised that he had survived this far. 'What does he contribute to the cause?'

There was a brief silence as none of the legionnaires rushed to explain what it was exactly that Aemilius did for them. 'He is… entertaining?' Taurio offered finally.

'From a solid Roman family,' Livia added, ignoring Ioana's scoff.

'And I don't think we've seen his full potential.' Aemilius could feel Abrax's eyes on him.

'Let's hope he remembers to breathe for long enough to get there.' She turned to Hanno. 'You, my friend,' she said gently, 'are a lucky little thing. I almost had to get my best coat on and go to Hades to fetch you.'

Hanno—a younger, fresher Hanno, wrinkle-free with a full head of sumptuous black curls, looking like he could barely contain his energy—beamed at her. 'And if you had come for me, I would have gone with you. You are, as always, a brook in spring.'

'Cold, strong and tasty, and likely to crack your ankle if you put a foot wrong?' Ioana shot back.

'Exactly!' Hanno's smile looked like it could split his head in two and his teeth shone in the gloom. He vaulted off the table and scanned the group. 'Oh, my friends! How I've missed you. Thank you for not just putting me in a hole.'

'We could hardly do that,' Livia said. 'Taurio has been trying to keep up the nonsense while you were out, but it's not the same.'

'The water is a puddle in the morning but sometimes it flows upstream unless you are a fish,' Taurio added.

Hanno blew out through pursed lips. 'You have suffered, my friends. You have suffered. But fear not! Hanno is here.' His eyes widened, and a shock of worry squeezed his brow. 'Where is our hissing hell-cat? Is she—'

'Next on the list,' Ioana said, turning towards the door. She snapped her fingers. 'Girls, you're coming with me for this one.' Wordlessly, the short sisters fell in behind her. Learning from experience, Aemilius had already taken a couple of steps back when she barged through the group and towards the door, noting with amusement that despite his tree-trunk frame, Abrax also had to hustle to get out of the way.

Moments later they were back in the corridor, half-running to keep up.

Rivkah's room was almost three times the size of Abrax and Hanno's, lined with bars, hooks with ropes through them, steps and sacks of different sizes. Something about it filled Aemilius with unease. 'There you are, you old hag. Right. Let's get this done.' She was reclining on a bench, propped up on her elbows. The short sisters flowed past the big healer to either side of the girl, and for a fleeting moment Aemilius thought he saw fear in her eyes, quickly replaced with fury. 'You two can get right up a horse's arse,' she growled, followed by a string of swears that melted into one another as the creatures grabbed an arm each and eased her back onto the bench. Wasting no time, Ioana had marched over to a side table with slim glass tubes full almost to the brim with water. She quickly removed a stopper. Light glinted on a drop of liquid on the point of a long, thin needle. Rivkah saw it too, because she thrashed on the bed—or tried to. Despite her best efforts, the short sisters did not budge. She barked something out in Hebrew. Ioana snapped something equally incomprehensible back at her—and a torrent of abuse was unleashed. Through the shouting back and forth, with neither woman backing away an inch, Aemilius watched transfixed as Ioana stepped up to Rivkah's bench, rolled up the material around her leg with a deft hand which was then clamped down onto her knee—and then the needle went into the purplish, two-palm-sized welt on the girl's thigh. As the leg spasmed, Rivkah screamed.

'Hold still, you little bitch!' Ioana screamed back at her.

'*I'm trying!*' Breathing heavily, her eyes squeezed shut and her jaw worked furiously. The spasming leg slowed down, then fell still. The roar started somewhere in the back of her throat, built up in her mouth and came out, growing in volume until suddenly it fell off, and as it did, so did she, collapsing back onto the bench. As one, the short sisters stepped back. After a moment, so did Ioana.

'You were lucky.'

'And don't I fucking feel like it,' Rivkah growled. A short sister wafted in silently, holding a cold compress, and gently mopped her face. The girl let her. 'How long?' she sighed.

'A day or two. It will hurt like a bastard. Test it slowly and build up strength and movement.' Ioana glared at the girl. '*Slowly*. Or I'll use the saw next time.'

'Thank you.' There was something in Rivkah's voice that Aemilius had only heard at the table of the Lord and Lady. *These are the people who care for her,* he thought, and a wave of feeling washed over him that he could not identify. He watched her swivel to a sitting position, legs dangling over the edge of the bench, take a breath and then push off, landing on both feet. 'Fuck,' she hissed, then stood up straight. She glanced at Ioana and got a raised eyebrow for it. 'Yes,' she muttered. 'Much better. But you won't have to tell me again. Slowly.' Then, more quietly, 'Thank you.'

The healer nodded, and there was a hint of a smile on her lips. 'Did you at least get him?'

'No,' Rivkah said, feigning sadness. 'I had to get out of the way as about a hundred wolves ripped his face off.'

'Good,' the healer said, as if she had been presented with an acceptable price for a sack of potatoes. Then it was almost as if she noticed the five other legionnaires, standing in an awkward bundle at the door. 'What are you still doing here? Mater's chambers. Right now.' And with that she turned her back on them and went to tidying her desk, and it was as if they'd ceased to exist.

VI

THE FORT

IT TOOK THEM twenty steps of walking in silence before Taurio spoke. 'She is a formidable woman,' he rumbled.

'The absolute best. An artist.' Prasta's voice was a whisper of hushed reverence.

'And a fucking cow,' Rivkah added with affection. 'I think she likes the pain, you know.'

'Oh, the river flows strong in that one,' Hanno chirped.

Abrax was already two yards ahead of them, his stride seeming to lengthen with every step. 'Come on,' he snapped. 'No hanging about.'

'Slow down, old man! Some of us have not had a sip of the good stuff,' Livia huffed behind him.

'Speaking of that,' Aemilius ventured as the group turned left and right, seeking every stairway up they could find. 'What was in the flasks?'

'Prasta?' Livia suggested.

'One of the reasons that the Legion has set up base here is that there was a rumour that these hills contained a tiny little trickle of the Fountain of Youth.'

'Oh, yes. I see,' Aemilius shot back. 'And Romulus sits by it and offers honey cakes? Try again. Was it some kind of magical medicine?'

'Yes,' Prasta said patiently. 'I said. Drops from the Fountain of Youth.'

Aemilius checked for the now-familiar and poorly hidden smirks when they were having him on, and there were none. Everyone was just marching, and there was no sign of dissembling.

'She's not lying.' The voice at his ear made him jump half out of his skin. From *somewhere* Cassia had melted into their group at pace and was now next to him and definitely within stabbing range. What was worse was that she clearly knew that she had scared him nearly shitless, and the twinkle in her eyes showed it. 'The Fountain is pesky, though. It only yields three drops a day. We gather them—*very* carefully—and store them.'

'We still don't know everything the water does,' Prasta continued. 'But it rolls back years, heals wounds almost instantly and gives a big boost of vitality. However… there is a snag. It always takes more of it to get the same results as last time.'

'So there comes a point where it is not worth the cost to revive someone, even the old man up front, no matter how important he is,' Livia joined in. 'Choosing where and when to use it is Mater's job. She decides who lives and who dies. It's pretty much all we have that they don't.'

'I wouldn't say that,' Taurio rumbled up front. 'It's only little and a bit hoppy at the moment, but we do have one monster…'

'Shut up, you fat sack, or I'll break my promise to Ioana and kick you with my good leg.'

'We figure their advantage is that they are gigantic and horrible and definitely don't play by the rules,' Cassia said. 'So it's only fair if we cheat a bit, too.'

This from a woman who probably hasn't been in a fair fight her entire life. Aemilius's mind boggled. *The Fountain of Youth*. This was an affront to reality that went a little bit further than the other infractions. He tried to think of sensible questions to ask, but it was easier to just accept that he was being marched along a corridor inside a mountain, beautifully crafted by two magi who had taken days and months off their lives to create a base for a secret monster-fighting army that was kept alive by magic juice. He closed his eyes and muttered an incantation to Mamercus, the founder of the Aemilii. *If you're there, old man—can you make any of this make sense?* He thought a bit, then tried again. *Mamercus—could you take the sense that this makes… and connect it to reality?* His ancestor might not have been paying attention, but the Gods must have been listening, because reality arrived in the shape of the door to Mater Populii's chamber. Without asking, Cassia ghosted to the front, opened it and swept through. The big table had been cleared of scrolls, save a grand, ornate map painted on vellum. *An awful lot of blue,* Aemilius thought. Memories of the Cetus below came back to him, and he shuddered. Hanno, he noted out of the corner of his eye, did not.

Standing at the head of the table, looking over it and at them, Mater smiled. 'On our feet,' she said, smiling. 'But wanting a bit more stew and sleep before we go, I wager.' *She is their leader. They are scared of her.* Aemilius forced himself to remember this, because if he didn't, he would just see a kindly aunt at a country farm, complete with apron and bread baking in the oven. The legionnaires made his task easier by all bowing their heads in unison. 'Now. Let us begin by remembering a fallen friend.' The silence seemed to spread from her and sweep all the world's concerns before it, out of the chamber and away, and behind it came a quiet space, and Aemilius could have sworn he felt Quintus walk past him. Somewhere in his mind he heard and felt Furibunda's cry when she knew, and he blinked and focused on remembering to breathe.

Mater Populii looked solemn and serious. 'He was a cranky old bastard.'

'He was,' Livia intoned. 'But we loved him.'

The quiet passed, somehow, and with it the memory of Quintus.

'I hope he is in Hades, kicking the shit out of Felix every other day.'

Mater offered a benign smile to Rivkah. 'Oh, he'd have to wait a while for it to build back up, my dear.'

Cassia grinned like a fox. 'He did not enjoy his last visit here.'

'Good. I wish to offer—' Abrax began.

'If you are about to try to apologise for not coming to me first…' Mater cut him off, and the twinkle in her eye suggested she knew exactly what Abrax had been going to say, and that this would be unwise. 'You are here now, all of you, and it is high time that you tell me everything. What has happened since you were given your mission? Spare no detail.'

And so, they told her. Of the flock of harpies and the three hydras. None of them wanted to, but then it was time to talk about Zeno, the one-eyed giant in the cave, and the demise of Quintus. They raised a glass in silence. When the cyclops's death was recounted, Cassia gave Abrax a nod of approval, but it was not enough to quieten Aemilius's burning shame. *It was my fault*. He just couldn't shake the thought.

Turning talk to the Mormo in Hispalis, Hanno's battle with Cetus and the chase through Alexandria felt like a relief. Livia 'accidentally forgot to mention' the clash with Caius Africanus and gave a glare that was nothing short of imperious when Cassia prodded at some missing details in the Alexandrian timeline and mentioned some very specific rumours. The showdown with Donato in the cave under the temple was meticulously recounted, with Mater asking short and pointed questions that pulled out details Aemilius had thoroughly forgotten. Their path through and escape from Sicilia warranted a raised eyebrow, as did Aemilius's adventures in wolf care. Somehow, while they were talking, someone had managed to enter the room with a tray of cups and a flagon of cool, watered wine, accompanied by a bowl full of roasted meats sitting on crushed chickpeas and a stack of flatbreads to go with it.

'Tell me more about this rune,' Mater commanded.

'I'm afraid I can't,' Livia said. 'It was too far away, and then Aemilius's silver spinner smashed it.'

'Oh, turd!' Eyes boggling, Aemilius became aware that not only had he said this out loud, but that the Hidden Legion's commander had not necessarily expected his input and was about to say something in response. 'I—uh,' he bumbled, as he stood up clumsily, grabbing the table to keep from knocking it over, all the while trying to ignore the voice in his head screaming that he was a dolt and about as thick as two planks. 'I—I've got something. In the cart.' Bumbling past the surprised legionnaires, he caught his foot on a chair leg and nearly fell on Cassia, who was there and then she wasn't, catching him by the elbow and half-pushing him out of the room.

'Do you know where you're going, chicken?'

'Yes,' he blurted out over his shoulder, turning to run down the corridor and begging his brain to bring up some—any—of the details he had been observing since they got here. *Hall, turn it around in your head, left—no, other left—steps, down, to the left—around the corner—there! Daylight!* He burst out, scanning for the cart in the small courtyard—*there!* He sprinted over, leapt up into the coach seat and found his bag, stashed safely. Grabbing it, he took care not to catch his foot again, as he didn't particularly want to come running back up with a bloody nose. Sprinting for all he was worth he barged back in, around the corner, up the steps and to Mater's chamber, bursting in. 'Here,' he said breathlessly to a rather bemused audience.

'And what might this be?' Mater asked kindly.

He emptied the bag out onto the table, and realised what he had done a moment later, and then Abrax fainted and everything, it seemed, happened at once.

Livia caught the big magus around the chest as he slumped, slowing him down enough for Taurio to be able to reach and support them, at the cost of her losing her balance and falling to the floor. The rune necklaces skittered onto the table and Aemilius could swear that he heard them hiss. The woman at the head of the table snapped both wrists out and up, fingers splayed, and spat out a quick five words he didn't understand. A gently shimmering shield appeared over the black and purple tokens, and Aemilius got an immediate and pressing wish to make sure he stood very, very still and did not move his hands at all. 'I,' he gulped, breathing carefully and speaking slowly, 'would like to apologise for my actions. I got flustered and didn't think about how he might react, and I meant no malice and please don't kill me.' The last few words were very carefully directed down towards the point of the knife currently sitting just below his jawbone and exerting an uncomfortable amount of pressure on his skin, pointing upwards. He thought he could feel a drop of blood oozing out.

On the other end of the blade Cassia scowled at him, then glanced at Mater Populii. Whatever she had looked like a moment ago had vanished, to be replaced again with kindly aunt. *They are afraid of her for a reason.* She nodded once, and the blade vanished as quickly as it had materialised. Aemilius deflated onto a bench, studied the intricacies of the flagstones and cursed himself for not stopping to *think*. Of course this had been a bad idea. There had been no rush. No rush! And what had he done? Dumped a lot of hostile, unknown magical items right in the lap of the commander of the Hidden Legion. He swore silently and passionately at himself, took a deep breath, gritted his teeth and decided—*no running, no flustering, no talking. I need to take my punishment like a man. Right. Get it over with*—then looked up to find that he was being comprehensively ignored. Abrax had come back round, Livia had recovered her dignity, and they were all gathered around the shimmering silver circle on the table.

'Better or worse?' The wiry old assassin had materialised at Mater Populii's side.

'Worse.' She looked with sympathy at Abrax. 'I can understand why these gave you a rotten headache, my friend. They are carved with anger and spite, and they bear the stench of death. We have been encountering examples like this recently, but these are superior in craftsmanship.' Under the silver shield, the rune marks seemed to snarl in reply.

'What do they do, exactly?' Woven into the horror in Prasta's voice was more than a bit of curiosity.

Mater Populii kept her eyes trained on the black disks, as if they were dangerous animals in a cage. 'They are wards, of a sort. The ones we have found until now just block the fire. Some of them protect against blades. These ones, though…' She narrowed her eyes and muttered something under her breath. One of the amulets hissed like a boiling pot, vibrated and fizzed. Mater exhaled through pursed lips. 'You were lucky, my friend. We looked at the runes on the collar of the wolf, and they simply deaden the fire. This one'—she pointed an elegant finger at the rune closest to her —'absorbs and charges. These seem to—' She stroked the air gently, formed an invisible ball between thumb and forefinger, and flicked it through the shield. Moments later, she winced. 'Yes. The power is magnified.'

'So, if Abrax had pushed through and fried the dog handlers or the one-eyed shit-sack before…?'

'You would have been bringing him home in a bag, Daughter of Abraham.' Mater stared into the shimmering light, as if the power of her gaze could wrench the truth from evil. 'A small one,' she added. 'A purse, possibly. Sit down.' As one, the legionnaires did as they were told. She turned to Aemilius. *So that's why we keep our hearts in our ribcages*, he thought. *Because it feels far too big in my throat.* 'Thank you.' *Wh—what?* 'You showed presence of mind, stripping these from the bodies. This will be an invaluable aid in figuring out where to go and what to do. We will send them up to the study and use the knowledge to hunt down our enemies.'

'Uh, happy to help,' he stuttered, completely avoiding looking towards where Abrax sat, ashen faced.

'But apart from that bastard Donato we don't know who they are!' Taurio snarled.

'Oh, but we do,' Cassia spat.

'All in its time, my dear. All in its time.'

'With the greatest respect,' Livia offered, all silk and honey, 'I feel like perhaps the time might be now?'

For the first time since he'd seen her, for a blink of an eye Mater looked mildly annoyed. 'I would *like* to decide where and when to use my information—' She glanced at Livia, and Aemilius felt a surge of pride that his friend showed deference, but no sign of surrender. 'But as you will be risking life and limb, I suppose it is only fair that you know what you are going up against.'

'Their leader, Donato, suggested there might be—' Prasta began, but an imperious raise of the hand from Mater stopped her.

'Donato is not their leader.'

The revelation fell like a boulder at their feet.

'Always another bloody monster,' Taurio muttered. Sitting next to him, Rivkah swore in Hebrew.

'There are, as far as we can gather, three of them. Donato is indeed one. He goes by many names, depending on where he is stirring up trouble. For a long time, he was responsible for attacks on Roman garrisons in Lusitania and Baetica. We knew of him, but he was not our problem. And then, perhaps five years ago, he vanished. And now he's back.'

'Where did he spend his time?'

'We don't know,' Cassia growled, suggesting she took this more than a little bit personally.

'We do not know yet where he went,' Mater took over, 'but we know that he was strong, and smart, and determined, and we can clearly see he has learned some new skills. I do hope that these'—she pointed to the runes—'will offer some wisdom.' She cocked her head to the side, hearing something no one else could. 'And on the subject…'

There was a silence that lasted for a few moments, and then a faint sound—voices, echoing off walls somewhere. They were drawing nearer, and very quickly getting louder. It was clear that an argument was happening, and closing in.

The door flew open, and two… creatures burst in.

It took Aemilius a moment to gather the information his senses were offering.

The new arrivals were human, or thereabouts. One towered over the other by about a head and a half, but the shorter one looked like they weighed twice as much. The lanky creature was wrapped in what looked like at least three blue-grey and layered capes, all scratched and covered in small holes. Big, dark and sunken eyes seemed to dart this way and that as the head swivelled to take in the room, balanced precariously on a body that seemed to be held together entirely by nervous energy. Somewhere around the tall one's elbow stood the short one—a cube of a man with a thick neck, thick arms, thick legs and thick fingers. Wearing a sleeveless leather jerkin over brown leggings and liberally stained in various shades of what might be blood or a variety of other fluids, he looked like he had been created by smashing together several different types of livestock.

And they seemed to pay present company no mind.

'...and *I'm* saying that your blind guesses are worth roughly your weight in bird-shit! You have no idea what's going on,' the short one snapped.

'Whereas *you* have no appreciation for *anything*, and you smell like the inside of a dog's stomach, and that is after you've cleaned up. Did *you* know we were going to be summoned?' the tall one squawked.

'Of *course* I did! I cleaned up, didn't I?'

The tall one looked down on the short one and made a sound somewhere between a snort, a cough and a caw. 'Paha! And don't you look fantastic? Bow down to the Prince of Tripe!'

The short one pouted. 'No fair,' he sulked. 'You *know* I haven't had a decent piece of tripe for ages.'

'Which is why I demand that *my* advice be heeded!'

'Well, you can demand what you like when we get there!'

Mater Populii cleared her throat gently.

The tall one blinked, pulled back and shook his head as if to dodge a fly.

'See what you've done, you oaf? You've embarrassed us.'

'You once spent an entire week designing special equipment to sift, separate and classify heron shit. I am not the embarrassment here.'

The tall one coughed nervously, then affected a ludicrously deep bow. 'Salve, Mater Populii. Your humble servant descends to serve the needs of the Legion, as—'

'Yes, yes, my dear Flaxus,' the woman said, waving away the rest of the salutation. At the sight of the lanky creature's crestfallen face, she added, 'I'll hear the rest of it later.' She turned to the shorter one. 'Well met, Egenny,' and received a curt nod.

'Right, you two,' Cassia snapped. 'What have you seen?'

'The swifts are uneasy. I have seen a flock of sparrows attack an eagle, and in the east the crested lark is moving far too early and way too far.'

'Ares speaks through the bull's entrails, and says thunder is rising in the north.'

'East!' Flaxus squawked. 'Hellas is trouble!'

'North!' Egenny snarled. 'Your flimsy feather-shitters—'

'Enough,' Cassia said, surprisingly kindly. 'Or I'll slice your groins open as you sleep.' This had an immediate effect, leaving Flaxus and Egenny glaring at each other, but mercifully silent. She turned to Mater. 'They might never agree, but they might both sometimes see different bits of the same picture. I have had word from some of my friends in low places that suggest they might have heard stirring in the east, and messages from the north as well. Nothing definite,' she added, 'but... suspicious.'

'Anything about our quarry?'

'Little.' Cassia looked annoyed. 'Suspiciously little.'

Aemilius looked around at the other legionnaires and found a little bit of pleasure in the fact that for once they all, in their studiously cool and dangerous ways, looked exactly as clueless as he did.

'Very well.' The shades of friendly country aunt seemed to just fade away, and Mater was once again the indisputable commander. 'You.' The two augurs snapped to attention. 'Dismissed.' As one, they shuffled out of the room. As the door closed, the legionnaires could hear the argument starting up again and fading away, along with the sounds of sandals on stone.

There was a pause in Mater Populii's chambers as the legionnaires recovered.

'I think maybe staring at birds and entrails all day makes you a bit strange in the head,' Rivkah said thoughtfully.

Taurio shrugged. 'Aren't we all a bit strange in the head? You carve up monsters for a living.' The young girl shrugged, as if to say *fair enough*.

'So,' Livia said, all business. 'Do we go to Graecia or vaguely to the north?'

'Neither.' Mater's look was calculating. 'Taurio, Prasta.'

'Yes, ma'am,' both mumbled.

'Go with Cassia. I need you to fetch me something.' Glances were traded among the legionnaires, but no one spoke as the big Gaul and the skinny Celt rose to move over to the door, where Cassia was already standing. *I wonder if she knows what Mater is about to say before it happens,* Aemilius wondered, and thought it likely. 'Send them down,' Mater said, receiving a curt nod in return. When the door closed, the old woman turned to them. 'Lucan is taking his team to Graecia, and Athalaric is taking the Pack to the southernmost part of Germania. No.' She paused for a moment. 'I have a different job for you, a little bit... closer to home.' Aemilius inched towards the relative safety of Abrax and Livia as Mater moved to a corner of the room that contained a tall box full of scrolls. Fingers moving quickly, she found what she was after and whipped out two of them, putting one down on a stool and spreading the other on the table, weighing it down with small pouches. It was a detailed map of Italia, sparkling with radiant blues and greens, gold thread marking the roads. Once she had the map laid out like she wanted, she motioned for them to gather round. 'I appreciate that you have been travelling far and wide for a long time, so it is best I ask. You are all aware that Tiberius has retreated to Capri, leaving Sejanus in charge. There are patrols in strange places, unease and unrest.' Livia and Abrax nodded, as did Hanno. Rivkah looked bored. 'But have you heard the name of Marcus Sulpicius?'

Livia frowned. 'Brother of Gaius the Grub? Ambitious little twerp, if memory serves.'

'There is truth in that.' Mater smiled. 'He has the ear of Sejanus and wields considerable power. Lately he has been given more responsibility in military logistics.'

'Even the most boring pebble can redirect a river,' Hanno chimed in.

'Correct. And this pebble directs quite a lot of river. He has retreated to his villa near Lavinium for two weeks. Cassia has heard the merest whisper of a rumour that some people have been asking questions, so she wants to send a team to make sure nothing happens.'

'Like what? He gets the wrong delivery of wine?' Rivkah huffed.

'The wrong delivery of wine can have quite an effect.' Mater smiled. 'In fact, I seem to remember a whole arm of the Minucii coming to an undignified and noisy end because someone'—the glance to where Cassia had stood was fleeting, but Aemilius caught it—'might have had something to do with a carefully selected amphora.'

'Was this when they were having some of their notorious parties?' Livia made a face like she had just smelled something. 'There were all kinds of stories. Some of them were... disturbing.'

'Perhaps.' Mater's mask had slid back on, and she was inscrutable. 'A tragic event, of course. But some might argue that they got what they deserved.' Livia raised one polite eyebrow, but did not challenge the statement. 'We do not yet know exactly what we are up against, but we do know that they have funds—funds that they have obtained through a variety of means. You are to go to the villa of Marcus Sulpicius, infiltrate and observe. We suspect that someone—possibly Donato's man— might be trying to weasel his way into either his graces or his coffers, and we want to make sure that we can keep both as closed as possible. If someone tries to turn his head, I want to know. As it happens, he has family that moved to Hispania Ulterior a long time ago. Recently, his cousin Martia has initiated correspondence, and has been invited to stay at the villa.'

'But what if Martia turns up?' Aemilius blurted out.

Mater smiled. 'If she does, I will be very surprised.'

'Martia doesn't exist,' Rivkah sighed. Beside her, Livia nodded wearily. *Another role to play.*

'And the letters…?'

'Couriers, most likely delivering straight back to Cassia. She loves messing with people.' Rivkah looked almost bored. 'I told you. They're dead sneaky.'

The commander of the Hidden Legion looked best pleased at Rivkah's judgment. 'We are, when we need to be.' She gave them the once-over. 'As evidenced in Hispalis, you still know how to carry yourself in polite company, but that was a rather more provincial situation. For this you'll need a little… reinforcement.' Looking towards the door, the tone of her voice changed to one of command. 'Come in.'

The door swung open, and two children entered. The boy was half a hand taller than the girl, but they looked every inch the older brother and younger sister.

They were perhaps eight, perhaps nine, perhaps ten. Immaculately dressed in expensively simple tunics, they were impeccably groomed, exquisitely mannered, perfect examples of well-bred and well-fed children of the very highest rank.

Aemilius hated them instantly.

Behind them a shadow of a man stepped into the room. He was slim of build but moved with quiet assurance, brown eyes scanning his surroundings quickly. Two steps in he came to a halt, stood perfectly still and somehow seemed to meld into the background, to the point that it started to hurt Aemilius's eyes to keep focus on him.

'I present to you: Flavius and Serena.' The children bowed in unison. The effect was unsettling.

'I am guessing they are my children, desperate to see Uncle Marcus?' Livia said, almost wearily.

Mater nodded, with something close to a smirk, and raised an eyebrow at Flavius.

'Caught picking pockets at five. Stood to lose at least a hand.'

'I was a window-monkey for a group of burglars,' Serena added. 'They used to throw me up on balconies. Would not have made my seventh summer.'

'Cassia... eased them out of a bit of trouble,' Mater continued. 'We have spent the last couple of years turning them into quite the convincing little nobles. But Cassia has also taught them... other skills.'

Aemilius caught a glance from Rivkah that contained about seven different swearwords in it.

'And...?' Livia nodded towards the spectre by the door.

'Carrick.' There was an almost imperceptible nod. 'He is your groom and coachman, porter and general hired hand. There is now significantly less chance that you will get taken by surprise.'

'By what?' Aemilius blurted out.

'By *anything*.'

'Fine,' Livia said in a tone which suggested gently that she felt anything but. 'But if I am to go mixing with the highest of the high, I will need—'

'Already taken care of.'

'Because I do not want to go into Rome—'

'You will go and see Brachus,' Mater interrupted again. 'We need to know, and he is our best chance at getting you inside. You will find he has been instructed very specifically to source everything you need. And I mean *everything*.' She inspected them again. 'So. Is your mission clear?'

'Yes,' Abrax replied crisply. 'We will endeavour to report back as swiftly as we can.' By his side, Livia looked down at the floor.

'Very good. Go, and may Vesta be with you.' She bowed her head once, smoothly.

Dismissed.

The effect was immediate. The legion rose to its feet—Abrax, Livia, Rivkah and Hanno all made for the door, with Aemilius, Flavius and Serena in tow. Carrick followed behind, and even though he was watching the slim man close the door, Aemilius could not hear it make a sound. They walked along the corridor, following Abrax and Livia down some steps and around yet another corner. Daylight crept towards them and mixed with the soft, magical glow of the discreetly mounted orbs, and before long they were standing in the courtyard.

'We'll need four mounts and a cart.'

Responding to Abrax's command, Rivkah quickened her pace. 'Froggy—you're with me.'

'As sure as sun follows rain follows cloud, the sea is never far from the river.'

Rivkah shook her head. 'I can't believe I missed your bullshit.'

'Hungry and thirsty ground will happily take some bullshit,' Hanno replied, grinning.

'Oh, shut up.' Rivkah's smile suggested that, unusually, Hanno's life was not in direct danger if he didn't do what she said. Aemilius watched them move to the left—and the feeling hit him. It was a warm, big feeling, an enveloping hug, a familiarity, a closeness—and then, suddenly, a sound, and he was running towards an unassuming building, hardly a building, a building front that seemed to have been tacked onto the hillside, with big, open double doors revealing half-lit stables that stretched on uncomfortably far, much further than the exterior of the house, and he ran and he knew that she was in there and then he saw her.

Furibunda!

The mare greeted him with a soft whinny and a snort, as if to say, '*and what took you so long?*' She stood at the edge of her stall, craning her head out to get close to him. When he was near enough, she nuzzled his hand once. 'Oh, I've missed you, too,' Aemilius muttered to his horse—*his* horse—and heard himself say it and knew that it was true. He was enveloped in the smell of her, and the warmth of her, and he felt like he could see himself with her eyes. Something about the shadows... He became aware that he was not alone and turned around to face the figure leaning against the opposite stalls, almost embarrassed. He had never had a chance to play games with the girls, but imagined he must have looked like a boy meeting his girlfriend. However, there was neither judgment nor scorn in Carrick's expression.

'Smart horse.'

'Uh… hah. Yeah. I guess,' Aemilius burbled. 'She's clever. Hah.'

'Saw me put down an apple.' The slim man gestured to a stool by the door, tucked out of sight. He smiled and looked at Furibunda like one would an old friend. 'Stole it.'

In the half-light Aemilius had to squint to make out the man's features. *Is he joking? Or mad? Or both?* When no answer was forthcoming, he searched for words and finally found a single one. 'How?'

'Bolt.'

As if on command, the mare gently head-nudged him out of the way, stretched, angled… and gently, ever so gently, put her teeth to the bolt on her stable door, sliding it out of the catch. He stared at her, and it hit him. *She is grinning.*

'Smart horse.' Carrick nodded once. 'Time to go.' Having said all that needed to be said, he turned and walked out without waiting for an answer.

As the initial shock of reconnecting with his horse faded into happiness, Aemilius watched the scout go and took in his surroundings. The stables were lit with the same hard-to-place orb lights, and if he looked carefully, he could spot where the building ended and the mountain began. The weight of it threatened to overwhelm him, as did the number of horses in the space. Suddenly the smell and the snort and stamp of it all became a lot to handle. Almost as if she could sense it, Furibunda nuzzled him again, her big head warm and comforting, pushing him towards the doorway. 'Come on then, girl,' he muttered. 'Let's saddle you up.' He realised that no one had decided who would be riding—and a moment later he realised that he didn't care. He would saddle up his horse, and he would ride, and there would be no discussion on this.

It did not take them long to be prepared and ready. A cart had been mostly prepared for them, with rations for the journey. Hanno, Flavius and Serena were seated comfortably in the back. Carrick had the reins. *It looks like the bloody thing has been built around him*, Aemilius thought. A moment later, another thought sidled in behind it. *Everything does.* He looked around and caught Rivkah's eye.

She shrugged back at him. *Here we go again.*

The thick wooden gates swung open.

The rattle of the wagon, the gentle rocking of the horses.

'Here we go indeed,' Aemilius muttered.

STANDING ON THE parapet, Flaxus looked to the clear blue sky and sighed.

'What are they telling you? Is Tiberius dead? Has Gaul risen to fight back? Is the sea boiling with blood?' The stout augur made a face at his beanpole companion.

'No.' Flaxus sighed again, deeper this time. 'No. They're telling me I'll have to take in my washing.'

'And?' Egenny rolled his eyes. 'You put it out two days ago! It'll be bone dry.'

'You will never understand anything that isn't covered in blood. It's plenty dry. That's not the problem.'

'Then what?'

'No flocks,' Flaxus said, staring mournfully at the sky. 'No swarms, no murmurations, no wakes, no murders.'

Egenny threw his meaty hands in the air. 'Are you seriously complaining that there is no bird-shit on your robes?'

'It's useful! Sometimes the patterns are vague, and may I remind you that unlike your slop-piles *my* information flies past at rather high speed, and a well-soiled robe can properly fill in a picture at times. You're so—' Flaxus flailed and squawked. 'Can you *stop* sneaking up on people?'

'It's my job,' Cassia replied calmly, having somehow appeared on the four-foot parapet without either of them noticing. A crocodile smirk ghosted across her face. '*And* my hobby.' She gestured to the cart trundling down the hillside. 'What did you make of your chosen one, then?'

From a widely disparate height, two very different faces displayed the exact same level of confusion.

'What are you on about?' Egenny's lumpen face was knotted in question.

'The boy.' When there was no understanding, she added, 'Aemilius. The one who brought the items.'

'What—the little chicken?'

'Don't you dare speak ill of chickens. They are beautiful and wise,' Flaxus snarled. 'The little, uh, young one? Face like a kicked puppy most of the time?'

'Yes.'

Flaxus looked down at Egenny, who looked back up at Flaxus. 'That wasn't him.'

'Nope.'

'No way.'

Cassia looked at both of them, dead-eyed, and took a deep breath. 'So you both—want to tell me,' she said slowly, 'that the prophecy you were on about a month ago, non-stop, about a keystone in the bridge, a missing piece of the mosaic, the arrow in the quiver and the trembling in the ground—was not, in fact, the boy we sent Abrax and his squad to get?'

Egenny shrugged. 'We say a lot. Some of it is true now, here, some of it isn't. Some of it is not true until it is. But that runt? Nah.'

'Seemed pretty useless to me.' Flaxus shrugged. Pivoting on a bony heel, he flapped off.

'Where are you going?' Cassia snapped.

'Have to take in my washing,' the augur said without looking back.

Egenny shrugged and walked off in the other direction, towards his grubby hut.

Alone on the parapet, Cassia watched as Abrax and his team disappeared behind a solid wall of trees.

'Shit,' she muttered to herself. 'She is *not* going to like that.'

VII

NOMENTUM

AFTER AN AFTERNOON spent in a hollowed-out mountain, the pine forests that had seemed so imposing on their approach now looked rather commonplace to Aemilius. Without anyone saying anything, the conturbium had arranged itself in what seemed to be its natural order— Abrax rode up front with Livia, Carrick drove the cart with the children and Hanno, and he and Rivkah brought up the rear. A companionable silence had settled over them the moment the fort was out of sight, and now they just chewed up the miles. *Is this how it happens?* he wondered. *Is this how they get used to it? One day at a time, one hoof on the ground, one turn of the wheel?* After the nonsense of the previous seven days the Fort had felt so… quiet. So calm. Safe. And then, it had been over and now they were on their way to another, unspecified terror. All he knew—if he could call it knowledge—was that whatever they were facing might be tougher than Donato. He looked for Taurio and Prasta, and missed them dearly. There had been no explanation as to why they'd gone, or where they'd gone to. They had just been there one moment, and then gone, and he had waited for anyone else to protest but no one did. He still could not quite believe the change in Hanno and Abrax, but it all seemed true, so it had to be accepted as such. As Furibunda trundled along sedately he realised that along all these thoughts the thing that had been niggling at him, the unfamiliar feeling, was neither alarm nor fear—but recognition. *This is the first time since the harpy landed that I have travelled the same road twice.*

Huh.

'Are you holding onto a fart or something?' Rivkah sounded one part annoyed, three parts curious. 'Your face is about to turn in on itself.'

He shrugged. 'Just… it's not easy. How long did it take you to…?' He flailed non-specifically at everything.

'A year. Approximately,' she added thoughtfully. 'Or thereabouts. I don't think I noticed when it stopped being strange.' They rode along in silence. 'Keep asking questions,' she said after a while, almost kindly. 'I promise I won't rip you. Well, not too badly, anyway.'

He felt a warmth in his chest and stifled a grateful smile. 'Do you know where we're going?'

'Brachus.' Rivkah's face twitched. 'Merchant. He sells… everything.'

'What do you mean?'

'*Everything.*'

'I see. Everything. Trees?'

'If you need them.'

'Clouds?'

'If you're thick.'

'So he's a merchant. That's what he's supposed to do.' When Rivkah didn't respond, he added, '…isn't it?'

'He's...' She shuddered. 'He is rich. Like, nearly Crassus rich—but he is not famous. He isn't even known. He's just... rich. And people don't get that rich by being nice. But I don't hate him for his sacks of gold. It's his eyes. There's nothing... alive in them. If I asked for apples, he'd sell me apples. If I asked for apples served in the hollowed-out abdomen of a vestal virgin, he'd ask to see the coin, and then he'd make arrangements, and a few days later someone would show up with a big bloody package. He's... dangerous.'

'Come now,' Aemilius blurted out. 'I have *watched* you stab a *Hydra*. *And* a massive snake. And that means you'd have to be close enough to them to do that.'

'Pfft. That's nothing. Those are just creatures. Big and lethal, sure, but they are creatures. I understand them. They see, they want, they act. Brachus... is different. I don't understand him, and I don't like it.'

She's actually squirming. 'I'm sure we won't have to deal with him,' he said meekly, glancing towards Abrax and Livia. Rivkah just shrugged. 'Uh, the cart,' he offered lamely. 'Is it the, uh, same cart we had in Hispania?' She looked at him, puzzled. 'Because—' He gestured to Furibunda and ran out of words. He had given up hope of ever seeing his horse again, and it had delighted and surprised him, but he could not get his head around any of how it had happened.

'Don't know. Don't think so. They've not told me exactly how that part works—mostly because I don't really need to know, but I do know that the carts we get are all'—she chose carefully—'equipped.'

'What do you mean?'

'Did you never wonder where all the *stuff* came from?'

Aemilius lit up. 'I *did!* There's no way there's space in the cart! I checked! But always—'

'They went and rummaged in the back and came out with something that wasn't there?'

'Yes!' He stared at her, willing her to give him the answer just a little faster.

'Every cart comes with a bag,' she said mysteriously.

Aemilius deflated. 'A *bag*. Oh. What a revelation.'

'I'm not finished.'

'Oh—what is it? A *special* bag? Just like a regular one, except it is really, really big?'

'Sort of. What are you getting all huffy for? I'm telling you a thing.'

'You're making fun of me.'

'Oh, if I was making fun of you, you'd know, Aemilius of *Hispania*. The bags were a gift from a magus whose brother was at Teutoburg.' Satisfied that she had piqued his interest, she continued, 'They look just like leather sacks, but they are a small gate to another layer of the world.'

He frowned and tried to arrange this information in his head. 'Like… Felix?'

'Sort of.' Rivkah frowned. 'I don't know if I can quite explain exactly how it works.' She looked around for words and found nothing but rolling fields in shades of yellow and green. Pinching her eyes shut, she thought hard—and then her eyes flew open. 'Pocket! It's like a pocket. Except the things you put in the pocket don't exist until you take them out of the pocket again.'

'I see.'

'What?' Rivkah snapped. 'You don't believe me? I'm trying to wipe the mope off your face, and you—oh, go shove your head up your own arse.'

'No,' Aemilius sputtered. 'It's not that I don't believe you. I do! I mean, uh, I do. Sort of? Maybe? Probably?' He felt the sense slipping away from him and flailed to get it back. 'It's just, uh, it's been a *lot*, you know. The Fort, and the monsters, and Hanno and Abrax doing magic and nearly dying and now being fine, and so knowing that I'm travelling with a magic bag is just a bit...'

'Too much,' Rivkah said. The fire in her eyes had dimmed, and she no longer looked like she'd rip his throat out with her teeth. 'I understand.' She looked at him, and saw the desperation, and the confusion, and the exhaustion and the question. 'Just ride,' she said kindly. 'Just ride. It will all be fine.' Along with her kindness, the slow, rhythmic hoofbeats started to calm him just enough for her to have the time to reconsider. 'Or we'll meet a horrific death at the hands of some unimaginable creature. Either way, you need to ride to get there.'

ALL ROADS, AS it turned out, did not lead to Rome. After a mercifully uneventful two days of riding, they crested a hill and looked down on a town nestled in a valley, sheltered from the elements and sitting astride a river.

'So this is Nomentum, is it?'

'It is.' Livia's mounted silhouette looked exactly like Aemilius imagined Julius Caesar must have looked just before he laid waste to most of the world.

'Since the fat bastard isn't here, I suppose it's my job to call it a shithole.'

Livia did not respond.

'Say what you need to say, and then be useful and alert. We have work to do.' Abrax spurred his horse and rode on, without checking that he was being followed. A heartbeat later, reins snapped and the cart rumbled on after him.

Rivkah executed a mocking bow to the big magus's back. 'My humble apologies, master. May I just ever so kindly request that you inform us next time something spiky crawls up your arse?' She shifted her hips and nudged her mount into a slow walk behind the cart.

Aemilius inched Furibunda closer to Rivkah. 'Looks like you might not be the only one who is a little worried.'

All he got in response was a contemptuous huff and a muttered grumble in Hebrew, but there was a slight softening to the scowl. Deciding to quit while he was ahead, Aemilius spent his time scanning the surroundings. It was much the same as what they had been travelling through—Umbrian farmland, fields of differing shades of green and gold, sliced up with tall, conical cypress trees. Pastures for cows and sheep. He breathed in through his nose and was filled with a quiet and a calm. This was not a place for big things—big scares, big monsters, big armies. He could imagine a full invasion of Italia completely missing this little town in its little valley.

They, however, were not missed. Long before they were within throwing range of the first houses that could be counted as in the town, a shifting mass of local children—three, then fifteen, then back down to eight— was underfoot and all around. One cheeky little boy tried to climb the cart, and showed no understanding of how close he was to immediate death when Rivkah growled at him. Instead, he made a face as he jumped off, and offered a hand gesture that Aemilius wasn't familiar with but guessed was the regional version of where exactly she could shove her command.

'Charming place.'

More muttered curses in Hebrew.

Once they got past the first line of huts and sheds, though, the town started taking shape. Two-floor buildings lined the broad, cobbled road, leading to a curved stone bridge across the river. Every twenty yards or so there would be an alley between the buildings, leading off to smaller houses and gardens. Across the bridge a piazza opened up, with a statue of Octavian as its centrepiece. It was here that Abrax led the legionnaires and motioned for Carrick to pull to the side. The scurrying children had vanished as quickly as they had appeared, save for a curious head popping around a corner to sneak a look and disappearing again.

'Livia and I will go in and source what we need. Carrick?'

Without a word he jumped off the cart and stood, somehow both stock-still and ready to dash at any moment. Abrax nodded.

'It would help if you fuckers actually used words,' Rivkah spat. 'So I take the brats, the toad and the cart, then? And the horses?'

'Find a stable run by a man called Mastroianni.' Livia's commands were clipped. 'North, past the butcher's and the vintner's. Tell him Mater sent you. He will keep what is ours without question until we come back.'

'And then, what? Walk back?'

'Yes. Aemilius, Carrick—you are with us.' Again, there was no question. Abrax and Livia turned and walked briskly towards the east end of the piazza. Aemilius looked at Carrick for sympathy, but there was none. The scout seemed to have anticipated Abrax's movements and was already ghosting ahead. *Maybe one day they'll*

ask me what I want to do, he thought wearily as he
followed the familiar shapes up front. *But I won't hold
my breath.* Reduced to trailing behind the leaders, he had
a little bit of time during the walk to think about what
lay ahead. *What on earth does the home of a creature
that frightens Rivkah look like? Skulls on spikes? A daisy
chain of spines? A garrison of murderers?* He pondered
this for a while, listing possibilities in his head that grew
increasingly outlandish—and all of them turned out to
be wrong. They walked, and then they walked a little
bit farther, and just about when he was getting bored
of looking for something remarkable, Abrax stopped.
It happened so abruptly that Aemilius almost walked
into the back of the big magus and Livia, and was close
enough to hear their muttered conversation.

'Are you ready for this?' A big hand, gently placed on
Livia's forearm.

'I… think so.' The uncertainty in the noblewoman's
voice sent a sharp shiver through Aemilius. He had been
able to ignore Rivkah's oddness—but if *Livia* was scared
of him, too? He could feel his heart start thudding in his
chest. Abrax moved to knock on the door when it swung
open on three hefty and well-oiled hinges. *And they'd
need to be.* The walls were double thick, and the door
was layered with what looked like inch-thick timber
bolted on either side of solid metal. They stepped in and
it swung quietly shut behind them. There was no bar on
the inside, but the unmistakeable rattle of sturdy metal
chains and a heavy thump suggested that something
big had slid into place somewhere. The antechamber
was just a square box, with doors leading off to the
left, right and up ahead. Lamps on tables in each corner
cast a yellow light on smooth, white and bare walls.

Aemilius was trying to make sense of the absolute lack of detail when a sharp elbow jabbed him in the ribs. Carrick was standing uncomfortably close, staring at him meaningfully. 'What?' he whispered. The skinny man did not reply. Instead, he almost physically pulled Aemilius's eye line to a spot on the wall, obscured by the table, where there was… absolutely nothing. 'It's a wall,' Aemilius hissed. 'Like the others.' Carrick shook his head and mimed holding a crossbow. *He's gone insane. We're trapped and he can't take it. But how do you help someone who won't talk?*

The door at the back wall swung open, quietly. The man who walked in was slightly below average height but built like a labourer. He was dressed in a plain, well-maintained brown tunic that would attract no attention in the street and well-worn but sturdy sandals. He looked them over and nodded by way of acknowledgement. 'I have been informed of your arrival.'

Somewhere, in the back of his head, an inner voice screamed at Aemilius.

Run away run away run away

'Well met, Brachus,' Abrax replied, in a voice that neither deferred nor commanded, but somehow also did a bit of both. 'Mater Populii sends her regards.'

The man in the tunic heard the name, and the weight of it, and was unimpressed. 'More importantly, she also sends her gold.' His attention turned to Livia, and Aemilius realised that from the moment he had laid eyes on Brachus he had been averting his gaze. 'Well met, Livia Claudia.'

'Well met, Brachus of Nomentum.'

Anyone who observed the exchange between them would have thought they were watching a merchant and a noblewoman exchanging pleasantries. But something set Aemilius's teeth on edge. *She is fighting hard to hide it, but she is terrified.*

And he could understand why.

There was an unsettling, quiet meticulousness in the way in which Brachus unhurriedly looked at her, from her face and down, slowly, to her toes and then back up. There was nothing lecherous about it, nothing aggressive, nothing contemptuous—and that was the problem. There was *nothing*. His gaze reduced Livia Claudia of the Claudii, holder of all values that were sacred to Rome, to nothing. To a problem that he needed to solve. Aemilius tried to imagine Rivkah standing still under such scrutiny and understood why she had shivered. 'You are going to Villa Sulpicia, and you need to pass as a noblewoman of a family that is doing reasonably well but is harmless and not at the centre of anything. Correct?'

Livia took a deep breath. 'That is correct. I thought—'

Brachus turned to his left and snapped his fingers. The door swung open and two young boys shuffled in with a rack on wheels. Aemilius looked at it and felt the punch to his gut before he realised what he was looking at. A tunic, beautifully woven, in the colours of Hispania. Red, purple and white embellishments framed a beautifully sun-drenched orange, bordered with gold thread. It was *his* home, and *his* sunset, and his soul cried out for it. Brachus looked at it dispassionately, then at Livia.

'No.'

With impressive speed, the helpers shuffled out with the garment. There was a brief moment of silence, then they came back out with another example on the rack. It was beautiful, and rich in greens and golds, and it didn't even get halfway into the room.

'No.'

The next example was wheeled in, and it was only because he was on high alert that Aemilius heard the sound Livia made. It was the smallest of in-drawn breaths—and then the front was back up, and she was implacable.

But Aemilius, it seemed, was not the only one who had heard.

Brachus turned and looked at Livia, at her and through her. 'Yes...' he said slowly, to no one in particular. 'Yes, this is yours, I think.'

'Thank you,' Livia muttered demurely. 'It is beautiful.'

And indeed, it was. It was grey, and it was silver, and it was pink. It was the colour of pearls and expensive wine. 'This is from two years ago,' Brachus said matter-of-factly. 'From the house of the Viccini. Are we satisfied?'

'We are.' Livia nodded.

'Good,' Brachus said. *The only satisfaction this man is taking is in the prospect of us leaving.* 'I have provided the other items on Mater's list. They are loaded in the cart.'

'Thank you,' Abrax said, bowing respectfully. 'Your service, as always, is of the highest quality.'

'You get what you pay for.'

'We certainly do. If there is no—'

'No more talking.' The weight in Brachus's voice was that of someone who was never contradicted. If the lack of emotion had not been so sinister, the shock on Abrax's face would have been almost comical—but Aemilius was not in any mood to laugh. Suddenly Brachus was looking away from the others and straight at him. Not through him—at him. 'We are finished. You may go,' he said, waving his hand vaguely at Abrax, Livia and Carrick. 'But the boy stays.'

'Like Hecate's pits he does,' Livia snarled.

There was the slightest hint of an amused twitch to an eyebrow, but apart from that, Brachus remained impassive. 'You three—go. The boy stays.'

The flames in the room flickered. Shadows danced on the wall, and Abrax seemed to *expand*. 'We all go,' he said, any suggestion of politeness gone.

Brachus sighed. 'I know you can burn me to a crisp, and that would be annoying. But I would like to remind you who I am. If I die, a missive I have already prepared gets sent to Sejanus, a regular customer, explaining that there is an army amassing in your precious little fort, ready to march on Rome.' He turned to face Abrax. 'And while I won't be alive to enjoy it, you will have somewhere in the region of eight legions of Roman soldiers descending on your position, eager to squash a rebellion that will pave the way for Sejanus to finally kick old Tiberius off his cliff in Capri. Do you think he will hesitate?' Abrax did not answer. 'And while I have no doubt that you could rain all manner of hellfire on the Roman army—is that what you want to do? Is that consistent with your *mission*? Killing little Italian boys?' Still there was no suggestion of emotion in Brachus's voice. He was calm, collected and… almost friendly, and every bit of Aemilius's sense of danger was screaming at him. 'I give you my word,' Brachus continued. 'And that is a very rare and valuable thing. No hair on this boy's head will be harmed. I just want to have… a conversation. Alternately, if you find that to be unacceptable…' There was the sound of stone sliding on stone, and a hole opened in the wall. Aemilius glanced at Carrick, who shrugged. *I told you so*. A crossbow bolt eased out of the hole, pointing at Livia.

Another cover slid back.

And another.

And another.

Within moments, six crossbow bolts were pointing at them.

'What you have here,' Brachus continued calmly, 'is called a negotiation. You have something I want. The boy. I have something that you want. Your continued existence. In my line of work, this is a fairly simple one.'

With a clenched jaw, Abrax eased his shoulders down and let his hands fall by his sides.

The flames that had danced in the lanterns steadied.

'A good decision.' Brachus snapped his fingers. The soft rattle of well-oiled chains was followed by steel on steel, and the door swung open.

Aemilius stared at Abrax, willing him to do... something. Anything.

And then the magus looked back at him, and the bottom fell out of Aemilius's stomach and his veins filled with ice water. *He is... ashamed.* Livia stared straight ahead, not meeting his eye. He could only see the back of Carrick's head, but the slim man's shoulders were hard-set as he moved out.

The door closed behind them with a soft exhale of breath, and Aemilius was alone in the room with Brachus. The man in the brown tunic looked down to the floor and seemed to think for a moment. Then he looked up, straight at him, and Aemilius had to fight not to take a step back. 'You are the son of Marcus Livius Sculla.'

Aemilius blinked. *What?* 'Um... that is correct?'

A brief flicker of irritation on Brachus's face. 'Of course it is. I am never wrong.'

'That must be quite annoying.' A heartbeat passed as Aemilius watched the words that had left his mouth in silent horror. 'I mean, uh, um—of course, I, didn't—'

'Be quiet.' This had an immediate effect. 'I will be brief. Your father owes me money.'

Aemilius's eyes boggled. 'Wait—what? My father owes *you* money? *My* father? Marcus Livius, about yay high—'

'If you speak again before you are spoken to, I will silence you for ever,' Brachus said calmly.

'But you promised to not hurt a hair on my head!' Aemilius squeaked.

'Yes. But I said nothing about ripping out your tongue.' Aemilius made a sound midway between a hiccup and a squeak, and closed his mouth as hard as he could. Brachus nodded once. 'Good. Thank you. Now—your father owes me money. And it is coming up on collection. It is an old debt, and one I am loath to collect, but I will. And if he doesn't pay me, here's what's going to happen.' The merchant fixed him with a cold look. 'I will make a list of his living family, going back one generation and then down two. I will pay bad men to hunt down the youngest first, and I will collect what I am owed. For one gold denarius I will take a hand. For five denarii, an ear. For ten, an eye. For fifteen denarii I will take both hands. I will have these parts sent to your father, along with details of where they were taken, who they were taken from, how they suffered and where his debt stands.'

'How much does my father owe you?' Aemilius whispered.

'Two thousand denarii,' Brachus said, matter-of-factly.

His knees buckled and he couldn't see straight. Fighting cold sweat, he squeezed out the words. 'So... when is it my turn?'

To his surprise, Brachus almost smiled. 'No pleading. No protests. Good.' The merchant seemed to eye him with renewed interest. 'You... might escape. And you might, in fact, save your entire family.'

The pressure on his chest, the thudding in his heart—Aemilius felt submerged, like he'd been sunk, and he kicked to the surface. 'How?'

Brachus's smile turned hungry. 'Marcus Sulpicius is in possession of an ornate jade dagger which he stole from Marcus Antonius. It was a gift from Cleopatra herself, and he believes it is part of what gives him the right to challenge for the Empire. I have a buyer for it, at a price which will clear your family's debt easily.'

Aemilius burst to the surface, gulping in the air, feeling the delicious pain of being alive. 'How do I get it?'

'Secretly. Your little friends may not know about this, because you will know—'

'—they'll tell me it will jeopardise the mission, and will not allow it. I understand.'

Brachus's shock at being interrupted was only tempered by the fact they both knew Aemilius was correct. 'Yes. I don't particularly care. But that dagger comes back to me, or your entire family line is extinguished. Understood?' There was no sneer, no fury, no threat in the man's eyes. There was only the cold promise of pain. He extended his hand.

Taking a deep breath, Aemilius shook it. 'Understood.'

He expected to be jolted by some kind of electricity, by a lightning strike of all the souls he had taken by his own hand, but there was only a warm firmness. A faint memory of a doorway in Alexandria flitted across his heart, and he had to fight the urge to pull back.

This hand has never held a knife.

No—this hand murders with a quill.

To his side, the invisible lock slid up and the door swung open.

WHEN HE STEPPED outside, two carts waited for him. One of them was an expensive affair—a well-made carpentum with a wooden roof and plausibly but not ostentatiously decorated panels. *Well off but not rich. Noble but not dangerous. Whoever Brachus employs knows their work.* It was pulled by four horses—solid creatures who stood placidly and awaited Carrick's reins. Livia was just about visible through a curtained window, dressed in her fancy tunic, flanked by Flavius and Serena who were equally tastefully attired. Alongside her rode Abrax, looking like he had never stepped out of his leather armour. It was clearly well-used, but the owner had survived his battles. He struck a perfect pitch of weary competence, as if he would be significantly more trouble than it was worth to bother him.

The second cart was a more rickety affair. Hanno sat up front, looking relaxed and pleased with his lot. Rivkah sat in the back, looking decidedly less so—and all of them were staring at him with a mixture of fear, concern and curiosity.

'Get in here,' Rivkah snarled.

Rather taken aback by the anger, he complied, and the carts trundled on.

They sat in tense silence as their convoy made its way out of Nomentum via a side road and headed south-east.

A couple of times Aemilius thought about speaking to Rivkah, but she practically radiated fury, so he thought better of it. They sauntered through fields, past workers curious enough for one glance but not for two—in his sellsword garb, Abrax did not encourage gawking, but there was also an odd, quiet menace to Carrick when the rangy coachman wanted there to be. Sat in the back of the cheap cart, Rivkah did not draw a lot of attention. However, the set of her shoulders and the sneer of her lip suggested to Aemilius that she might be slowed down by a full-grown hydra, but not by much.

'Here.' There was more than a hint of Mater's absolute command in Abrax's voice as he gestured to a road that led into a copse of trees. It was big enough to tuck the wagons out of immediate sight, but too small to hide unwanted surprises. The moment the wagons stopped, the big magus led his horse to Aemilius's cart. 'Now. Talk.'

Livia leaned out of the window of her luxury cart, and Aemilius felt like he could *smell* the children eavesdropping. He was about to speak, when—

'How about *you* talk, you jumped-up old shitbag?!' Rivkah was up and on the balls of her feet, looking like it was taking all the strength she had to hold herself back from leaping on Abrax and biting his eyes out. 'You fucking *leave*? And then demand that *he* talk?' The big man in leather armour suddenly seemed a lot less imposing.

'We had no choice.'

The girl shrieked, a sound of pure fury. '*Listen to yourself!* Is this the way of the Legion? "We had no *choice*"?! We *never* have any choice! We're *always* looking death in the eye! Tell me,' she growled. 'Tell me now.

Next time I risk my life, and you have the chance to risk yours to save me. Are you going to *walk?* Are you going to say you had no *choice?*' Her voice was thick with raw emotion. 'You left him to *die!* You—' The words arrived to her, faster than she could speak them, and Aemilius realised that he had noticed movement from the corner of his eye and suddenly Livia was there, fancy tunic be damned, leaping quickly via the spokes of the wheel, over the side, and into the cart, and within a blink of an eye she had Rivkah in her arms, embracing her like there was no tomorrow and the future of the world relied on there being not a single inch of space between them. The girl thrashed and howled, and it was the sound of fear and heartbreak, and still Livia held on for what seemed like a small eternity.

Eventually Rivkah's sobs diminished, and she melted into the older woman's embrace, and Aemilius remembered to breathe and looked around. He did not know what he was expecting, but what he saw still surprised him. Hanno, Abrax and Carrick all watched with solemn sympathy, and the children stayed out of sight.

This is what is underneath. The realisation hit him. *This is what gets put to the side.*

'I'd just gotten used to him.' Rivkah's words were half-sniffled and half-muttered, and there was no note of apology in them, but they were unmistakeably directed at Abrax.

'I understand.' The big man looked serious. 'And I miss the old bastard, too.'

'Fuck off,' Rivkah muttered by way of agreement.

And then Abrax turned to him, and Aemilius wished that he was a hundred—or possibly five hundred—miles away. 'If you wouldn't mind,' the big man said, almost kindly, which was somehow more terrifying. 'I *would* like to know why you are still alive.'

Looking away from Abrax he found himself standing eye to eye with Livia, who watched him with cold determination. 'Brachus had four of my family members killed because they *heard* of a business deal. They didn't do anything. They didn't spoil anything. They were just in the wrong place at the wrong time, and they disappeared. Eventually, a selection of their body parts was found. And you were in with him, alone, at his command, and yet here you are with not a single ruffled hair.' There was no question in it, no request for information. There was just a simple command. Talk, or you will be wearing your organs like a cape.

It wasn't much of an effort for him to blush. 'Uh…' he stammered. 'I… don't want to.' Now it was Rivkah's turn to hold Livia back. It was gentle, and subtle, but Aemilius definitely saw the hand on the noblewoman's dagger arm. 'It's… embarrassing.'

This, as he had hoped, was not what they were expecting. 'Explain.'

'He, uh'—*look down*—'he asked… uh… he said… he asked if I wanted a little bit of extra spending money for the road.' This was *definitely* not what they expected. Their incredulity was stretched… too far? In his mind, the dice tumbled from his hand. 'In return for certain… services.'

The word hung in the air for a moment.

And then another.

And then another.

And then, like a pregnant thundercloud, it was Rivkah who burst first. It wasn't a laugh, really. It was more of a shouted '*Hah!*'

Hanno, on the other hand, cracked up. 'Oh, monsoons and typhoons!' he wept. 'Brachus is a flying fish!'

Even though he was doing his best to pretend to be embarrassed, he still caught the quick glance from Livia to Abrax, and the brief flash of suspicion on the face of the big magus.

'And what?' Rivkah said, eyes sparkling with glee. 'Are you buying the drinks all the way down to Sulpicius? Do you need an orange or something to take away the taste?'

'I said no,' he replied, rather tersely. 'Or, at least, made it clear that I wouldn't know what to do, and must have looked miserable enough about it.'

'And what? Brachus—*Brachus*—just let you go?' Livia said. *She is not buying it.*

'I don't know, do I?' Aemilius snapped. 'I was rather too busy expecting my head to be ripped off my shoulders or something. I don't know what he was thinking. Maybe he thought I was a Lupino, and lost interest when he found out I wasn't legal. He just seemed to shrug and then the light switched off in his eyes.'

'He usually takes what he wants.'

'Probably, yeah.' *Play it softly. Speak like you just thought of this.* Aemilius forced himself to slow down. Livia looked suspicious enough already. 'But… I think… it's a crime, isn't it? Forcing yourself on someone?'

'Most of the time,' Livia said coldly. 'Depends on who your father is.' She rallied. 'But Brachus could buy any sort of judgement. Why would he care?'

Hold it softly. Let them grab it and run away with it. 'If I came out looking like I'd been… you know, I don't think you'd be quiet about it. Maybe he worried that his enemies might find out?'

Another exchanged glance between Livia and

Abrax, quick and unreadable. 'I suppose there might be some powerful players who could use that kind of information...' Abrax mused.

'It's easy to fish if you know the bait,' Hanno chimed in.

'True.' The noblewoman looked serious. 'Well—maybe Aemilius of Hispania escaped with his honour—'

'And the skin on his knees,' Rivkah cackled, and proceeded to deliver an obscene mime with full sound effects.

Yes. It was all he could do to not sigh with relief. 'May a randy troupe of satyrs come and thoroughly fuck you all with a log-strap,' Aemilius said with a smile and as much mock annoyance as he could muster. Abrax turned his horse back towards the path out of the copse, and once Livia was back where she needed to be, Carrick followed.

His secret was safe.

For now.

VIII

VILLA SULPICIA

VIA FLAMINIA CRADLED the carts and sent them rolling smoothly towards their destination. The new mission and new configuration of legionnaires did not seem to matter—Aemilius watched them fall into the same, mile-eating rhythm. They did only what was absolutely necessary, conserved energy, travelled in silence for half a day if needed. *Travelling to them is like breathing.* And even though he felt himself getting better at it, better at letting the mind wander and the body relax in amongst the vistas of beautiful green and gold hills, sharp lines of trees leading up to some nobleman's summer villa and fields tilled by ant-like swarms of workers, he found his mind wandering to the same question over and over. He glanced at Rivkah, who with her closed eyes and sneer-set mouth looked somehow both asleep and annoyed.

'What?' she snapped.

'I didn't say anything,' he replied nervously.

'You're thinking it. I can smell your staring.' Her eyes popped open fast enough for him to recoil and wince as he banged his elbow on a wooden corner. 'Go on. Ask.'

'Where did Prasta and Taurio go?'

Rivkah rolled her eyes. 'I don't know. Behind a bush to smash.' She slung it out, then chortled at the shock on his face. 'I'm *joking*. You look like you've seen about three flavours of ghost.'

'I, uh, yes. Didn't need to imagine that, thank you. And now I can never look at them again.'

'Odds are you won't have to.'

'Oh,' Aemilius said, crestfallen.

Rivkah rolled her eyes again, like one would at a dim younger brother, then glanced over his shoulder, over the road they'd travelled. Her expression changed. 'Something's up. Abrax!'

The tone of Rivkah's voice made explanations unnecessary. The magus stood up in the stirrups and stared backwards. 'A full turma,' he snapped. 'Sounds like they are coming in fast.'

Cavalry?

But Aemilius didn't need to ask the question.

He could feel it. There was a tremor in the ground, and with it he could feel the running *and the racing and the thumping and*— Pinching his eyes shut, he pushed the sensations out of his head. It was hard, and they didn't go away, but he regained use of his own senses. Up ahead there was indeed a small cloud of road-dust, rising gently. Livia's head was out of the carriage, conferring with Abrax, but it was impossible to hear what they were deciding—until Abrax gestured, just as Carrick started nudging the carpentum off to the side of the road. This was followed by a string of mild swears by Rivkah as she sought to emulate the move, nudging their considerably less manoeuvrable manure-shifter in behind their mistress at a respectful distance and doing her best not to end up off the road altogether.

'The old fart wasn't lying,' she muttered once they had cleared the road. 'Reckon Brachus changed his mind?'

Aemilius shot her a look that said *I'd punch you but you're not worthy*, much to her delight.

The cloud of dust was now significantly closer, and they could hear the thunder of hooves approaching. It took no time at all for the horsemen to approach at a gallop, all thirty of them, hollering as they went past. A while later, Abrax signalled to go. 'If they were after us, they'd have come back by now,' he said to no one in particular.

'They'd also not have called us little snail-shits,' Aemilius added helpfully.

'What?' Rivkah sounded one part offended and three parts bemused.

'Lusitanians, by the sound of it.'

Rivkah shrugged. 'Horse boys. They're all the same. Well, almost all.' With that settled, she diverted her attention to getting the cart back up on the road. Up ahead, Aemilius couldn't help but notice that Abrax looked a lot less dismissive of the horse patrol.

THEY SAUNTERED ALONG at a respectable pace, with Carrick driving the luxury wagon and the three of them taking turns with the old cart. The silence was companionable, and Aemilius found his mind drifting to nowhere in particular, just observing the well-maintained farmland undulating into the distance. It did not take long for it all to blur into one—hills, fields, lines of trees—and he found himself marvelling at the order and precision within the empire. The Via Flaminia carved straight through the land, broad enough for other carts and travellers to pass easily, and as flat as a tabletop.

'I know what I and the mighty Aemilius are doing when we get there,' Rivkah said, breaking the silence. 'But how about you, froggy?'

Hanno had somehow managed to make himself look as if he was reclining on a royal couch, tucked away in the corner at the back. He waved a hand imperiously. 'I shall be dusting my hair with the finest flour to affect an air of wisdom and donning some reasonably expensive robes courtesy of Aemilius's special friend'— he winked conspiratorially at Aemilius, who made a face at him—'and presenting myself as her exaltedness' pet philosopher from lands far away.'

'Moloch's balls,' Rivkah groaned and rolled her eyes theatrically. 'Will you give us notice so we can be somewhere far, far away?'

Hanno very carefully ignored her request. 'In fact, I thought I might start practicing. In Syracuse—'

'Please take the reins so I can go wring his neck.'

'You asked,' Aemilius replied, delighting in the glare from the girl.

'—in Syracuse, it is said that a man with two heads walks the streets. How does he look? In all directions at once.' Nodding sagely at his own wisdom, Hanno stretched his legs out and smiled. 'It is a blessing and a curse, wisdom. It really is.'

'Tell you what's a curse,' Rivkah muttered, and silence descended once again. Their shadows grew smaller on the left, then moved to the right as the sun inched lazily past midday and into afternoon. They passed a smattering of travellers on foot; others passed them on horse.

A convoy of riders and carts, laden with grain and lumber, passed them heading north. 'The river flows,' Hanno remarked, sitting on the driver's bench. 'Rome is a thirsty place.'

'A stinky one, too. Ever been there?'

'I am a Roman born,' Aemilius replied, more haughtily than he had intended. 'We lived there when I was a child but had to move.'

'Ah. Yes.' Rivkah's complete lack of interest almost made him laugh. 'From Sardinia, to Hispania. Well, it sucks. Full of shite-bags and praetorian guards and old men stuck so far up themselves that they can see out of their own mouths.'

Hanno chuckled. 'That is a beautiful image, even for you.'

He got a genuine smile in return. 'Thank you. I've sometimes wondered whether you could do that, you know. Shove someone so far up—'

'Probably not,' Aemilius interrupted. 'They'd, uh, suffocate, probably.'

Rivkah nodded slowly. 'You're right. You'd have to cut air holes all the way up first.'

'And that would probably mean they would give back some of the blood they so selfishly hoard,' Hanno chipped in. 'Possibly enough so that they would not actually be able to see out of their own mouth.' Studying his hand intently, he tried to form it into a curve, then twist it around his wrist. 'Also, I imagine that their spines might be unhelpful.'

The petite girl beamed. 'That's assuming that they *have* a spine! Hah!'

'Very good, Daughter of Abraham. Very good.' They lapsed back into silence.

Well, nearly. *Is she… humming?* Not for the first time, Aemilius wondered at his new life and his strange companions.

Up ahead, Abrax's arm rose, palm flat. *Stop.* He pointed forwards, to a pole with attached signs, too far away to read. 'Turn left up ahead.'

'Aye,' Hanno barked back, in perfect mimicry of a life-long teamster.

It did not take long to get to the crossing, and Aemilius found himself sighing with sadness.

'What?' Rivkah snapped.

'Just… the road,' he mumbled, nodding towards the turn-off.

'The road is fine.'

'I know. But it's just not… oh, never mind.'

'He who defeats the mighty Roman empire shall be he who gets in amongst them and jostles them about a bit,' Hanno intoned. 'But do not worry, sapling. The unknown isn't always as bad as you think.'

And indeed, he was right. The road they turned onto was as good as it got, short of a properly laid Roman road. 'Someone has paid good money for this,' Rivkah observed.

Aemilius had to agree. 'It doesn't seem like Marcus Sulpicius likes being jostled about either.'

They rode on in a silence that was three parts rest and one part apprehension, through orchards and fields, over a meticulously maintained bridge and farmhands who all knew to look the other way. Towards sunset, a beautiful breeze carried the hint of ocean with it. 'Company.' Carrick's voice betrayed no emotion as it sauntered past the steady clop and wheel-rattle.

Tearing himself away from appreciating the evening, he struggled to see what the scout was on about. *But there's something.* The others had the look of keen hunting dogs about them. There was a pause, a dip and a turn, and an access road became visible in between the trees. Sitting by it was a small troop of bored-looking men. Rivkah swore in Hebrew. 'How—*how*—did you see them?'

'Didn't.' Now the scout's voice did betray emotion, and it was a glorious smugness. 'Smelled 'em.'

'Remind me not to fart in your presence,' Rivkah muttered.

'...again?' Carrick shot back, gleefully.

'Shitty Celt bastard.'

She likes him. For some reason he couldn't quite understand, this made Aemilius relax. If Rivkah trusted the shadowy creature...

'Hail Tiberius, Emperor of Rome. Identify yourselves, if you would be so kind.' The group, which looked to be about a dozen, seemed to have a leader who was lazily getting to his feet. There was an accent to his voice that Aemilius couldn't quite put his finger on except to label it as unpleasantly familiar, layered with a tone that was definitely not as respectful as the words would suggest.

'Just a dozen?' he whispered quietly.

'Bet your left nut there's another dozen in the trees,' Rivkah whispered back.

'And what do I get if I win? Three nuts?'

'Two, if you're lucky.'

Up ahead, the carpentum had become the stage for a small play. Livia appeared at the driver's window, a ghostly shadow, then drifted back out of sight. When Carrick's voice rang out it was all Aemilius could do not to burst out laughing.

'Domina Sulpicia Martia, with her two children and party, to see her beloved cousin Marcus Sulpicius.'

The speaker cocked his head to the side, crossed his arms and made no move to get out of the way. 'Well met, Sulpicia Martia... and party.' On some invisible command the others rose, and Aemilius got a sinking feeling. *These are not your everyday guards.* He did his best to observe the men in front of them without being seen. They looked lean, sharp and aware, to a man, and not a one of them seemed like they had been intimidated once in their life. *A pack of wolfhounds, this.*

With every heartbeat, the tension rose—until Sulpicia Martia spoke.

'What is happening?'

Aemilius risked a glance at Rivkah, and even in the fading light he could tell that she was taken aback. In three words, the voice from the carpentum had communicated contempt, authority, irritation and threat all at once. Carrick was equal to his part in the play.

'Guards, Domina.'

Like the voice, the pause—two beats of a worried heart—was perfect. 'Well, ask them what they want.'

Carrick performed the most authentic, sympathetic look over at the leader of the guards complete with a shrug. *The rich, eh?*

The response was not worth the performance, but a fraction of a silent nod from the man in charge sent three of his men to either side of the wagons. Aemilius did not have to lay it on thick to act nervous around the guards. Like trained dogs they flowed to the side of the carts, checking quickly underneath and within. He noted that they did not open the doors of the carpentum, merely satisfying themselves that there were no concealed weapons or other unwanted surprises. He felt the eyes of two of them scan quickly over himself and Rivkah—an old man with a white, thumb-thick scar across his left eye and a young, rat-faced one with thin, blond hair tied in a tail—and sighed with relief when they moved on. A couple of them sized up Abrax, but he, too, seemed to be assessed as manageable. The inspection took very little time, and then they were nodded onwards. Marcus Sulpicius's guards melted to the side, silent and efficient, and let them pass up the access road.

It felt less than pleasant to watch them flow back across the road.

Our escape is well and truly blocked.

Once they were out of earshot, Abrax leaned in to confer with Livia up front, then eased back to their cart. 'We think those were Germanes.'

'Shit.'

'Why is that bad?' Aemilius found himself squeaking. After the events of the last two weeks his realm of experience now covered a variety of things, and considering what he knew about Rivkah, anything that made her this annoyed should be considered at least a serious threat.

'They are, on average, tough as nails and most of them don't like us very much,' Abrax rumbled.

'But they have been Romans for ages!'

'Can I kill him? Just once?'

'They have,' Abrax conceded. 'But most of them are not happy about it. Much like Armenius.'

'Oh. Yes.' Aemilius felt the colour rise in his cheeks and was glad of the fading light. *How could he have been so stupid? And why did he always have to ask about things?*

'And we think if Sulpicius is hiring Germanes, then

there is a reasonable chance that we'll find more than a trace of Donato and his lot.'

'Shit and shit and shit again. I was hoping this would be easy.'

'Does the river ever flow upstream?' Hanno half-sang, head covered in what Aemilius assumed were his philosopher's robes.

'Do you ever shut up?' Rivkah shot back.

'Only when I have something to say.'

The lithe girl groaned. 'I don't know if I am more happy to be rid of you or sorry for the poor bastards who will be forced to listen to your mad ramblings.'

'Then think less and look more,' Hanno replied gently, still tangled in his robe. 'We approach greatness.'

And even in the falling light, it was clear that the Sulpicii had done well for themselves. They turned a bend in the road, inclined upwards—and suddenly the Villa Sulpicia was there, above them, glinting like a jewel in sunlight. The approach road was steel-straight and set with a mosaic of white, red and purple stones that caught the dancing lights of big, mounted torches set in brass circles. Shadows draped over statues of a variety of heroic figures—a gladiator with a trident, a warrior brandishing a shield and short sword, a general on his horse, a wise-looking scholar holding an armful of scrolls—surrounded by the outlines of carefully tended trees. Behind the sculpture garden rose majestic columns that guided the path into an atrium. Even from a distance the light caught on brilliant sparkles of gold and silver in painted vistas on the walls.

Rivkah whistled.

'The might of Rome.'

'Too right, frog. Too right.'

'I wonder what Taurio would have had to say,' Aemilius ventured.

Rivkah sniggered. 'Glad he's not here... but I would have loved to hear it. He'd struggle to decide which one to piss on first.'

'We would be quite dead quite quickly,' Hanno offered. His appearance had changed significantly, and he now no longer looked like a simple traveller. A simple, white robe with a blue sash upon which were written the words *Sapientia super omnia* sat snugly on his shoulders, and Aemilius watched him practice poses. Nose up, nose down. A gently raised eyebrow. He placed his thumb and forefinger on his chin, as if to signal deep thought, and frowned. 'Much like Achilles at Troy,' he said slowly, 'I do hope they buy this crap.'

'We're about to find out,' Rivkah said.

Valets ghosted out of the shadows and approached the carpentum obsequiously. Carrick handed them the reins, jumped off and went to open the door for Livia—but he was too slow. A well-dressed and well-groomed servant had swept in and was already bowing and showing her to an immaculate carpet that had been rolled out. To her credit, "Sulpicia Martia" did not hesitate for a moment. Instead, she swept across, her two dutiful and perfectly well-behaved children in her wake, and Aemilius marvelled at her ability to turn people invisible with her gaze. Hanno had somehow managed to swing off the cart and fall in behind her, looking just as much like he belonged. *These... people,* he thought, shaking his head. There was a very real risk of all of them being killed, but his travelling companions might be the best chance anyone could have. Without wasting a single motion, Carrick had drifted back to the second cart.

'Shift it.' The scout yanked a thumb in the direction of their mistress, who was well on her way to disappearing out of sight.

Rivkah did not need to be told twice. She leapt down from the cart and strode after Livia, forcing Aemilius to scramble to keep up. He only barely managed to land on his feet and stumbled into a brisk walk behind the lithe girl. She looked every inch the servant—head down, combined with the odd watchful glance to ensure that she was going the right way and not about to cross paths with someone far superior—and he tried to copy her without being too obvious. It was hard work, though, and particularly looking down and away. If the villa of the governor in Hispalis had been new money and poor taste, this... palace was anything but. No expense had been spared anywhere. In the middle of the atrium, a seven-foot statue of an almost obscenely muscled Mars stared out into the settling darkness from a man-high plinth, his commanding features and clenched fists promising to beat seven shades out of anyone who looked at him wrong. Mounted torches cast a generous light over the marbled floor, and fleet-footed servants emerged from and disappeared into porticoes to the left and right. At the far wall elegantly studded and iron-bound double doors, wide and high enough to drive an elephant through, swung open, spilling out light, laughter and music.

A man emerged, and Aemilius had to steel himself to look away.

Oily.

He was too far away to get a good first look at him, but something about the man made his stomach turn immediately.

'Sulpicia Martia,' he intoned. 'Cousin. How *marvellous*.' His voice was nasal, reedy and unpleasant.

'Marcus,' Livia purred. Out of the corner of his eye, he saw her gesturing towards the columns, torches and the back end of Mars. 'This is *wonderful*.'

'Oh, *don't*. I'm sure you have seen much in the provinces.'

'Yes, darling.' Liva paused artfully. 'And it is all covered in sand.'

Marcus Sulpicius's laugh was a braying "hnyech-hnyech-hnyech," and immediately added to the list of contemptible vices in Aemilius's head. 'Come in,' he squealed. 'You simply must refresh yourself. I have a small number of guests, and I am sure they will be *riveted* by you. Sand.' He cackled to himself, and Aemilius risked a glance.

The back of the lord of Villa Sulpicia was lit by a torch and covered in a deep, dramatic blue sash slicing over a tunic that looked soft to the touch even at forty yards away. He struck a tall figure, almost a head taller than Livia in her guise as Sulpicia Martia—and then the doors closed on Livia, Hanno and her two "children" and the magic disappeared.

A blink, a breath, followed by a loud and impressively directed snap of the fingers. 'Service.' The words sounded like the flick of a whip. Following Rivkah's lead, Aemilius turned smartly and looked up as far as he dared. Abrax had somehow snuck up behind them, as had Carrick, and the owner of the voice addressing the four of them sounded like she wouldn't have cared if they'd brought the first four of Tiberius's legions with them. 'You are with me. Servants' quarters. Get rinsed, get ready. I am Augusta, but you may refer to me as Domina. At Villa Sulpicia we have standards, and if you don't meet them…' The threat was an invite to look up. Aemilius did, and wished he hadn't. The woman staring at them had a countenance he had come to recognise. There was a family tree somewhere which featured Cassia, Livia and Brachus, and this woman was somewhere on it. She was wearing the immaculate robes of a majordomo, but they were the least remarkable thing about her. She was about as tall as he was, but nothing about her suggested that he'd survive in a fight for longer than it took to drink a glass of water. She had the bearing of a trained gladiator and a gaze that could cut through stone. '…I will cut your throats in your sleep and feed you to my dogs. Understood?'

Rivkah the Fierce, the deadly Carrick, Flame-lord Abrax and Aemilius of Hispania all came to the same conclusion and spoke in unison.

'Yes, Domina.'

Augusta gave them a withering once-over. Then she turned and walked away briskly to the left, disappearing through a nearly invisible side door. The four shared a look.

'What are you smirking at, you skinny-arsed ghoul?'

'That's my future wife.' Carrick's smirk broke into a full grin.

'Wonderful. Just tell us where you want us to bury your remains.' Aemilius turned to follow Abrax, who was already heading for the baths, noting that Carrick's shoulders were shaking ever so gently with silent laughter.

BEHIND LIVIA AND Hanno, the door closed and cut the world in half. Outside was Italia, nature and stars taking over a darkening sky. And inside, in the wake of Marcus Sulpicius, was the mastery of man. Even someone like Livia Sculla, born to the most noble of patrician families and raised in all the finest that Rome had to offer, did not have to try too hard to find nice things to say.

'Oh, *Marcus*,' she purred. 'This is *sublime*.'

Marcus cast a glance over his shoulder. 'Mm,' he said, revelling in the praise. 'Commissioned it especially. Atlas holding the world. Just like the Sulpicii carry the Empire.'

'Quite, quite.' Light from artfully inset bronze lanterns in place of planets bathed the towering figure of the muscular God in a very flattering light, playing over his bulging muscles and caressing his noble but pained features. 'He even looks like a Sulpicius.'

'A coincidence, I'm sure,' Marcus said breezily as they made their way through the atrium.

'The water flows where the water will, and there is little we can do about it,' Hanno added thoughtfully. 'Well, except aqueducts, of course.'

'A practical philosopher!' Marcus chuckled nasally. 'A rare breed.'

'As rare as an honest senator.' Hanno bounced back and forth, heel and toe.

The quick reply brought a bark of a laugh out of the nobleman. 'Oh, he's *precious!* Where did you find him?'

'In the land of the Moors. I followed darling Publius on business there last year and heard him conversing on various subjects with some travelling academics. He completely and utterly ruined them. Reduced them to calling him a savage.'

'Some men like shouting at the rain.'

'Indeed,' Marcus said slowly. 'Indeed. Now, friends— come with me! We were just settling down to a little snack.' He turned sharply and walked off. As she moved to follow, Livia glanced at Hanno and gave him an almost imperceptible wink. The short philosopher flashed her a brilliant smile. Serena and Flavius ghosted in behind them, well-drilled and dutiful, having already finished cataloguing the most valuable items and the best shadows to hide in. From the atrium Marcus led them through double doors and into the triclinium.

'I wonder what he is compensating for,' Livia muttered under her breath.

The dining room was no modest affair. Easily forty feet by thirty, and with doors at the far end, it was richly decorated with scenes of gods and wars lined by dark blue curtains, but the main feature was couches angled to fit twelve people reclining on three sides around a central space. Six of the spaces were already taken, and Livia's party was being sized up by its occupants. Marcus clapped loudly, once, and a matronly woman appeared from behind them, standing to attention. He glanced over his shoulder at the children, and the woman swept over to them, putting hands on their shoulders. A question in the form of a raised eyebrow to Sulpicia Martia was replied to with a gentle nod and a smile, and Flavius and Serena were summarily whisked away. Marcus gestured to two available reclining spaces, and Hanno and Livia got to take in the "snack" that their host had referred to.

A table had been built to fit the couches, with space for servants to walk into. It was covered with a vibrant blue tablecloth, on which floated a variety of dishes in miniature bowls. Thumb-sized prawns in a rich, red sauce. Bowls of vibrant greens pulped with oil and nuts, surrounded by fist-sized bread rolls. Two legs of meat—

pork, roasted and thickly sliced, glistening with syrup, and something that must have been off an ox twice the size, cut so thin that it could almost have been moving with the wind. Three whole cooked flounders, dressed with lemon, herbs and enough butter to swim in. A stuffed partridge, skin golden and crisp. Sparks of light danced on white wine in crystal goblets as big as a man's arm.

'Oh, but I've missed real cooking,' Livia said huskily.

'You probably don't get this in Hispania, do you?' Marcus said smugly.

'We certainly don't, cousin.' Feigning surprise, she "discovered" the other diners. 'Greetings, and profound apologies for interrupting.'

'Please. No apologies. Any relation of Marcus Sulpicius is a friend of mine.' The deep bass voice of a thick-set, thin-haired old man, clean-shaven and clearly used to being told he was correct: a senator, Livia guessed. Next to him, what had to be his wife nodded demurely, revealing a lifetime of agreeing with her husband.

'You must be exhausted, poor darlings.' A woman, perhaps in her late thirties, expensively dressed in a low-cut dress of green satin. Her companion, a handsome and athletic young man, smiled along in a way that suggested he might have understood that new people had arrived, but would definitely need to be reminded of who and why.

The fifth and sixth diners did not say anything. One, a dark-skinned man, lithe and bright-eyed, shot them a bright smile. The other, at least a decade older and hardened by the sword, tall and thin, short-haired and tough-jawed, acknowledged their presence with a curt nod.

'So wonderful to have you, cousin,' Marcus prattled as Livia and Hanno settled into their custom-built reclining sofas. Silent child-staff appeared with plates and seemed to magically read every slight glance, leading to full plates within moments.

'Oh, the pleasure is all mine.' For emphasis, Livia grabbed a prawn and sucked the sauce off it, making a sound that only just escaped the obscene. 'Oh, heavens above and all the gods in them. Who cooks this?'

Marcus Sulpicius seemed fit to burst with ill-deserved pride. 'They have been with us for twenty years now, and I have told cook and her kitchen team that they must sign a contract that guarantees me the right to their offspring.'

'Mm! Clever!' the senator's wife exclaimed. 'It's *so* hard to hold on to decent staff, and one must surmise that they beget good staff themselves. That's just logic.'

'Too right, Clarissa, my dear. Too right,' her husband rumbled.

'If I find them, I'll try to tempt them across the valley,' the woman in green purred.

'*Don't*, Octavia,' Marcus warned playfully. 'You have the best grapes in the region—'

'Cheers to that,' the senator rumbled, raising a glass.

'—and the fattest pigs, and it is only fair that I get to keep *something*.'

Next to Octavia, the handsome man seemed to register that a threat had been made and prepared to rise. A gentle hand on his hulking frame settled him back down. 'You're no fun.' Octavia pouted. 'I am but a poor widow, and you seek to deprive me of the daily joy of a well-cooked meal.'

The senator snorted. 'Last time we were at yours we had seventeen courses. I couldn't move for a week. I wouldn't say you're deprived.'

'But if I got to have him, we could let my cooks fight it out. It would be fun!' There was a sparkle in the woman's eye that suggested her idea of "fun" was intimately connected to direct and immediate pain.

'No—you can't have him, and that's that.' Marcus raised a finger to stall Octavia's protests. 'You may not be used to the word, my dear, but it does exist. No.' He turned to Livia. 'Tell me tales of your travels, cousin! Where have you been? What have you seen? Barbarians? Tumblers? Strange patterns in the sky?'

Livia smiled demurely. 'Oh, I don't know whether I've seen anything much of interest, really. I just wanted to come home, really. Set my foot on Italian soil.'

'Where from?' Clarissa leaned forward.

'Hispania.'

The lithe, dark-skinned man's voice was cold and smooth, and it slithered in the dark. 'Hispania, you say?' He sized her up, then glanced at his companion. 'Interesting...'

IX

VILLA SULPICIA

THE HISS OF water on hot coals from the next room jolted Aemilius out of his stupor. He had been sitting on a wooden bench, staring into the middle distance with robes half-off and half-on, and while he wasn't asleep, he wasn't far from it. Carrick and Abrax must have gone on ahead, because tendrils of steam were drifting into the doorframe—slender at first but growing thicker. *Like a beckoning finger.* The thought came from nowhere and gave him a sharp chill, so he bit down and undressed, quickly wrapping the towel around himself and walking through into the baths.

He could feel the road dust fight a losing battle against the steam heat as he moved further into the gloom. The servants' baths were functional, with minimal decoration, but well-made. Through the steam he could see Carrick, a corpse-white twig next to the dark mass of Abrax.

'Bath's over there.' A pointed finger towards a big, circular structure in the corner. 'Should still be reasonably warm.'

'Thank you,' Aemilius muttered awkwardly. Having grown up a governor's son, he had never given much thought to bathing in the company of others. Trying to cover his modesty and neither show his front, back or profile to the men, he whisked the towel off quickly and plunged himself in, only barely holding in a scream. The bath was more than reasonably hot. He could feel his skin reddening and almost yelped when it enveloped his testicles. He'd not felt this kind of heat since—

'It's nice to travel with a fire magus.' Even though Aemilius couldn't see Carrick's face he could hear the smirk on him.

'You're welcome,' Abrax rumbled. 'And be thankful that Hanno isn't here. I've seen him play some awful tricks on people bathing naked.' Aemilius twitched in reflex before he realised the bathwater was not, in fact, going to assault him in any way.

And then, the heat started working its magic.

Inch by inch Aemilius of Hispania found himself unravelling. It started in the fingers, in the tips of his fingers, which suddenly felt almost heavy, unwieldy, like they belonged to someone else. He could feel his toes relaxing, his hips, his knees—he thought himself lucky to have propped his elbows up on the edge of the tub because his spine suddenly seemed to be made of butter, and slowly his legs, which he remembered thinking looked scrawny and weird, like on some kind of reed-bird, drifted upwards and he was floating and his hips felt heavy and light at the same time, and all he could manage was a sigh from the very centre of his being.

'Thank you,' he whispered hoarsely across to Abrax, or what he assumed was the fire magus, sitting in a cloud of steam.

Time passed, and Aemilius could not have told anyone how much, but way before he wanted it to, Abrax's deep voice said, 'We must move. We are servants, and we do not have the luxury of freedom.'

With great difficulty Aemilius levered himself out of the bath and stepped to the floor on wobbly legs, wrapping the towel around him as an afterthought. The other two were already moving into the dressing room, and he hurried on after them with everything above the neck. The rest of his body took its sweet time. When he got back to his bench, clean and folded tunics had appeared in place of their travelling gear, and Abrax was already fully clad. Carrick stood with his back to them, holding up his tunic in silence.

'You need to wear it, friend,' Abrax said gently.

The scout shot the magus a look that was sharper than most blades Aemilius had seen. 'Slave cloth,' he spat.

'I know,' the big man replied. 'I have met many of my people caught in it. But we fight a different fight, and the ones we hunt will not care about the colour of your tunic.'

Carrick looked about to snap back at the big man but thought better of it. 'I know,' was all he offered before pulling it over his head. However, Aemilius had time to see that the tunic covered what looked like a lot of whipping scars.

RIVKAH WAS WAITING on the other side of the baths, wearing the house tunic and looking her usual blend of bored and furious. 'Took you long enough,' she grumped. 'Did you stop for a cuddle?'

'Of course we did,' Aemilius shot back. 'We just couldn't handle how much we missed you.' A quick snort-cackle from Carrick gave him an unexpected flush of pride. 'Have you checked where we're going?'

Rivkah nodded down the corridor. 'Saw some runts disappear down that way, and there's food. Reckon that's our best bet.' The men didn't need to be told twice, and they moved as one along the corridor. A pool of bright light was spilling around a corner, with the occasional and familiar sound of metal clanging or a warbled shout—the song of the cook.

The kitchen at Via Sulpicia was impressive, even compared to what Aemilius had grown up with. Two ovens, each big enough to stand a child in, blazed on opposite sides of a square room, easily sixty feet to a side. Workbenches hugged the northern wall and three big islands, covered in a variety of knives, boards, animal remains and piles of chopped vegetables, created an obstacle course to get to a long, simple but sturdy dining table, seating at Aemilius's estimate some twenty people at a time. It took a moment before they were spotted in the doorway, so they had the chance to observe.

At either end, close to the ovens and the heat, two sturdy figures moved with the force and authority of ownership. *Command always looks the same.* The cooks—one male, one female, Aemilius guessed, although they were both of a similar height, width and general shape— bossed, prodded, poked and jostled a handful of helpers, who seemed more busy tidying than cooking. *They must have just served a meal.* The occasional runner would appear at the door, mutter something to one or the other of the cooks, and a series of orders would be barked out, at which point the others would jump to and whisk something away on a plate. Finally, they were spotted, probably because they were standing still. An angular woman who looked like she had not wasted any time in her life ever and wasn't about to start, snapped her fingers and pointed towards the table before marching over to deal with some carrots. Being quite comfortable with the chain of command, the legionnaires accepted their orders and went to sit down out of the way.

Within moments, three Germanes all cut from the same cloth—brutes and attack dogs, square of shoulder and cruel in the eye, smaller than Abrax but not by much—barged in through a side door, nearly knocking over a servant who rescued a plate of lamb meat with some astonishingly quick footwork. Unlike the legionnaires, the Germanes did not hesitate. They marched straight to the far end of the long table and proceeded to beat upon it with their fists—slowly at first, then harder, louder and faster, shouting for food.

Just before the noise became unbearable, a servant appeared with three bowls of stew which he deposited in front of the soldiers and spun away at speed. The Germanes fell upon their food, slurping noisily. It took two spoons' worth before one of them howled for mead, swiftly joined by the others, and flipped his bowl. Thin, brown liquid with unidentified chunks spilled out onto the table.

'That'll be mostly spit, I reckon,' Rivkah muttered.

Aemilius had to blink twice to notice Carrick. The scout had gone dead still, so much so that it actually took some effort to notice him, and Aemilius had a chilling premonition. *In three more blinks he'll have melted into the shadows. Another five, and he'll emerge from behind the brutes, and then there will be blood.*

'There is no love there,' Abrax rumbled, raising an eyebrow towards the staff.

'Cats in a kennel,' Rivkah agreed. 'All on high alert.'

Except the girl who came in, holding a tray that was too big for her. She swerved towards the Germanes and one of them, a scruffy square-jaw, launched an arm out, hooking her in by the waist. She screamed, first in surprise and then in anger as the brute pinned her arms to her sides and roughly squeezed her breasts and arse, shouting something in a coarse language that had his friends hooting with laughter.

Time changed, and slowed and sped up at the same time, and the noise of Aemilius's chair scraping backwards was somehow much louder than he thought it would be, and his voice sounded much louder than he thought it would, and when he shouted, 'No wonder you're barking loudly because the mothers of all Germanes are bitches,' for a moment he did not realise that he had said it out loud.

The pause, and then the sound of all three of the warriors standing up at once, though, was about as loud as expected. The girl staggered away, retreating to safety behind one of the cooks, who had taken the tiniest of steps towards the rack of short, heavy meat cleavers.

'Say that again?' another of the Germanes said, a darkly expectant note in his voice.

Out of the corner of his eye he saw Rivkah tense and he thought for a heartbeat, then held out a hand behind his back. *No.* A part of his brain screamed at him, quite loudly, too, but there was some certainty in him somewhere. This was the right thing to do. The part of his brain that had screamed at him just then promptly demanded an explanation, which was drowned out by his own voice saying, with confidence he did not quite understand, 'I'm just saying, that when your *vater* fucks your *mutter*, your *mutter* goes *woof*. Just like you did.'

They were on him in a flash.

He blocked the first punch. Well, sort of. He got his arm in the way of the first punch, and his own arm smacked into his face. Then he doubled over for a moment before he realised that he had been hit in the stomach and heard himself make the sound 'hrrrrbhgh'. He tasted the blood in his mouth with the deafening smack of a backhand that spun him around, and as he was falling a vicious kick was levelled, heel-first, at his hip bone, which connected perfectly and sent him twirling to the ground with a crunch. Everything was upside-down and sideways, but he saw big feet closing in on his face and then a swing and he was airborne thanks to the foot in his stomach and he heaved and retched and landed and another kick hit him in the chest and his face smacked into a table leg and he could taste more blood, and then there was a moment and he looked up and up and up towards the far-away face of the massive warrior and he saw the foot lift slowly up, and up, and up, and then there was a whip-crack voice from somewhere and the foot came down slowly, and Aemilius heard a hocking sound and then something wet landed on his face, and then a broad, stinging pain as he was kicked in the bollocks and then the Germanes left.

A silence followed, and then a scrape of a chair and Rivkah was next to him. 'I can't *wait* for you to explain this one to me,' she hissed in his ear as she hoisted him to his feet, ignoring the whimpering. 'You'll live, and nothing's broken, but you're fucking lucky Augusta came in. The big one was just about to rearrange your face, and it might even have been for the worse.' Every part of his body screamed at him, but Aemilius didn't particularly care. He wasn't listening. 'And why the fuck are you smiling?'

'Just wait,' he whispered back, allowing her to ease him into a chair.

Everything had gone back to normal in the kitchen with remarkable speed. It was as if they had turned invisible, sitting at the table. And then three servers walked past, and somehow big plates heaped with offcuts of roast pork, raw beef and cheese appeared on the table. Nobody said a thing, nor did they mention why a flagon of expensive wine had been accidentally left on their table with four cups. Fresh baked rolls fell off a tray, and a bowl of roast vegetables was not there and then it was.

Aemilius glanced at Rivkah and raised a swollen eyebrow.

Shit for brains, she mouthed back at him, tucking into the food.

He winced in return, feeling for his teeth with his tongue. Everything was sore, but the throbbing was getting easier to deal with. Nothing broken. *Good.* He touched his cheek and felt wet and sticky. *Not so good.*

He noticed Rivkah's glance, followed by a twinkle in the eye. He saw and felt no presence, but somehow, at his elbow, a bowl had appeared with a clean, wet cloth in it. He looked over his shoulder, but there was no one there.

'MAY ALL GODS praise you, but mostly your cook,' Livia sighed, leaning back. 'That was simply divine.'

The senator belched in agreement. 'Perfect, Marcus. Just perfect.'

'Beautiful,' Octavia purred. 'Simple'—she let the word hang in the air, then continued just before the pause became an insult—'and beautiful.'

Hanno smiled and nodded. He knew that quiet waters were sometimes the most dangerous, so he had held his peace during the dinner, and he had listened and he had watched. And there were some crocodiles in these waters, for certain and sure. The man Ismael was still and long and slim and quiet, and the only thing that moved was his eyes, and he wanted to eat them all. Hanno smiled. There was beauty in the old ones, the floating ones. Cold and cruel, but a beauty, nonetheless. And so Hanno watched, and waited, and waited and watched, and then, just as the animals at the watering hole were making their happy noises, bellies full of happiness, he moved.

'A fine meal indeed, Marcus Sulpicius. Easily the equal of anything that Rome has to offer.' He paused artfully, and added apologetically, 'Well... *almost* anything.'

'Oh, I've had more *elaborate* things,' the senator huffed. 'A swan baked into an elephant's leg and whatnot.' He waved his hand dismissively at the best efforts of the world's most refined chefs. 'But this—it is just *right*. We are away from the hustle and bustle, and there is just the right number of dishes, and the room is just the right size and the recliners are comfortable and the company is entrancing.' He swept over the women of the room with a suggestive glance that the senator was unaware had lost what little charm it ever had several decades ago. His wife tittered dutifully.

'Oh, absolutely,' Ismael agreed. 'Everything is as it should be.' And Hanno watched as the jaws closed, almost gently, and the weight of the old one started dragging the antelope to its drowning death. 'But imagine... if you could have this kind of space, and quiet, and still be within a comfortable walk from everything that Rome had to offer? Imagine if you didn't have to choose either or.' He nodded to Octavia, who was watching him with hungry interest. 'Imagine if you *could* hire three top chefs, at your whim, and have them show up to your door before noon to stage an epic battle of dishes that would last all night and into the morning.'

The senator scoffed. 'Easily imagined. Sounds like some of Diodorus's stories about Crassus. And no one will ever be that rich again.' He smirked at the other guests, but... Hanno smiled. The thrashing of the beast only made it go down faster. The old man had mentioned the richest Roman of all time. Ismael hadn't needed to— and now the idea was there, it was mighty hard to ignore.

The lithe, black man glanced at Marcus and flashed a brilliant, conspiratorial smile. The host smiled back. 'Maybe...' he said, drawing out the pause artfully, '... and maybe not.'

The senator's face turned angry. 'Marcus—what is this?' he demanded. 'Have you brought me here to sit with a *street vendor*?'

If the barb was meant to outrage Ismael, it was unsuccessful. Instead, their host smiled benignly and held out his hands to placate the senator. 'Listen, Tarquin. My friend. How long have we known each other?'

Tarquin scowled. 'What? Uh...'

'Twenty-three years,' his wife said quietly.

'We have played the game together for a long time.'

'We have,' the old senator huffed.

'And have you ever seen me be dishonest?' Marcus said, grinning.

Tarquin laughed sharply and looked straight at the host of the party, searching for information in his face. 'Of course I have.'

'Of course you have,' Marcus agreed. 'And have you ever seen me bend the rules?'

'Yes! Twice last month!'

And Hanno watched as another old one joined the hunt, jaws closing around the antelope's neck. Marcus Sulpicius stared straight and hard at Publius Tarquin Cornelius, and any trace of jocularity vanished from his voice. 'And have you ever seen me let go of a chance to get an unfair advantage?'

Anger and haughty authority drained from the senator, who for a flash just looked like an old man. However, he had gotten to be an old man because of well-honed instincts for personal benefit. 'I have not,' he said slowly. 'In fact, I have known you to be a vicious blood hound for anything that can move your ambitions forward by even an inch.'

'And likewise, my friend,' Marcus said, grinning and raising a glass. There was a moment—a heartbeat—and then Tarquin did the same. 'And we know, of course, that opportunities to do so are more or less exhausted wherever we set foot.'

'Everything is squeezed,' Tarquin agreed mournfully. 'All posts are gone, all routes are taken. Everything is owned.'

'Some of it by us, granted. And, of course, your late and lamented husband, my dear,' Marcus offered an inclusive sweep of the arm to Octavia.

She put an entirely insincere hand on her heart and sighed. 'He would have loved to be here.'

And Hanno smiled. There were more crocodiles than antelopes in this river.

'So,' Tarquin said. The dinner guest was gone, and in its place was a bloodless operator. 'Talk.'

Marcus Sulpicius reclined, popping a grape in his mouth and savouring both the taste and attention, before glancing over at Ismael. 'Would you like to tell them?'

Ismael bowed his head obsequiously. 'In your house, my friend? I would not dream of it. Why would I speak when I could benefit from the oratorial power of the great Sulpicius himself?'

Flattery is a crocodile's trick, thought Hanno. This one has hunted well. He is going to let them convince themselves and drown each other. And just so, Marcus started doing Ismael's work. 'As we know, much of Aethiopia remains unexplored. And in the case of the land of my friend Ismael's father, this is by design. He comes from a place he calls the Silver Heart, due to its abundance of precious metals. It is an inaccessible valley, approachable only through a treacherous jungle, over harsh mountains and through killing waters. His father ruled there and was by all accounts a wise and judicious king, kind and generous to his people but wary of invaders.'

'When you say abundance,' Octavia said. 'How much?'

'They do not have the need to dig out the ore from the mountains,' Marcus continued. 'They simply pick up the nuggets they find on the ground.'

The woman in green gasped, cheeks flushed with greed.

'And why have we not heard of this magical land before?' Tarquin pressed. 'You'd think someone would have told the tales.'

Marcus nodded to Ismael, who smiled almost apologetically. 'All trades are done through a series of intermediaries. We buy most of what we need in Alexandria, at which point any sign of our riches has vanished. It is only at home that our streets are lined with silver and gold.'

'But surely someone would have seen this?'

'They have.'

'And why didn't they bring back tales?'

Ismael did not raise his voice. He did not rise to Tarquin's challenge. He simply stated a fact. 'Because when they tried to leave, we killed them.'

There was a brief pause, but in a room full of viciousness and greed no one saw a reason to challenge this. 'Right,' Tarquin said. 'So why are you here now, asking for our help?'

'Because my father...' And again, Hanno smiled. He did not look over at Livia, for he knew that she would have her eyes trained on Ismael as indeed Sulpicia Martia should, as he was a man speaking, but he knew that she would be smiling as well, inwardly. They were being treated to a display by a master craftsman. 'My father was murdered by my treacherous uncle.' Behind him, Ismael's companion hocked once, angrily, and spat on the floor. 'And now my uncle wants to stop his people from enjoying the riches of our valley and keep them all to himself. I only escaped with help'—the faintest nudge to his companion—'and I feel it is my duty to find good Romans who will help put me on the throne and restore order in the Silver Heart.'

'And what's in it for us?' Tarquin snapped.

'Silver and gold worth an initial twenty million sesterces, divided between us based on our contributions,' Marcus Sulpicius shot back. 'Followed by a mining contract worth six million sesterces a year, for as long as your family line lasts. It's not Crassus... but it is a start. Think of your situation, my friend. Think of your estates, your standing and your reach, which is formidable.' Tarquin stared intently at him. 'What could you do with, say, an extra ten million? Who could you crush? Where could you gain a foothold?'

Next to the calculating senator, Octavia looked positively ecstatic. 'Oh, *Marcus*. This is incredible—'

Tarquin interrupted. 'Precisely. I have learned and learned well that if something sounds too good to be true, it usually is. What do you want?'

'I want to be the ruler of my—'

'Yes, yes, yes,' Tarquin interrupted. 'Save your people and all that. What do you want from *us*?'

'Funds.' Ismael smiled, and waited for half a heartbeat, until the senator made to speak again, at which point he interrupted. '—and I should hope, senator, that you are about to request proof.'

Off-balance, Tarquin huffed. 'Of course I am. How do I know that you are not some dice-rattling, snake-charming, two-bit Aethiop?'

'You don't,' Ismael replied. Tarquin frowned in confusion. 'In fact, I could have waited, and watched, and chosen a prominent Roman known for his avarice'—next to him, Marcus Sulpicius looked utterly torn between offence and pride—'wormed my way into his good graces and convinced me to introduce him to his rich and powerful friends.' Ismael allowed this to drift between them, waiting for his audience to catch up. 'But...' he looked at them each, in turn. His face was gentle, and open, and happy. 'You will possibly agree with me that Rome suffers no shortage of greedy patricians.' There was just one smile in the room, and it was slow, and it was spreading across the faces of Octavia, Tarquin, his wife and Marcus Sulpicius. Next to Octavia, her companion was snoring gently, laid at his mistress's feet like an over-bred hound. 'And so, I daresay if I was indeed just a dice-chucking Aethiop—' The smile, and the confidence, turned the slur sideways in Tarquin's mouth. 'I could have picked myself some significantly easier targets. Greedier. Dumber. *Weaker.* No, my honourable Romans. I chose Marcus Sulpicius because his reputation as a tough man who gets things done reaches far further than he could comfortably travel. I asked him to invite the two of you because you have a unique combination of ruthlessness and resources. We may be isolated in our Silver Heart, but for a decade now I have been my father's ambassador and trade overseer, and I have walked among the wealthy all along the African coast. I have heard what they say, especially when they assume the two-bit Aethiop isn't listening. I know how you came by some of your lands, Publius Tarquin—' The senator blustered, but Ismael was quick to cosh him. '—and I applaud it. I need men like you. And as for you, Domina Octavia—' The black man turned his focus to the woman in green, and something lightning-quick passed between them that made Hanno thankful that the young companion was sleeping, for even he would have understood. 'I want my uncle to die like your husband died.' She looked him straight in the eyes and neither of them wavered, until he smirked and added, '…in a tragic case of ill health.'

'Such a shame, that was,' she purred.

'And so we are here. Publius Tarquin—you have asked, understandably, what I want. I want funds to hire and train a small company of the toughest soldiers we can find. A hundred and fifty will do. It is almost impossible to get anything much more than that to my home, but luckily our location means that we have not had the need for a big army, and those who do guard duty are complacent. The kind of men I want will not come cheap, and there will be assorted costs for getting them there and paying them to stay, for once they enter the Silver Heart they will not be allowed to leave.'

'How much?'

Ismael turned away from Octavia and towards Tarquin, fixing the senator with a steely eye. 'If I was indeed a chancer, now is where I would suggest a number. The number would be too high by a third. I would make you bargain me down to the number I wanted to fleece you of, which would be *just* under what you'd be comfortable with.' The old senator huffed, but did not speak, instead inviting Ismael to make his next move. 'And I would be a fool.'

'You've got that right,' Tarquin spat.

'So, I am going to ask you to tell me instead. How much does it cost to raise and equip a troop of mercenaries?' Ismael grinned like a crocodile. 'Marcus Sulpicius—raids on rival grain supplies in '28. Burning down warehouses in '31. Publius Tarquin—thirty years of funding a variety of pirate operations out of Sardinia, Sicilia and the Baleares, picking a beautiful collection of his competitors' ships, just enough to cause damage but never ruin.' Both men sputtered, but Ismael just grinned and nodded. 'Obviously none of this is true. Vicious rumours always abound about successful men.' Palms up, he smiled. 'So, let's push that to the side and instead engage your famous problem-solving skills. *If* you were to ever indulge in such things—for the first time, obviously—how much do you think would be required to recruit and fund such an enterprise?'

Eager to have something else to think about, Marcus and Tarquin went for the bait. 'You'd need more than a hundred and fifty soldiers, for a start,' Marcus said.

'Doctors, cooks... horses?'

'No horses,' Ismael said. 'They'd get eaten alive.'

'Infantry, then,' Tarquin continued. 'How long might it take?' He shook his head. 'No. You said. They are in this forever. A soldier—'

'We don't need soldiers.' They jumped at the harsh, heavily accented voice of Ismael's companion. 'We need *fighters*.'

Tarquin nodded. 'Good. Trained soldiers come at ten denarii a month, food excluded. Fighters you could get cheaper. But if we say, for argument's sake, that we are going for rather more skill...'

'...you could end up doubling that,' Marcus added.

'And you get what you pay for. So, let's double it. Three thousand denarii for the first month. That again for travel and food. Add another thousand denarii to equip them.'

'And another three thousand for bribes,' Livia added sweetly.

Marcus's head snapped round and he blinked. 'Cousin!' he exclaimed, not able to get anything else out.

'My honoured husband does a lot of business in Africa. If you are wanting to transport a company of one hundred and fifty men—which I would split into fifteen groups of twelve, auxiliaries included, and have them travel from at least six different directions, converging as far up the Nile as they dare go and following the river upland—I will warn you that the Africans will do their very best to divest them of every single bit of precious metal they carry, including the buckles on their belts.'

The silence after her entry was followed by a guffaw from Tarquin as he slapped his couch. 'She's a Sulpicia, all right! Blood doesn't lie. Absolutely right on all counts.'

Ismael now turned his attention to Livia. 'My humble apologies, Domina. I have quite forgotten my manners. I should have known that from your family, your standing and the company you keep that you'd be a force to be reckoned with.'

And Hanno watched as the undercurrent of Livia's grace and quickness flowed beneath the burbling waters of Sulpicia Martia, creating a canny Roman noblewoman who had sat at the table during the making of decisions and listened carefully all her life and was, here, just a *little* bit out of her depth, and he thought to himself that sometimes, when a new species of fish makes its home in the water, the ones with the biggest teeth have to work harder to keep themselves alive. 'Oh, I don't know about that,' she demurred. 'I have just heard a lot of talk, is all.'

'As have I,' Ismael pressed. 'And in the big game, those who listen often beat those who talk.'

'Oh, I'm awful at games.' Hanno stifled a chuckle, knowing full well that Livia Sculla had personally redistributed the wealth of at least five branches of three significant patrician families in various gambling dens in the less salubrious parts of Rome. 'I can never get the numbers right.'

'But you still think three thousand sesterces is right for bribes?'

'Probably,' Livia said, making a show of thinking. 'It does depend on your companies, though. Bring some canny negotiators and you can probably cut that down by a tenth. I think—'

'Travel by night, hire some quiet ones who don't mind wet work and you can cut it down by half,' Tarquin interrupted.

In a fantastic show of self-control, Livia managed to make Sulpicia Martia look both impressed and happy to be corrected. 'Of course,' she said. 'But I know nothing of such things. If my honourable husband has ever used such methods, they have been negotiated while I have been otherwise occupied.'

'The details can be arranged later,' Marcus said, somewhat impatiently. 'The most important question is—are you in?'

'Yes,' Octavia snapped immediately. Next to her, the sleeping hunk stirred but did not wake.

'I think my husband would definitely be interested,' Livia said with a beautifully calibrated mix of caution and greed.

Marcus turned to Tarquin, who scowled. 'I don't know,' he huffed. 'It all sounds incredibly shaky. We don't even know what we are going for. And I have not heard a single peep about this Silver Heart. I would have expected to—'

The bag clinked softly as it landed on the table in front of Ismael. 'I understand. These are family heirlooms. They belonged to my mother, and some to my father. I would like to offer them to you as thanks for your valuable time'—he nodded to Tarquin—'and your help.' Smiles for Marcus, Octavia and Livia. He pulled the bottom of the bag up with a flourish, and out tumbled a galaxy of stars.

A necklace, woven of the blackest silk, adorned with silver panther claws set in between finely polished blue-black stones.

A bracelet crafted of knuckle-sized orbs of silver, engraved with sharp, angular lines.

A whisper-thin leather choker with strands of spun silver cascading from it, evoking a waterfall.

Octavia gasped loud enough to wake the hunk. He rumbled, but she shushed him. 'Oh, by the heavens,' she whispered. 'They are *spectacular*.'

Ismael nudged the claw necklace towards Tarquin. 'This belonged to my father, a proud warrior of—'

The senator pushed it back. 'I will sleep, and I will ask my ancestors,' he said coldly. 'If your idea sounds as good in the morning light, with a headache, I will consider it. I thank you for your efforts.' He stretched, farted loudly and found some of his dinner guest charm. 'But now an old man must go to bed.' He clapped twice, and servants appeared from the shadows as he clambered to his feet. 'Thank you, Marcus. The food was spectacular.' And with that he left, trailed by the dutiful wife.

The others watched him leave. 'I am sure our friend will return in the morning with a favourable outcome,' Marcus said nervously.

'Do not fear,' Ismael said. 'He is a wise man. I am sure you are right. Meanwhile,' He fixed the women with a gaze. 'Will you bring the strength and wisdom of Diana to our cause?'

'We will,' Octavia replied breathlessly. 'We will.'

'I—yes,' Livia said, matching her excitement. 'We certainly will!'

'Excellent!' Marcus grinned. 'This calls for a celebration!' He clapped his hands three times, and within moments a tray had appeared on the table, set with a glittering crystal goblet full of a maroon liquid. 'This I have been saving for a special occasion. It is seven years old, and from the Emperor's own vineyard. He gifted me with an amphora for services to Rome, and I promised myself it would have to be a beautiful night for the cork to come out of this one. And what could be more beautiful than this?' While he talked, quick hands had filled up seven goblets. One by one, the guests were offered theirs, which were dutifully raised. 'To freedom for the Silver Heart!'

'To freedom!' the guests echoed.

And Hanno marvelled once again at the flow and the ebb and the flow of it all.

X

VILLA SULPICIA

THE DARK PURPLE sky enveloped the Villa Sulpicia as stars twinkled overhead. Inside, wall-mounted bronze lamps cast a soft, gentle glow of light that kept the night away and lit the corridors just enough to orient its guests. Striding on after their ghost-like servant girl, Sulpicia Martia, better known to her fellow travellers as Livia Sculla, wasted no opportunity to marvel at the ornate walls.

'Ooh! Look! That's Hercules fighting the Hydra!'

'That's a big one,' Hanno the Wise remarked.

'Yes,' Livia laughed. 'Hercules was famously a rather big boy.' Silently, she turned to glare at Hanno, who smiled impishly and stuck his tongue out at her. 'I am so glad that Hydras don't exist,' she added pointedly.

'They don't anymore—but who is to say what hides under our beds?'

'A pot, I'd hope, and nothing else.'

The servant had stopped by a door and silently swung the door open. Livia stepped in without even remotely acknowledging their presence. Hanno nodded solemnly in recognition as he passed. The girl stepped in behind them, moved to a door at the far end of the room, past the bed, and opened it, again without making a sound.

Livia glanced at her. 'Are they in bed?' she said curtly. The girl nodded once. 'Good. I will speak for a while with my philosopher. You may leave.' The girl nodded again and vanished into the corridor, closing the door behind her.

'Your cousin is a wise and generous host.' The moment the door shut, Hanno walked around the room as he talked, studying everything in the room carefully as he spoke. A dresser with a generously proportioned candle set upon it in a bronze dish stood next to an elegant but sturdy chair. 'He has treated us well.' Glancing at Livia, he shook his head and mouthed, *safe*.

As Hanno worked from east to west, Livia worked from north to south. 'He is. Most of Rome I cannot give two flips of a sesterces about, but I have always liked him.' A large, wall-mounted mirror. Floor inlaid with a patterned mosaic—intertwined lines and squares in blue and gold, with a silver border. 'He knows his mind.' She nodded back to Hanno. *Safe here*.

'He certainly does.' A bar to hang clothes on. A solidly built bed with delicately carved bedposts. Hanno tilted his head to the side and sniffed the air, a hound on a scent—then he shook his head. *Still safe*. 'And his friend is quite the crocodile.'

'Not seen the like for a long while. Made me feel quite... excited.' A playful smile danced on Livia's lips, not unlike the last thing a mouse ever sees.

'If there are unwanted ears here, I cannot find them,' Hanno said quietly.

'You can speak.'

'Oh, f—' Livia managed to choke off the rest of her swearwords. Her darling children had *manifested*, like sibling ghosts, at the door to their bedroom.

'We swept it. Snuck out after bedtime. Naughty,' Serena said, grinning impishly.

Flavius nodded. 'Every inch. Stuffed a sheet in the air duct under the bed, but that is about it.'

'Very good,' Livia said, regaining her composure. 'What did you see?'

'Mater's plans were broadly correct but did not account for detail.' He spoke quickly. 'The art room is shuttered during the day, mostly dark—but it's big pieces. The Sulpicii are rumoured to have a vault somewhere, but we'd need more time to find it. The Germanes roam the place freely, and the staff gives them a wide berth. Marcus's study oversees the triclinium. The majordomo looks like trouble.'

'Good,' Livia said. 'We'll try to get you more freedom tomorrow. Now, sleep.'

In unison, the children nodded and disappeared back into their bedroom. When the door closed, Hanno made a show of shuddering. 'Now we know what Ismael is after,' he mused, 'how would you go about stopping it?'

'I don't know.' Livia's gaze was far away, but a smile played on her lips. 'But I look forward to finding out.'

'SAY THIS FOR rich people's servants—they can drink, the fuckers,' Rivkah chuckled.

'I was impressed with the efficiency and confidence with which they drank wine that must have cost at least a year's wages,' Abrax warbled, watching their guide to their quarters walk away somewhat unsteadily. 'And the expertise with which the rest was watered down.'

'Years of experience,' Carrick slurred. 'They're all at it. Used to run an operation for a corrupt majordomo. He bought it in from vineyards for his master's money, halved it, sold off the excess to tavernas at night and kept the change.'

'And no one noticed?' Aemilius found to his surprise that despite the company he kept, and despite the fact that they had lied themselves into the heart of the Villa Sulpicia and would be executed without so much as a sniff of a trial if anyone found out, he was mildly outraged at this ill treatment of the patricians.

'All wine tastes the same after the first three goblets,' Carrick replied, grinning like a fox. 'You just need to make sure they are taken from the right amphora.'

'After three goblets of wine you are downright chatty,' Rivkah quipped.

'Seven,' Carrick smirked.

'What happened to your majordomo friend?'

'He got greedy and thought he could water down the third glass. Served it and found he could not. He was dragged out of bed in the middle of the night and drowned in a wine barrel, in front of the entire household.' The half-drunk scout drew an index finger slowly across his throat and made a thoroughly unpleasant sound not unlike a cat preparing to get rid of a hair ball.

'Hah,' Rivkah spat, leaning up against the door frame. Aemilius watched her and felt a warm glow that he convinced himself was only mostly expensive, stolen wine. *None of us wants to go to bed just yet,* he realised. *This is a good moment, and we don't want it to end.* It went some way towards making him forget just how much pain he was in. 'Our Augusta clearly knows better. Obviously, I would have turned at least two of those three bastards into soup for kicking off at my people...' She gave Aemilius a look that could, in the right light and with a lot of generosity, be interpreted as sympathy. 'But if you can't do that, I'd say keeping a pot of dishwater on the go and serving it as stew every day is a close second.'

'What were the chunks?' Abrax yawned and moved towards his room.

Carrick wheeze-chuckled. 'Something thick. Like our Germanes.'

'Right. It's nice of them to tuck us away here in the shit bits—'

'They called it the original servants' quarters,' Abrax admonished.

'Like I said. The shit bits.' She made a face at him and burped so loudly she made herself wince. 'And right now I am going to *fully* enjoy having an entire room to myself and not needing to listen to any of you lot snoring. Go to bed. You're old.'

'Hey!'

'And you.' She glared at Aemilius. 'You are an idiot, and you should not do that, and...'

'...and?'

She glared. 'And it worked. We are *in*. But in order for your'—she laced the words with razor-sharp sarcasm—'*heroic sacrifice* to not have been in vain, we all need rest. Good luck finding an angle to sleep on.' With that she kicked the door open and disappeared into her room.

Aemilius turned to find that Carrick had not waited to hear the end of his insults. His door was already closed. A couple of yards away Abrax stood by his door, looking down. 'You keep surprising me, Aemilius of

Hispania,' he said quietly. 'Just… make sure there aren't *too* many surprises.' Pushing through, the big fire magus disappeared out of sight, leaving Aemilius alone and blinking in the corridor.

What's that supposed to mean?

Confused, he amble-shuffled into his own room and took in the surroundings as well as he could, being exhausted, confused and in several different sorts of pain. The lodgings were simple—at some point they had been rooms for high-ranking servants, so they offered comfort, but not space. By the torchlight in the corridor, he could make out a table and a chair. A dusty mirror and hooks on the wall. And, most importantly, a bed. He shuffled towards it, closing the door behind him and wincing with every step. His ribs hurt from the kicking, the entirety of his face hurt from the punching and his back hurt from landing on the floor, and while Rivkah had cooled down some things and patted down others with the experience of a trainer used to various states of gladiator, Aemilius still felt like he was most likely to lie down and instantly perish. Easing himself onto the bed, hissing and cursing, he thought of his mother, sitting by his bedside after he'd fallen off a horse for the first time. He thought of Ioana, bustling from bed to bed, followed by the Short Sisters. Muttering a string of half swears and full curses, he lay down and squeezed his eyes shut, focusing on breathing in through his aching nose and out past the stinging cuts in his lip.

And then there was a faint glimmer of the corridor light, and a whispered breath of the door closing, and he realised that he was not alone.

And immediately after that, he realised that whoever was in there with him had him at their mercy.

So I'm dead. This is it. Finally.

He tried shouting, but his voice caught in his throat so that he couldn't make a sound, and calm settled upon him and he waited for the pillow over the face, the weight on his chest—and it did not come.

Feeling brave enough to finally face his death, he eased one eye open.

He could see the faint glow from a candle.

The Germani is taking his time about it, he thought, and had a brief tinge of amusement at his own annoyance. The words echoed in his head, brave and strong, and he spoke the challenge to his would-be killer. *Come on, then! Charge at Aemilius of Hispania and see what that gets you!* What came out was a faint, sagging '…eeeuh.'

'You didn't need to do that.' A girl's voice. Admonishing, almost annoyed… and something else.

He opened both eyes.

The candle she must have brought was mounted on a bronze holder with a cup that had been opened, casting a gentle glow on the room. He could see the outline of her—a slim shoulder and neck, hair bound up in a servant's bun. Her face was mostly in shadow, but her voice sounded… young. Maybe his own age. And Aemilius of Hispania—who had faced a hydra, foiled a cyclops, crushed the skull of a mormo and seen more death in two weeks than, he guessed, anyone he had ever known—had no idea what to do or say. 'Uh…' he mumbled.

'Shush.' She moved towards him, light at her back. The set of her shoulders suggested she was holding something. He gave up on trying to see her and focused instead on his other senses. Her footsteps made no sound, so she must be wearing something—cloth?—on her feet. The scent of her reached him, and Aemilius suddenly found it a lot harder to think. She smelled like lavender and warmth, and then there was a gentle weight on the bed as she sat down. 'I was stupid,' she said. 'I should have watched where I was going.'

'No,' he croaked, finding to his horror and surprise that his voice had suddenly gone dry. The blood rushing to his face in the dark brought a wave of pain that he had to bite down hard to overcome. 'He shouldn't have grabbed you like that,' he managed to whisper.

She huffed, but did not reply. 'I think I saw where they kicked you,' she whispered. 'But I don't want anyone to see a light under the door. So I am going to try...' Her voice trailed off, and then a warm, light hand landed on his ribcage to the left, just under the heart and pain lanced through him. He drew a hard breath through clenched teeth. 'Sorry,' she whispered urgently. 'But that's it, isn't it? That's where it hurts.'

'Yes,' he managed to mutter without squealing.

'Good,' she whispered back. 'I mean—not good, obviously. But...' The touch lifted, and he felt an intense loss, wanting it to come back but not daring to say anything or move at all in case she left or he did something wrong. 'I think...' He could feel an almost imperceptible, tickling sensation as his tunic moved, the gentlest touch pulling at it, exposing his stomach and his ribcage to the cold air. He sensed the warmth from her as she felt for his skin, moving upwards, taking care not to touch him until—

Cold.

The surprise of it made him twitch, which in turn made his body hurt in at least six different places.

'My auntie's mixture,' she whispered, almost

apologetically. 'She took the recipe to her grave. This is my last pot.' And the cold spread, like a ring in a pond, and with it a beautiful feeling of numbness. He gasped as the throbbing in his ribs faded. 'It works.'

'Yeah, it does,' he whispered, wincing at the pain when his face moved and hoping vainly that she wouldn't notice. 'Thank you.'

'Ssh.' The pressure of her fingers lifted, and he ached but in a different way, and then her hands moved downwards and Aemilius found it momentarily quite hard to breathe and then his tunic touched his skin again and her hands disappeared and then she shifted forwards a little bit and he could sense her moving, ever so carefully, and then he felt the warmth of her hands again, this time closer to his face.

'No...' he half-hissed. 'Hurts,' he added apologetically.

'It's okay,' she whispered back. 'I'll go as soft as anything.' The realisation hit him. *She is as nervous as I am.* And then the cold of the salve was on his skin, and he forgot words, and the numbness took away the pain in his cheek and the throbbing in his chin and all the while she was whispering like you would to calm a skittish animal. *Which one of us is she soothing?* 'The women talk about men like that and how you keep your eyes and ears open at all times, and how you carry something small and sharp in case they get you alone and which spots to strike and I've thought about it and played it out in my mind a hundred times but when he grabbed me I froze and couldn't do anything but squeal and I think if I'd fought back he'd just have enjoyed it more but then you shouted at him and I still don't know why, and you are such an idiot and they gave you such a beating and it's all my fault for being stupid and—'

'Ow,' he managed to hiss.

'Oh—I've hurt you,' she gasped, snatching her hands back as if she'd been burnt.

'No,' he blurted out. 'I mean, a little. But it was good,' he added quickly. 'It was pushing the pain away. It's just a little bit sore.' Ignoring the thumping pain in his face and feeling like his heart was about to burst out of his chest, he sought every ounce of bravery in his heart and felt, very carefully, for her shoulder. When he found it, he moved his hand slowly down towards her elbow, then her wrist, and guided her hand as gently as he could back towards his face. 'Please,' he whispered. 'Go on. It really helps.'

For a moment he could have sworn that everything stood still, including the tiny flicker of candle flame— and then her fingers started moving again, as gentle as an evening breeze. After a while she spoke. 'Martia Sulpicia seems a good mistress, and the household thinks you and yours are decent sorts.' She hesitated. 'I hope you understand that I won't be able to speak to you when we meet—Augusta would have my hide—but...' There was a pause, a hesitation—and then the fingers stopped moving and she shifted and leaned and suddenly she was *there*, and her lips were on his and she kissed him, and he felt and smelled her and then, as suddenly as it had happened she pulled back, and stood up, and moved away from the bed. 'Rest now,' she whispered as she picked up her candle. 'And don't do any more stupid things,' she continued, and he thought he could hear a smile in her voice, but he had no time to think about it because the moment the door closed, sleep took him.

* * *

THE ROSE-GOLD RAYS of the morning sun caressed the Villa Sulpicia, painting an idyllic picture that was only slightly marred by the far-away cries of a particularly loud argument between circling gulls down by the bay. Ushered forward by the silent servant who had brought their breakfast and waited while they ate, Livia and Hanno turned a corner to the atrium to find Octavia standing by the double doors looking bored next to her consort. Publius Tarquin Cornelius looked decidedly less calm, and the only thing that was stopping him from working himself up into a lather seemed to be his wife constantly asking his opinions and evaluations on various bits of artwork.

The moment she saw Livia, the stone-faced majordomo opened the doors and guided them out into the yard. Outside, Marcus Sulpicius beamed at them, flanked by Ismael and his quietly furious companion. 'What do you think, eh? A hunting party fit for an Emperor.' He gestured to the force assembled before them. Four strong men ahorse, clad in leather armour and carrying thick lances, looking serious. A little bit away from them stood three Germanes, looking bored. One of them had a big, cone-shaped horn slung over his shoulder and a battle-hammer in his belt. The other two carried sturdy hand-axes. Standing to the side, the majordomo looked almost statue-like in her stillness. 'Behold—my venatores.'

'And what fine specimens they are.' Livia smiled politely.

'A hunt!' Olivia's muscle-bound companion exclaimed. 'Oh!' He stared at her with a purity of want only seen in children and dogs. 'Can I go? Can I?'

She smiled indulgently. 'Of course, my love.'

The youth clenched his fist in triumph. 'Praise Diana! I'll have to get my—' and then some of the facts caught up to him. He looked at Marcus Sulpicius, and a cloud of confusion passed across the clear blue skies of his intellect. 'What are we hunting?'

Eager to play his hand, Marcus only just allowed him to finish the sentence. 'Boars,' he cut in. 'I have taken the liberty of sending for some things for you. My hunters have captured six wild boars and set them loose on the estate. My hunters tell me that one of them, in particular, is a nasty old sort.'

'Much like you, Tarquin.' Octavia smirked.

The senator eyed her coldly. 'I am too old for your charms, girl, and I have earned a reputation for remembering very well every slight and snide remark thrown my way. However, I will happily come for the exercise.'

'Oh, cousin,' Livia said sweetly. 'I would love to come, too, but I fear I may embarrass myself at the sight of blood. Could I please bring my philosopher with me? I trust him with potions and such things. And I am sure my myrmidon would not want to miss the fun.'

Marcus waved her request away. 'Of course.' A glance to the majordomo, who snapped a command to the shadows, where someone moved swiftly out of sight. 'Now—equipment. I had Augusta source some kit for you.' A cart appeared, followed by two women. 'Paulinus. Breastplate, gladius, greaves, vambraces. Javelin.' On command, the women held up solid-looking metal pieces with thick leather straps. Grinning at the delight on the youth's face, Marcus continued, 'I reckoned you might want to get up close. Tarquin—what would you like?'

'Lance,' the old man snapped. 'Leather jerkin. A knife with a blade thick enough'—he shot Ismael a hard glance—'to go through a hog's neck.'

The black man showed no sign that he had even noticed a threat of any sort. 'I respectfully decline, Sulpicius,' he said with a smile. 'I have all the protection I need.' Next to him, the tall warrior allowed himself a twitch that was not quite a smile.

'And for you, the fair and wise, who will not play silly games for boys—' Marcus clapped his hands, completely unable to hide his smugness. A decorated cart rolled into view, drowning in cushions.

'Ooh! Delightful,' Octavia squealed and turned to Livia, a glint in her eye. 'Is that your man, there?' Carrick sat in the driver's seat, dressed in a servant's uniform that hung loosely on his bony frame. 'He looks rough.' She glanced over at Abrax, sitting in credible imitation of the mounted hunters. 'They both do.' The tone of her voice was almost exactly opposite to the judgement in her words.

Hanno stood behind them and marvelled at the lessons the water had taught him. He had often felt the presence of sleek predators knifing through the blue, completely confident in their abilities and completely dead when a bigger beast came along. And so, he admired the fraction of a heartbeat that Livia left before her reply—*just* big enough for an idea to squeeze through—before replying.

'They serve me well.'

'Oh, I bet they do,' Octavia purred.

And Hanno thought about how the water spoke to him and he spoke to the water, and how he turned it and twisted it and made it do his bidding and he watched as Livia effortlessly created an ally in the heart of enemy territory, a woman who seemed to want nothing more than a cold-blooded and like-minded hunter to share her victories with. "Sulpicia Martia" had not explicitly stated anything, but Octavia had been allowed to hear what she wanted and create from that a truth which suited her.

Livia smiled a demure but suggestive smile. 'Shall we?' She inclined her head to the caravan and offered her arm.

'Oh, please, sister.'

'I am delighted to finally be in such civilised company. And I am sure Hanno the Wise will entertain us while we wait for the boys to run themselves ragged.'

Knowing a signal when he heard one, Hanno traipsed after her, only just stopping himself from barking like a dutiful dog.

NOBODY HAD SAID that he had the day off, but Aemilius couldn't help but note that the sun had come up a long time ago and no one had turfed him out of bed and told him to do anything or be anywhere. He still felt sore—there was no doubt that last night had not been an unqualified victory—but the salve and the memory of the application had done him a powerful lot of good. Through his window he could hear the whoops and hollers of the hunting party receding in the distance, and in its wake followed a beautiful wave of quiet. There was the occasional sound of industry—wood being cut, a door closing, someone hollering—but the spaces in between were peaceful. *Maybe I'll have myself a villa in the country when I am a senator*. He smiled, rolled his eyes and thought about how he would go about sitting up.

'Slowly,' he muttered to himself, easing one elbow under himself and pushing. Expecting a sharp pain, he almost flopped back onto the bed when there was none. He could feel a hint of something, but his side was much less of a mess than he had remembered. A twinge in his neck reminded him to save gymnastics for later, but soon he found himself sitting up properly. He felt for his face, looking for cuts, bumps and bruises. 'Witch,' he breathed with admiration. The swelling in his face was almost gone, and there was only the merest hint of a scab where he was sure his cheek had fully split open from the Germani's backhanded slap. Without warning, Prasta came to his mind and his soul wrenched with missing his friends. *Where are you now?* He hoped they weren't staring down the gullet of some over-toothed monstrosity... but when he thought about them, the imaginary threats were much less detailed in his mind's eye than the real people. 'Friends,' he mused. 'Real ones.' He'd always gotten on reasonably well with the boys at his father's villa, but there was a gulf between them, nevertheless. He had always been the governor's son, and as such could not be thrown about or given a kicking, even when he deserved it. They had always been... careful with him. Whereas he had no doubt that now, if he actually did something that deserved a kicking, Rivkah would gleefully dispense one and then organise a queue for the others. The thought of it reminded him of last night's adventures, and he winced as he put a foot down slightly too fast.

The room was, as it had been last night, modest and not designed for spending much time in. The door swung open and he was out in the corridor. Sunlight coming from the far end gave the stone walls a dusky grey colour, and dust mites danced in the air. It had an old feel about it, the feel of a place that sees no thoroughfare. The art on the walls was faded and dated, and he guessed it might be at least a couple of generations old. Generals he didn't know and tales he couldn't tell bounded alongside him on frescoes done in the style of yesteryear, and Aemilius just wandered along, idly stroking the wall with his fingertips as he went, towards the light. The corridor opened into a small atrium, flooded in sunlight from window spaces set under a central cupola. Blues and golds dominated on the walls, and someone had gone to an awful lot of effort to paint the stars in the night sky onto the curved bell of the ceiling above him. A set of discreet pulleys connected to bronze balls were suspended high up above his head. *This must have looked quite magical in its time.*

Three portals led away from the atrium. On his left, he looked straight to a medium-sized dining room, the right led to the gardens, and the third took an immediate, sharp turn. With the help of his nostrils, Aemilius's stomach decided swiftly and dragged him through the last one. The moment he turned the corner, the smells were unmistakeable and vague, wine-coloured memories from last night did the rest. He remembered stumbling through this with his friends, away from the kitchen—and even if he hadn't known where he was, the cooking grease, smell of broth and baking waft lining the walls would have told him where he was going. It was easy to imagine the servants scooting through with laden trays straight to the diners beyond—but when he crossed into the heart of the villa, he had to take a moment to orient himself. He had come in from the same passage the Germanes had entered from last night, and he looked down the length of the kitchen. The table was still there, all lined up like nothing had happened. Beyond it sat the giant pots in the fireplaces, the counters for cutting and slicing and the big island in the middle. A short, shuffling figure was busying itself with something in the sink, and the only sound was that of sloshing water and a song, tunelessly hummed with snatches of lyrics that made little sense.

Propelled forward by an increasingly loud rumbling in his stomach, Aemilius shuffled towards the benches. A question formed on his lips, but then he saw two crates of oranges and a basket of bread rolls tucked to the side, and before he knew it, he was on his way out again, through a third exit, clutching his stolen bounty. If the potwash had noticed him, he had not cared.

A few swift steps took him out into the main atrium, and he gasped. Above him a far superior piece of wall art spread, wisps of silvery cloud scattered before sun rays of gleaming gold, a beautiful depiction of a Tuscan summer sky. The Sulpicii had clearly done well for themselves in recent times as well. *I wish my mother was here to see this. She always loved pretty things.* The words appeared suddenly in his head, out of nowhere, and brought with them a tinge of sadness. He had not spared much thought for his parents, what with being nearly killed by supernatural monsters quite regularly, but the moment's respite without mortal danger, safe in a villa that, although significantly more opulent than his father's mansion in Hispania, was still familiar, tightened his chest. *Will I ever see them again?* He thought back on the conversations around the campfire, and how none of his legionnaires ever mentioned their families, or anything from the past that wasn't a near-death experience. They had all been very focused on getting him away from Hispania and back to the Fort in one piece. *That was supposed to be very important,* he mused, *but...* Oddly, no one had mentioned

much about it since they came here. They had all been
much too busy thinking about—

Family.

The memory of it hit him like a sledgehammer.

Brachus. Death. The jade dagger.

If ever there would be a moment to find it—

Looking around surreptitiously, Aemilius very
carefully quickened his stride. *Walk like a servant with
a purpose,* he chided himself. *Be invisible.* Traversing the
length of the atrium he turned and paused for a second.
A perfectly manicured square garden lay in front of him,
flanked by columns, framing a stunning view of cliffs
and beyond, the velvet smoothness of a cloudless sky and
the sparkling blue of the sea. For a moment he thought
he saw a monstrous shadow twitching in the depths and
shuddered. *It will be a while before I'll be at ease in a
boat.* From somewhere within the house, someone in
command of something called out to an underling who
was clearly in some trouble, and Aemilius hurried away
before he could be found and put to work.

Ducking in amongst the pillars he found a side door
that led into a disconcertingly dark room. The contrast
from the sunlight made his eyes hurt, and acting on
instinct he froze on the spot, squeezed them shut to get
the light out and opened them ever so slowly.

Razor-thin lines of sunlight high above suggested
that there were window openings up high that had been
shuttered. He could follow the slender strips of light
down to where they caught on the shells of copper lamps.
The dimensions of the room were hard to puzzle out—
it felt high, and long, and full of strange shapes in the
twilight—and on top of that he had an uneasy feeling.

Like he was being... watched.

XI

VILLA SULPICIA

MOMENTS LATER, THE words just appeared in his head. In the dark he reached up to touch his ears, just to try to see if he could feel it—but there was nothing. He wasn't hearing any sort of voice.

And who are you?

At least not a human one. It sounded… different. Drawn out, calculating, delighted. Almost lazy. 'I am Aemilius,' he whispered into the darkness, heart thudding and cheeks swiftly reddening. 'I travel with Sulpicia Martia.'

In some way that he did not understand, given that he could neither see nor hear whatever was watching him, he felt the wave of disdain. *I do not care.* The statement was imperious. *I ask not for names. I care not for names. You… are always naming things.*

'It sort of helps with talking about them,' Aemilius offered meekly, and felt immediately a lot worse, and he hissed at himself. *Stop being an idiot!*

Another wave from the dark, this time one of delight.

Ooh, the voice purred. *You smell of blood and hurt.* A pause, and then—*I like it.*

'What is your name?' He stared in disbelief at the darkness and wanted to scream. *Was that the best you could come up with? You don't even know what you are talking to, you stupid—*

The voice-feeling in his head chilled him to the bone, and he couldn't escape the sense that he was in the presence of something more terrifying than any three monsters he'd met thus far combined.

My name is he who stalks the night. I am shadow, and I am terror. They call me Silent Claw. When they catch my scent, they scurry. I speak in pain and fear and death. A twist of my jaws will snap your neck, and my glorious teeth will rip you open and feast on your entrails. I am the ruler of this house, and none dare oppose me.

'I see,' Aemilius said humbly, and added, 'your exalted highness.'

A moment later—*food. You—food.* A half-moment after that—*feed me.*

In the dark, he patted his pockets. The voice had sounded—no, felt—hungry, and the part of his brain that was planning a rapid exit through his ear wondered idly what kind of slavering beast he was about to be set upon by. He had focused so upon the enemy in the dark that he had gotten badly turned around and lost his sense of direction, so escape was not an option. He patted his tunic—*there!* The wax-cloth he'd swiped from the kitchen. He unwrapped it swiftly. His fingers and his nose told him immediately that he was holding a particularly delicious chunk of salami.

Give it give it me want it hungry Aemilius jumped almost completely out of his skin as he felt something touching his calf. Something light. Something… furry. *Friend want it hungry friend* the vibrations echoed in his head, and he could feel the soft, warm touch of a purring cat winding around his feet. Kneeling down, he dug his nails into the sausage, tore a chunk off and dropped it. In a flash, the cat twisted around and caught it in his jaws, in the dark, before it hit the floor. A wave of contentment washed over Aemilius, and he felt warm at the thought that he had caused another creature to feel like that.

Ooh, that's good. The voice appeared in his head again, and the whole thing caught up with him.

'Wait—what? *You* are the terror? The Silent Claw? I suppose that makes sense. But you can talk? *You* can talk? Are we talking? I can't hear you. Can I?' he whispered with increasing speed and pitch.

The cat rubbed its head up against his leg once again and purred. *No. But you can…* A small pause. *…think me*.

Aemilius forced himself to slow down, breathe and take stock. He pinched himself and winced. He was not losing his mind, and this was not a dream. And when he felt around with his mind, he could… sense the cat. Or something cat-like, in the darkness.

See? You understand.

'So, uh—' Several questions crashed together on the way out of his mouth, and came to nothing. He could feel the warmth of the body up against him, and fancied he could hear the smug grin on the creature. Truth was what was needed here. 'I don't understand,' he muttered, meekly.

Understand. The word hung between them, unspoken and alive. The voice in his head—the silent sound of it— was warmly superior. *Do not worry about understanding.*

Just know. You can feel the thoughts of us. None of the others can.

'So… I *can* talk to animals?' Aemilius asked incredulously. 'I can actually do it?'

A wave of irritation hit him.

There is no need to shout. Keep your ugly, smelly mouth clamped shut and try again.

Chastened, he closed his mouth, and tried to think.

Can you hear me? he thought, feeling ridiculous and awkward.

Yes, the cat replied, in the manner of a patient teacher. *That wasn't so hard, was it?*

No, Aemilius thought back. *It wasn't. I just… thought you.* He felt a swelling of pride, and smiled in the dark, receiving a firm head-nudge on the calf for his efforts.

Ask.

What? Aemilius replied.

The stench of curiosity is so strong on you that even humans can smell it.

Now. Think. *Think!*

How do I, uh, call you?

You do not realise how loud you are, the cat replied with haughty amusement, and Aemilius felt like a mix of dim student and prey with a very short life span. *We can all hear you.*

What do you mean, all?

…all of us. The cat's mind felt confused. *All of us?* When Aemilius did not reply, there was a pause. Then the cat spoke again. *Quiet your thoughts,* it commanded. Aemilius did his best to think his way inward, to not think questions and to breathe. In, out. In, out. *Good. Now—listen. You can hear me. Yes?*

Yes, Aemilius offered hesitantly.

Snorri Kristjansson

Good. Can you hear anything else in the room? Listen. Listen carefully.

Straining hard, he felt like he was trying to reach something using his ears. Nothing—except...

One note, he whisper-thought. *Very high.* He tried to imagine what it could be. It felt low to the ground, and light, and... *mouse!* Feeling like a fool, he tried to point to it with his mind.

A purring at his calves. *Good. Good. Now try talking to it. Ask it to come. But nicely, and quietly,* the cat added. *It has... small ears.*

Come here, Aemilius whisper-thought as softly as he could. *I am a friend.* A thrill coursed through him as he felt the mind of the animal, felt it react to him, its high pitch changing, reaching out to him. A faint something—a question? In reply he stretched out his arm slowly, extending it hand up. *I have food.*

Now, listen, the cat thought. *Listen to its travel. Imagine where it goes. Feel its warmth.*

Doing as he was told, Aemilius sent out a thought-feeler to the mouse. He could feel it now, in the tight places, sticking its nose out to sniff the air, could feel a tension like wires, like... whiskers. The slow, careful, measured touch of a small claw on hard stone.

A stroke of a tail on his calf and the cat was no longer there.

Flushed with panic, he reached out to try to sense it, and felt simultaneously weightless and powerful and terrified and then, somewhere within, he felt the raw, panicked, primal thoughts of the mouse, and felt them blink out of existence with the snap of a finger. Eyes wide open, Aemilius shook his head and flailed in the dark to push the coldness away. He had felt something die.

211

You—killed him!

Thank you, the cat replied smugly from somewhere in the dark. *I've been hunting that little scrape for a week.*

But couldn't you have sensed his thoughts?

A derisive snicker. *If cats could do that… do you think there would still be mice?*

But—but—you used me!

There was a pause. *Yes,* the cat finally replied.

Why?

Because he annoyed me, came the matter-of-fact reply. Before Aemilius could answer, the cat continued, *But this is boring. I am curious. Can you hear human thoughts?*

No, he stuttered, feeling inept and furious at being tricked by a cat.

But you can smell them, right? Especially the big and stinky ones?

No. Why?

A wave of irritation hit him. *Because two of them are coming. I'm not sure they are the ones you like.*

What? Panic flared in him. He could just about make out the lights around a door, but it was too far away. He would never reach in time. The cat had showed the good sense to vanish—and then the meekest light dribbled into the room. It was small, covered, and coming up from a crack in the floor. A world of angles and lines opened up. Plinths. Columns. He dove down and compressed himself into the first corner he could find, making himself as small as possible. Peering round the corner of the plinth, he searched for the light—which seemed to stream in from a crack in the floor that widened slowly. It was coming from a covered lantern that was set to give its holder just enough light to see. The tiny point made it hard to make out shapes behind it, but the whispered language behind it was unmistakeably harsh and guttural. Aemilius watched as the darkness changed shape and a hatch opened slowly. He strained to listen and decipher. Language had never presented a challenge to him, which had infuriated his tutors as this meant he had never put in any sort of effort. In the darkness, he groaned inwardly. *Fine, fine. Education might after all be the difference between life and death. I will grant you this.* He had to remind himself that the Germanes crawling out of whatever place they'd been to were not expecting him to be there, and as such he was probably not in mortal danger as long as he made no sound, and had a bit of luck.

The third shape followed the first two up through the floor.

'It's ready.' A rough voice, with a heavy accent.

'Yes. We go tonight.' The other Germani spoke in stilted Latin, as if he was searching for every word.

'We have to make sure he has the right one, though. Or she will not come.' The third speaker, most likely the last one, was a native. 'You know what you need to do.'

Affirmative grunts followed as the three men clambered to their feet. The swinging light set their shadows dancing.

Stand still, you bastards.

But wish as he might, it was impossible to make out what they were doing, or how, or in fact, where. All he heard was a smooth, heavy *thunk* as stone slid on stone, followed by a click. The three shadows made their way to their left, into the villa, and their receding footsteps brought a deafening silence in their wake.

How can you not smell them? The cat in his head

sounded disgusted. *I don't know what hunts your kind, but in the wild they'd be dead before sundown.*

I know what hunts our kind, Aemilius thought. He wondered about sending a mind-picture of the things he'd seen but decided against it. Some things did not need to be shared. *Do you know where they came from?*

Follow the scent, the cat replied sardonically. *No— wait. You can't.* A small pause, then—*this way.* Trusting in newly awakened senses he was far away from naming, Aemilius let his feet guide him in the dark. He could sense the cat, and could feel himself drawing closer, but he lacked the words to explain to himself how that worked. *This.* And suddenly he was standing where the men had stood, and had to admit that yes, there was a smell. Oddly, the smell was... salty.

Is there a hatch of some sort here?

What's a hatch?

It's, like, an, uh—never mind. He looked around, hoping his eyes would somehow draw in the tiny little sliver of light he could see through a crack in a shutter way up high, and saw absolutely nothing. Reaching down, he felt very carefully for something—anything— that would mark his place.

There! His fingertips landed on something cold, ridged and bumpy. A pattern of some sort, in the stone... a mosaic! Feeling around a little more quickly, he extended his sensing search. He could feel bumps mixing with the smooth texture and thought he might be able to feel a curved line, but any guesses at what he would have been looking at were useless. 'I'll have to come back here with lights,' he muttered. He tried to send out his thoughts to find the cat—but he was alone. 'Arrogant bastard,' he added under his breath. His mind was dizzy with possibilities, and he felt a headache coming on from the intense thinking, but he still couldn't shake the feeling of being a dim-witted pupil. Carefully stepping out, hands in front of him, he saw a sliver of light under what promised to be a small side door. Why did all his teachers have to be the same?

THE GENTLE SQUEAK of the cartwheels stopped, and Hanno looked around. They had rattled along the approach to the main villa, turning to their left through the trees and moving up a well-camouflaged road. In the distance a hunting horn sounded, and a moment later another two responded, further away. They had watched the back of Abrax and the other horsemen as they galloped up ahead, led by a huntmaster that looked tough as old boots and half as charming. At the time Hanno had said thoughtfully that perhaps they should usher old leather-face into the woods by himself, tell him to smile and then send a group to pick up the dead animals, which had gone down rather well. Well-crafted sentences were like rain in the desert. Rare, and appreciated.

But now they had stopped, and no one had explained anything, and he was growing tired of this game. He knew their mission, and to an extent they were watching Marcus Sulpicius and making sure he came to no harm—but the man Ismael was a slippery one.

Just behind the driver's seat, where Carrick sat stock-still, Livia had successfully engaged Octavia in chatter that ranged far and wide, touching on patrician gossip, then flitting to fashions and across to business and how to run a household. Anyone who would have chanced upon their conversation would believe the women life-long friends catching up on five years apart, rather than two people who just met last night. She had somehow also managed to engage and enliven the older woman, Clarissa, who now sat with them and hung on their every word, offering regular agreement. Hanno marvelled at his friend's craft, and thought that if anyone would want to drive a wedge between these women, they'd have to thrust quite hard. The men—Marcus, the young and strapping Paulinus, scowling Tarquin and the man Ismael and his guard—were grouped about ten yards away from a clearing in the trees, talking among themselves and gesturing.

'No!' Marcus said, loudly, glaring at the young man. 'We wait here, and exactly here.' In response to a remark by Paulinus, he continued, 'Because this is where they'll drive the boars, you lump.'

This caught the women's attention, and they shared a titter and a conspiratorial glance before Octavia shouted, 'Go easy on him, Marcus. It's his first.' A muttered comment from Livia, a glance to her new friend and a dirty, twinkle-eyed laugh from the dark-haired woman followed. Hanno thought back on the first time he saw a python kill—how slow and strong and almost gentle the big creature had been, as it sank its teeth into its victim and then twisted itself around its body, slowly pressing and squeezing and crushing until the prey was no more. He looked at Octavia, and he knew that she would be used as Livia saw fit, and when she was of no further use, she might live, or she might not, but the woman who thought herself in charge was not in charge at all. A solid thirty yards away from the entrance to the clearing, the men had taken up fighting positions. Paulinus and

Marcus on either side, Ismael and his man in the middle, Tarquin in front of them. A hunting horn sounded close by, and again the call came from other parts of the forest, hanging over them like an ominous bird call. There was a moment of absolute silence...

...and then there was the sound of hard-smash hooves, and Abrax and two other hunters came riding through the clearing, yanking on the reins, turning their horses sharply and jumping off, blood-stained javelins in hand, dashing to stand in front of the noblemen.

'*Two coming!*'

Tension rippled through the men, and Hanno imagined he could see dots of white on the knuckles clenching around their weapons. The hunting horn, again, closer— and a creature thundered into the clearing, straight into the half-circle of waiting spears. A boar, a sizeable one at that, but bloodied and dazed.

'*Mine!*' Marcus shouted. Like dancers, the hunters at the front leapt to the side. The boar, sensing the opening, dashed through—and with agility belying his age, Marcus Sulpicius dashed in front of it, drove the butt of his spear into the ground and lowered the point to the right angle just as the animal barrelled towards him, pushing off a blink before the tusks swiped at where his legs had been. There was a sickening, wet sound followed by an ear-splitting shriek as the point drove through its shoulder, a spasm and then the boar keeled over, momentum carrying it past the nobleman and towards Tarquin. A moment later the two men descended on the fallen beast, knives flashing in the air as they hacked down into its throat, roaring with bloodlust. Shouts from the men as the second boar met its fate by the clearing's entrance.

Hanno noted that the man Ismael had gently shifted his position to be just a little farther away from the blood and the death and thought that sometimes water is still and quiet and smart.

The hunting horn, again—this time so close it almost made him jump. 'I am Hanno the Wise,' he sniffed to no one, watching in apprehension. Somewhere close the hooves thundered—and two creatures came crashing through the undergrowth.

'*Mine!*' The voice was young, and bright, and fierce—and Paulinus charged towards the boars. He was a statue come to life, a fresco from a wall. His arm raised, javelin levelled, sent the spear flying hard and fast and true towards the lead boar's snout. The beast could do nothing but follow its path. The steel tooth sliced its maw open, lodged in its throat and it shrieked and shook and tossed its head. The butt of the spear caught on a root and the boar, powered by back legs and terror, was tossed in the air by its own force. Half a heart-beat, followed by a thud as the boar landed, with a sickening squelch as the back end of the spear drove up into its head—but Paulinus did not need to look, for with the soul of a hunter he knew the spear would find its mark the moment it left his hand, and had drawn his gladius with his next target in mind. '*I said mine!*' he roared at the venatores in his path, and the older men dutifully stepped aside. Confused by the shifting patterns before it, the boar's eyes darted this way and that.

The young man's gladius flashed as he made to strike from the right. The boar, angry and confused, snorted at him and swung its head, each movement a potential disembowelling, but Paulinus planted his weight on his right foot, leaned then leapt forward to his left, easily clearing the boar's head, switching sword-hand in mid-air and landing with a ferocious kick to the animal's side. As the animal staggered under the impact, he pushed off again and dove after it, point-first, driving his blade deep into its neck and twisting away before the tusks swung at him again, ripping a gash in the flesh and getting his face sprayed with blood for his troubles. Half beneath him, the boar struggled to rise and get away from his giant tormentor, but it was too little and too late. The legs gave way and it collapsed on its side, staring brokenly into the distance. Hauling himself to his feet, Paulinus howled in triumph before sinking down again to hack frenetically at the boar's neck, ripping and pulling, until he roared with furious delight and rose to his feet. 'Did you see that? Did you see me?' he shouted towards the ladies on the cart. Joy radiated out of every fibre of his being, and his bulging muscles glistened with boar's blood as he raised the severed, lumpen boar's head high. He drew a deep breath and howled. 'I *am* the *Lord* of—'

The impact sent him spinning like a wooden child's toy as something dark, angry and massive crashed past his hip.

'*No!*' Octavia screamed.

The beast that had arrived in the middle of the clearing, surrounded by a host of terrified hunters who levelled javelins uncertainly at it, was a number, and a large number at that. It was easily the biggest boar Hanno had ever seen, looking like it had the bulk of a prize pig and the temper of a particularly furious attack dog. Its three-finger-thick tusks were coated in blood, and its hide looked like it would easily withstand any weapons currently pointed its way and most others known to man. A stubby snout led to a wrinkled, scarred face with vicious, beady eyes that seemed to be choosing its next victim.

'Come on, men! For the Sulpicii!' Marcus Sulpicius shouted, stepped forward—and slipped in blood-slick grass, his leg sliding out from under him and chucking him flat on the ground.

It was all the creature needed. With horrifying speed it coiled and sprang, powerful legs pushing its bulk into motion as it went for the gap, straight towards the edge of the clearing—and Ismael.

Who did not move, despite the hell-boar charging him.

With the smallest shift of his body, his warrior stepped in front—and as quickly as the boar had burst into a run, it hammered its front legs down and ground to a halt again. A moment of absolute silence as the boar stared at the warrior, who stared back. Hanno saw the man's lips move ever so slightly, but whatever passed between man and beast could not be heard from that distance—and then the boar tossed its head angrily, turned in a sharp twist and barrelled away through the underbrush.

A meek honk of the hunting horn, coming from nearby, broke the spell and suddenly everyone was shouting at once.

'See to the boy!'

'Go after the bastarding hog!'

Octavia was off the cart and running across, holding her skirt in rough bunches not for protection but for more speed, barging past Marcus's hunters to dive down next to where the youth lay and cover him with her body and her kisses and her words. The huntmaster's horse trotted into the clearing, with the huntmaster hanging half out of the saddle, bare-chested and pressing his rolled-up, blood-soaked tunic to a vicious tusk-slash on his thigh with less and less force, face turning closer to white with every heartbeat.

'Move,' Livia hissed at him, and Hanno jumped off the cart, ready to make himself reasonably—but not too—useful.

The grass under his feet was fresh and smelled like dew and soil, and Hanno found himself tingling with the life of it all. Around him, though, was slightly too much death. The boars lay strewn like stinky rug-lumps, their entertainment value swiftly diminished. At the far end of the clearing Marcus Sulpicius was working on gently lowering his huntmaster to the ground with the help of Abrax and another grim-faced venator.

Closer was the supine form of the king of the hunt, young Paulinus. He seemed to be very busy pretending to not be in excruciating pain, but judging by his posture and the lack of screaming Hanno judged the risk to life to be minimal.

And then he noticed that about thirty feet away Tarquin seemed to have fallen and was not getting up, and because Hanno the Wise had earned his nickname, he did not shout out nor draw attention to himself. Instead, he thought about what he learned from the water, and looked up.

The man Ismael was staring right at him, waiting and assessing.

Feigning fear, he pointed at the body. 'The senator—' he began, pretending to run out of words because adding '—is now your problem' did not seem entirely appropriate. Then he moved towards the old, fallen man, as carefully as his lowly position demanded.

'Your excellence…?' he offered carefully.

The senator did not answer.

A few steps later Hanno established that that was because Tarquin was, in fact, almost exactly as dead as the boars.

As WAS BEFITTING of a woman of her stature, Clarissa grieved beautifully. She approached her dead husband quickly but not too quickly, knelt by his side with kindness and grace, and closed his eyes gently. She said to him words that were only meant for the two of them, two souls who had walked the earth together through hard times and good, braved life's challenges and faced the world bravely, holding and supporting each other when the clouds grew dark overhead. She shielded her face from view as she walked back to the two women waiting for her at a respectful distance—blood-stained Octavia and her new friend Sulpicia Martia. The dark-haired woman embraced her, as did the newcomer. They stood there, in silence, three women braced against the cruelty of life, love and loss. And in this moment of sisterhood, of beauty and care, repeated through time immemorial, Octavia whispered, 'So it worked.'

'Heart attack,' Clarissa replied. 'Dead as an absolute stone. Just like you said. Three drops in his cup last night. And no one will find the vial.'

Sulpicia Martia looked equal parts shocked, terrified and excited.

'Welcome,' Octavia whispered huskily, 'to freedom. I'd recommend waiting for half a year before you… make arrangements. Make sure they see you mourn like a dutiful little servant.'

'Don't worry. I have been waiting a while for my chance to wear the black of a mourning widow,' Clarissa replied coldly.

'How long?' Martia blurted out.

Clarissa smirked. 'Fifteen years.'

Octavia quickly pulled the women closer to stifle the giggles from the group. 'Breathe,' she hissed happily. 'And put up your masks of sorrow. Remember—we can only think and act for ourselves as long as they don't believe we can.'

And to anyone watching, a moment of quietude passed between bowed heads, and then the women returned to their lives—mothers, maidens and wives, prepared to stand behind and support their noble and infallible husbands through whatever might come, till death did them part.

'WHERE HAVE YOU been?' Rivkah glanced sideways at Aemilius, leaning up against the wall just outside the kitchen, with half a smirk on her lips. 'Getting... *seen to?*' The half-smirk blossomed into a fully formed one at his discomfort. When he stepped into the light, she appraised him. 'That being said—someone did a good job. Did you?'

'Wh-what?' he stammered.

Rivkah offered some very suggestive hip movements. 'Ooh, big strong traveller, thank you for sa-ha-haaaving me,' she squealed.

'Shut up,' he hissed. 'Not funny.'

'You say that, but *you* can't see your face.' Taking another look at him, she jabbed him playfully on the shoulder. 'Calm down, lover boy. I have no doubt that you'd never ram an innocent little servant girl just for the sake of it.'

He was about to say something when Rivkah's eyebrows rose just a fraction, and something about her stance changed subtly. His own body responded immediately, and he was about to try to notice where the threat came from, when their eyes met. They'd both felt it—a ripple of energy through the house. It came in the way a door was slammed in the distance, the tone of an indistinct shout somewhere, the rhythm of running feet.

The hunting party was back.

'We should be out by the front.'

'Yeah,' Rivkah grunted. 'Can't understand how people live like this and just not kill someone every day.' She pushed off the wall and Aemilius fell in behind her, watching as danger and threat somehow melted away with every step until all that was in front of him was a scrawny girl who looked like she'd be knocked over if you opened two windows in the wrong place. 'Watch your step,' she said over her shoulder. 'I've learned from hanging out with the mighty Aemilius of Hispania that there's a good chance I'll either get knocked sideways by grunts who want to smash your face in or young women who want to slather you in salves and have their wicked way with you.'

'To the left here. That one leads to the triclinium. You know the difference between you and a bitch?'

Rivkah puffed derisively. 'What, stud?'

'A bitch *occasionally* stops yapping.'

She did her best to hide it, but he saw the smile—and then they heard it.

The wails of mourning.

XII

VILLA SULPICIA

THE VOICES ROSE and fell, pushed and pulled, soared in grief and sank in lament. Trying hard to contain rising panic, Aemilius hurried towards the big double doors. He couldn't make out the words, or which gods were being called for, but it sounded proper. *Someone rich.* Unbidden, his mind offered images of Livia and Hanno, gored and bleeding, a group of hunters standing over their bodies and looking down impassively. *Shame. Accident. Couldn't help it.* Or worse still, a Germani warrior wiping the blood off a nasty blade. *She slipped and fell. Nothing for it.* There were all kinds of possibilities here, and none of them good. He was so deep in thought that he nearly bowled Rivkah over.

'Watch it!' she hissed. 'You are a servant. And a thick one, at that. We do nothing, we see nothing, we just wait until we are called upon.' They had arrived at the front doors, and his heart thudded in his chest. What would they see? Knowing that the death had already happened was almost worse than facing the possibility that it was about to happen. The doors opened, and he had to fight hard to keep his impassive servant's mask up.

Somehow, a group of mourners had already been dressed and prepared to meet the hunting party. The mounted venatores were leading the way, slowly, heads bowed. The carriage followed, and the first in view was Marcus Sulpicius, walking with his hand upon the driver's bench, almost as if to lead it home. *Not him. Pity.* Behind him walked Ismael, looking serious and sad, and at the back of the cart, his bodyguard. Aemilius had to fight hard not to scream for Livia.

Where was she?

A woman sat in the carriage, alone.

The part of his brain that wasn't busy screaming started adding things. *Body—in carriage. Marcus would have been Sulpicia Martia's next of kin… so…* And then the carriage curved ever so slightly on its approach, and he saw the people on the other side. Octavia, the limping lump next to her—and then, Livia and Hanno. He had to fight to hold down a whoop of joy, and then a chortle, as they looked almost comically sincere. *We survive, again.* He desperately wanted to look to Rivkah, but she was staring up ahead with a firmly set jaw. Her absolute lack of acknowledgement radiated command. *Wait, you idiot. Just—wait.*

The carriage slowed to a halt, and Marcus Sulpicius stepped forward. The oleaginous charm had vanished, and he was every inch the sombre statesman. 'Today, Rome lost one of her noblest sons. We bow our heads and remember Publius Tarquin Cornelius, and salute the Gods, for now he walks with them.' The mourners— who Aemilius now recognised as people he had seen just yesterday scuttling about the household doing chores—

responded with a plaintive lament to Jupiter, to Juno and to Saturn, to guide Tarquin through the afterlife and up to where he deserved to be. Porters arrived in step towards the back of the carriage and hoisted the makeshift stretcher with the old man's body upon their shoulders. *They are well drilled,* Aemilius mused. Out of the corner of his eye he saw Augusta staring eagle-eyed at the procession, willing her staff to do the right thing at every turn. The hunting party fell in behind the porters, who walked slowly towards the main entrance. He drifted to the side with the other staff. Nobody told them to—they just parted to make way. *Death will come to us all.* And he remembered, despite himself, the cold terror of the harpy. He remembered the frothing water under the monstrous cetus. He remembered the stench of Xeno's cave, and the cyclops's child-like cruelty. He remembered—

An improbably sharp toe in his calf jolted him out of his own head. He tried to respond, but Rivkah was already shuffling ahead of him, following the crowd. He seriously debated kicking the back of her legs anyway but thought better of it. Judging by the pure intensity of Augusta's blazing eyes, he could not even begin to imagine what punishments would be in store for two servants who started fighting during a funeral procession.

THE KITCHEN WAS rammed full of people, and terrifyingly silent. He felt the warmth and gentle pressure of bodies up against him on all sides—big and small, soft and bony—and for a moment wished he could be pressed up against the girl. He hadn't seen her anywhere since the night before and had arguably not seen her then either as the room was almost completely dark. *Would I know her?* He was sure he would. But there was still an ounce of survival in him, so he pushed thoughts of her to the side and focused on the table.

Augusta stood on it, a general surveying her troops. There was a moment of silence, and then—

Orders. Each one barked with a snap like a teamster's whip. Each one eliciting a short, sharp response that sounded the same whether it came from one voice or ten. And with precision and discipline that would have put an army to shame, the household sprang into action.

'You! Corner. Peel.'

He felt the heat of Augusta's eyes on him for a split-second and responded with the same affirmative he'd heard from the others. Fighting rising panic and the feeling that everyone was looking at him, he forced himself to turn towards the corner and see if he could find anyone—*there*. At a table tucked out of the way, someone sat hunched over large buckets of vegetables with their back turned. Peel was already flying. He picked his way through the suddenly bustling kitchen and sat on a stool that was wordlessly shunted towards him. A well-used peeling knife appeared out of nowhere, and he did his best to slot in. *I know how to do this. I do it all the time.* He repeated the words in his mind, a calming mantra, but he still couldn't shake the feeling that he was walking through a pride of sleeping lions with a steak hung around his neck. *They'll know. They'll know I'm an imposter. I'll slip up and they'll know.* He stared at his hands and breathed out once, twice, three times to stop the shaking.

A carrot appeared next to him.

'Thank you,' he mumbled.

'Don't worry.'

The voice hit him like a punch in the gut. He glanced over, and—it was her. There was no denying it. She was younger than he'd thought—might even be younger than him, by a year. Auburn hair, tied up in a bun under a head scarf. Twinkling, green eyes and a rising colour of red in her cheeks. Sat as she was, she looked shorter than he'd thought. He caught himself staring at her, remembering—

'And thank you for the salve,' he blurted out.

'It was nothing. But start peeling or she'll peel you.' With that, the girl looked away from him and fell back into a rhythm of quick, sharp strokes, sending the peel flying into an empty bucket. Watching her, he copied the movements. He could not match her speed or dexterity but found himself able to peel a carrot without losing any of his fingers. He was about to start on his fourth one and had almost built up the courage to speak when he heard a familiar voice.

'Oi. Punch-bag. She wants you to go with horse-face over there to do some stuff that requires people to be tall. Scoot.' A familiar, lithe shape stood over him, grinning and glancing meaningfully at the girl, who was looking intently at her carrots. He made a face at Rivkah, and she smirked back. The moment he was up she sidled onto the stool and grabbed the knife off him. The last thing he heard was Rivkah's voice, sweeter than he'd ever heard it.

'Hey. I'm Rebeckah. What's your name?'

Aemilius hurried towards the gangly youth who was waiting for him. He was not hard to find, because he was the only one standing still in the kitchen and his face was remarkably similar to that of an ill-gotten foal, laden with a bucket and a tool belt that seemed to come with its own air of self-importance. When he got there, the boy grunted at him. 'We're going to light up the gallery. Two-man job. You stand back and watch me. Got it?'

'Yuh,' he grunted back, in his best workman's voice.

The boy didn't wait for any further conversation. A sharp heel turn and he was heading off, forcing Aemilius into a half-run to keep up. Once out of the kitchen, the sound of the house was completely different. The atrium was filled with a stifling silence, the wails of the mourners only just intruding on its edges. Ahead of him, his guide turned once to the left, then right, through a colonnade and back in towards forbidding, reinforced double doors. *This is it!* Aemilius realised with a buzz. Unbidden, his mind raced out to find the cat—but he felt nothing. Following the boy through the doors he tried to take in all the things he'd missed on his first, rather panicked visit.

The light from the open doors only just managed to illuminate a beautiful marble floor. Arrow-straight lines of rich pink cut through radiant white, leading the visitor into what felt like a sizeable hall. He could see plinths on either side, but only shadowy impressions of what stood on them.

The boy had disappeared from view.

Aemilius stood stock-still, counting in his head to keep the panic at bay. *One. Don't shout. Two. Don't shout. Three—*

'You're not doing much, are ya?' The boy emerged from the darkness, holding a pole that was easily twice his height. 'Here. Hold this.'

He thrust the pole at Aemilius. It felt light but strong, and he could feel it sway in his hand. 'You said to stand back and watch. Besides—I can't really see.'

The boy grinned, turning his face from equine to vulpine. 'Scared of the dark, are ya? Well—how do you feel about—'

He paused dramatically, putting his hands on his hips—and then he clapped them together, loudly, and fire sprang from his palm, fluttering down into the bucket. '*Fire!*'

Aemilius thought about Xeno, and the harpies, and the dead king of wolves. He thought about the feeling of the fireball passing him at head-height, and how the Greek fire of Prasta's clay pot had enveloped the mormo and his hand, and the smell of charred flesh.

'I'm okay with fire,' he replied, watching the modest flames rise from the bucket.

'Gimme the end of the pole,' the boy huffed, his thunder well and truly stolen.

Aemilius did as he was told, lowering the long pole towards the boy and watching horse-face take some sort of cloth off his belt and wrap it around the end with expert movements. A moment later the lanky boy dunked the end of the pole in the bucket, watching with troubling levels of joy as the fire spread. 'There we go—biggest candle you'll ever see.' He worked his hands backwards, away from the slow-burning flame at the top, raising the pole higher and higher until it was standing straight up in the air. 'This is where you want to be careful,' the boy said. His voice wasn't quite strained, but Aemilius could hear the effort it took to hold the pole straight. 'There's a couple of very expensive curtains in here. If you drop this—whoa!' Everything slowed. Aemilius watched the pole start toppling over and falling towards him—and then it stopped. He quickly checked—and horse-face was staring at him with delight. 'Hah! Your fucking face. Bet you pissed yourself. It's not hard to hold at all. I've been doing this job for eight months now. Best in the house. So you just stand back like I told you and try to learn something.' He sneered and turned to his task.

It only took a couple of moments for Aemilius to leave the thoughts of asking every insect in the house to eat the boy's eyeballs. *Give horse-face his due,* he thought. Watching the fire glide through the room at twice a man's height was mesmerising. One by one, lanterns mounted on the walls and hung from the ceiling sprang to life after a kiss from the fire-pole. And orb by softly glowing orb, they illuminated a world the like of which Aemilius had never seen before. He trailed horse-face slowly, drinking it in.

The walls were covered with rich, vibrant frescoes depicting heroes in a variety of battle-poses, bordered by the "very expensive curtains" horse-face had mentioned. Octavian surveying the battlefield, flanked by someone who looked very much like a Sulpicius. A beautiful depiction of Romulus, with more than a passing semblance to a Sulpicius, founding Rome. A scene from the battle of Antium, so realistic that he thought he could smell the sea, feel the crunch of clashing ships and hear the swords in the distance. Beneath each scene the floor was inset with beautiful, swirling mosaics that stretched the pictures and gave him the sense that he was standing in the landscape, moving with the gods. *The Sulpicii have done well for themselves indeed.* And that was before he got to the statues.

The room was dominated by a road of sorts set in the marble, a path through the centre in the whitest of white, bordered by thin, pink lines. On either side stood statues designed to tower over the human spectators—heroes and scholars, statesmen and goddesses, all with varying hints of Sulpician features.

'Bet you haven't ever seen anything like it.' Horse-face was stood at the end of the room, watching him. There was a new note in his voice—defiance? Pride? 'Bring the bucket.'

Focus! Aemilius hissed at himself. He had completely lost his concentration in there, and it would only be because this particular servant was dim-witted and smug that he'd get away with it. He hurried to get the bucket and rushed towards the fire pole—and just as he moved past it, he saw it out of the corner of his eye. The mosaic he'd seen—or felt—last time. Waves! Glancing up, he just caught a magnificent scene of Neptune rising out of the sea. *That one.* Dragging himself past it and fighting down the urge to go and inspect, he instead focused on his annoying taskmaster. 'Sorry,' he muttered. 'Got distracted.'

Horse-face looked at him with undisguised disgust. 'You are not worthy of serving a Sulpicia,' he snarled, dunking his pole in the bucket and snuffing out the fire. 'You are a useless little bag of shit.' The boy stared at him, hard, daring him to disagree. *This is how it goes,* Aemilius thought. *You hand down the beatings.* Either he could rise to it, step out of line and be given a thrashing which would in turn beget a telling-off—or he could bow his head, take the abuse and accept his place in the world.

'Sorry,' he muttered, staring at his toes.

The boy hocked loudly and spat in the bucket. It hissed when it landed. 'Limp-wristed fuck,' he snarled. 'No wonder the Germanes kicked the shit out of you.' When no response was forthcoming, he stomped past Aemilius, tried to shoulder-barge him and missed, muttered something under his breath and marched to the corner behind the door, where the pole must be stored. Deciding to not tempt fate any longer, Aemilius grabbed the bucket and followed horse-face out through the doors. On the way he had an idea, and had a thought, and asked a polite question inside his head.

* * *

THE MOOD IN the dining room was sombre. Marcus was busy conferring with his majordomo, and Ismael and his man were deep in conversation. Clarissa was being looked after by Olivia and the bandaged and wincing Paulinus.

It had not taken them long to get to their chambers, where black clothing had already been laid out on their beds. Olivia wore a dress that was pulled, tucked and tightened to display all that there was to display. Clarissa's robes spoke of class and wealth. Without shifting her focus or making any show of it, Livia muttered to Hanno, 'Pretty sure that's the fashion from two years ago. She has been waiting for this day for a while.'

'If the river flows for long enough, it eventually reaches the sea,' Hanno replied.

'True.' She glanced over at Ismael. 'Keep your eyes open, old friend.'

'For what?'

'Opportunity.'

Their quiet reflection was disrupted by an angry shout from outside. Augusta's head whipped round with a glare that could have burned a hole in the door and was out in an instant. Just as she passed through there was another sound from the same voice, this one far beyond rage and into blind fury. The door closed behind the majordomo and there was the faintest sound of a hissed command, followed by a much louder slap. Moments later, the woman returned, looking like someone trying very hard not to roar.

'What was that?' Marcus Sulpicius sounded mildly curious.

Augusta looked disgusted. 'An idiot boy howling because he somehow got himself shat on by three pigeons in quick succession. However, the hall of the Sulpicii is now lit.'

'Wonderful.' Marcus turned to his guests. 'Please— come with me. In times of sorrow, I go to the place in this house that most feeds my soul and reminds me what it means to be a true Roman.' They followed him into the atrium and through double doors to a spectacular hall, decorated with the most glorious artworks.

'Wow. This is… pretty.'

'Thank you, Paulinus. My family has been building this collection for—'

'Generations,' Clarissa breathed. 'Tarquin told me of it, but he was not a lover of the arts. Is that—' Her eye alighted on a street scene—modest next to the battlegrounds and the gods, but magical in its simplicity.

'Peirakos. My great-grandfather had the chance to acquire some of his works. Traded most of them off, but he kept this one. To remind us where the Sulpicii came from.'

'He was a wise man,' Livia said solemnly.

'Thank you for showing us this beautiful collection, Has anyone hazarded a guess at what it's worth?'

Marcus smiled at Octavia. 'More than you and I will ever have, I reckon. They should never be sold.'

'Treasures that belong to a family should remain in a family.' Livia had somehow sidled up to Ismael and laid a calm and understanding hand on his forearm. Hanno saw the twitch in the bodyguard as she inched in between them. He also saw the tiniest hint of a glance from Ismael and almost took a half-step backwards himself. The command was clear. *Sit. Good boy.* 'It is such a shame that Tarquin will not have the chance to fully join in our efforts to free the Silver Heart—but I think he believed in the cause. Don't you, Clarissa?'

'Oh, I do,' the older woman agreed. 'He said so to me, the morning of the hunt. Clarissa, he said. I don't know why, but I trust that man. He seems like he has gone through a lot, and he is very brave to come here and ask us for help. And are we not good Romans? Do we not help those in need? That's what he said.'

'Thank you,' Ismael muttered. 'It touches my heart that you will help me in the struggle of my people.'

'The struggle of your people touched his heart, too,' Clarissa said, nodding sagely. 'Really touched his heart.' There was a small pause that Hanno didn't quite understand, after which the other women both seemed to agree very much.

'Please,' Livia begged Ismael, gently guiding him by the elbow towards a seating area that offered a magnificent view of sculptures, frescoes and mounted pottery. 'Tell us more from the Silver Heart.'

The burly warrior grunted something at Ismael, who dismissed him with another curt nod.

Opportunity.

Hanno fell in at a safe distance behind the tall man as he made his way to a door at the far end of the grand gallery. A couple of moments later they were outside, in a square surrounded by columns. The big man moved to a bench in the shade and sat down with his back to Hanno, fishing something out of a fold in his tunic and chewing on it for a moment before spitting out a wad of black. 'What do you want?' he grunted.

He hasn't looked at me once. This one knows the tides. 'Oh, nothing. Just thought I'd heard enough for one day about being a good Roman.'

This earned him a derisive snort from the big man. 'They like to talk, the Romans.'

'They do.' Hanno inched into view at a respectful distance, found himself a place in the sun, sat down and soaked up the joy and the life of it, allowing his problems to not exist for a while.

'Death.' The big man spat again.

Now we see where we are. Hanno opened his eyes, and let the man see that he was being looked at. Ismael's bodyguard was tall, maybe almost a whole head taller than Hanno. There was something of the panther about him—the way he sat, he looked strong and supple at the same time, but also like he would not make too much noise in the night. It made Hanno think of the hunters in the water—the eel, the crocodile and the beautiful shark. There was nothing on this man that wasn't made for killing. The man saw him look, and looked back. His jaw was covered in close-cropped beard, and blue eyes twinkled with dangerous intellect. *Not only chosen for his brawn, this one.* 'Hello, Death. I am Hanno. Hanno the Wise.'

The man looked at him with annoyance and just the right amount of amusement. 'Save your parlour tricks for the paymasters. I am Ioannis.'

'Well met, Ioannis. Tell me more of Romans and Death.'

'They are better at giving it than taking it.'

'This is true.'

Ioannis scowled. 'Their *empire* has pushed it so far away that when it happens to one of them, in the heart of Italia, they speak of it as something strange, something grim and cold and unfair. For them, the day their friend dies is a day of great mourning and salt water spilled. It is a day of contemplation, of sorrow, of wailing at the skies.'

'But for us, their loyal and savage subjects, it is a day like any other,' Hanno finished.

Ioannis nodded slowly, and now Hanno felt he was being inspected—searched over with those ice-blue eyes for hidden weapons, deceit and trickery. The warrior's hand extended. 'Liquorice?'

He didn't need to help it much. The smile spread from the centre of himself and touched his ears on both sides. 'Oh, absolutely. Wakes are dreadfully boring.'

'Dead,' Ioannis said.

Hanno chuckled. 'Enough of death. Tell me more of life, Ioannis Liquorice.'

Overhead, a seagull squawked once, despondently, but no one replied.

THE SOUNDS AND smells of food preparation carried through the corridor as Aemilius walked back, stifling a smirk at the fate of horse-face. The boy had been sent back to the baths to wash off the shame of a stinging face and an impressive amount of bird-shit. It had been surprisingly easy, too. He had allowed his mind to wander outside his body, reach up onto the rooftops and find there some bored pigeons that did not question his motives. There was maybe a hint that his intended target was recognised by the birds, and not in a good way. Watching the righteous yowl had been treasure enough for one night; seeing Augusta storm out in a fury, hiss at the boy and watch him unthinkingly shout back at her had felt like he was twice blessed. And that was not counting the slap. The movement had been so fast that he hadn't even seen it—he only heard the sharp smack and saw horse-face recoil and try hard not to cry. A quick turn, and he was in the kitchen—and the part of his brain that had been trying to gain his attention through the smug reminiscing caught up. *There's something wrong. Approach with…*

…caution.

The rough voices of the Germanes were layered on top of the noises of the kitchen, shouting for drink. And he had, unwittingly, approached the kitchen from the corridor that led directly to the table.

There was a moment—a single moment—where he had noticed them, but they hadn't noticed him. He saw it—and saw it flitting away from him, as the gangly and pock-scarred one turned and roared at his mates.

Chairs flew as the warriors all sprang to their feet. One of them somehow managed to leap in between Aemilius and his escape, and he found himself encircled, and death had come to Aemilius yet again. It was in their eyes. It was in the flexing of their fingers. It was in the absolute lack of fear, of worry about any of the kitchen staff intervening. They had caught their prey, and they were going to have their way with it.

'You.' The leader, the lanky and scarred one, spat on him. 'Little shit. I am so sorry about last night.' He smirked, showing off sharp teeth. 'We were interrupted before we could finish.'

A cold feeling filled him, like the warmth of life had drained away. 'It's a shame that didn't happen to your parents,' he replied levelly.

The soldiers laughed. 'Funny little shit,' the leader snarled. 'Big balls. Maybe I'll cut them off and feed them to my dog.'

Reaching for a witty remark, he found... nothing. *Right*, Aemilius thought. *Now what?* He thought about easing down into a fighting stance, like Rivkah. *They might laugh so hard they died*. No—this was a time for thinking less. 'Look.' He tried his best to sound like someone reasonable. 'It's all just for fun. I—'

'Shut up, little shit,' the Germani growled. 'We're going to teach you—'

And just the smallest moment he took to glance at his friends was enough for Aemilius to shove his hand in his pocket, grab what he could find and throw it at the man's face, launching himself forward to get into the inevitable gap as the Germani's hand would instinctively fly up to block the blow.

But he was nowhere near fast enough.

Because it didn't.

The impact on the back of his head sent him sprawling on the kitchen floor to the roaring laughter of the soldiers. The pock-marked one stood over him. 'You think you can kill me with a bread roll, little shit?' he drawled. Aemilius felt the yank of a rough hand, and suddenly he was vertical again, suspended two inches above the ground, staring into the face of the Germani, so close he could smell the man. 'I am going to kill you slowly,' the soldier growled. 'Maybe choke you on your fucking bread roll. How would you like that, little shit?'

It took him a moment, but Aemilius noticed that the kitchen had gone deadly silent.

'Put him down.' A woman's voice.

The Germani looked over his shoulder, and his scowl of frustration turned to defiance. 'No,' he snarled. 'He has insulted my honour. He's mine.'

'I will say it one more time. Put. Him. Down.'

And Aemilius was airborne, and then his back exploded in pain, and there was the crash of splintering wood, as he stared up at the underside of the table. 'There, bitch. I've put him down. Happy?' the Germani snarled. But Augusta, the majordomo of Villa Sulpicia, was not happy. Not even slightly. Aemilius saw her take one step towards the Germani soldier... and then everything faded into a garbled mess of blurred shapes and sounds.

WHEN HE CAME to, he was being carried on some sort of stretcher. He grunted in pain.

'Welcome back, punch-bag,' Rivkah said, looking down on him and sounding delighted. 'You're fine. You got winded and passed out. He threw you on a chair, which smashed, but I checked you over. There's nothing broken, and there are no major holes in you.' He tried to reply, but very little came out. 'It was a shame, though,' Rivkah continued. 'You might have enjoyed the show.'

'What... happened?' Aemilius managed to groan.

'Augusta absolutely and comprehensively kicked five different flavours of shit out of your friend with the scars,' the lithe girl replied with glee. 'That boy is not walking again for a week, and his face has *not* improved.'

'Tell you,' Carrick wheeze-laughed from the front. 'Wife.'

'Mate,' Rivkah said. 'She would *break* you on your wedding night.'

'Fun way to go,' the scout chortled.

'Did you see how hard she kneed him in the nose, though? It was a sparrow's fart away from a killing blow.'

'She pulled it.'

'Think so?'

'Oh yes,' Carrick said. 'Knew exactly what she was doing.'

'Man,' Rivkah replied dreamily. 'I want to be like her when I grow up. And the way she stomped on his crotch—'

'His friends couldn't wait to get out of there.'

Aemilius groaned. 'Hate to interrupt,' he mumbled. 'But where—'

Rivkah cut him off. 'I reckon they'll go fast and hard on you next time they see you, so I told Augusta you needed rest. But honestly? I think you made even more friends getting thrashed the second time. The staff needed someone or something to push her over the edge.'

'So, what happens now?'

'They're cooking an obscene amount of food for the grieving widow and her sad, sad friends. Once the sun sets, they will feast in the dining room, and tell stories, and probably fart a sad song.' The creak of a door and a moment's pause in the jiggling of the stretcher suggested that they had reached their destination. 'Now get off and go have a lie down, Aemilius of Hispania,' Rivkah said, not unkindly. 'And try not to do anything stupid for a bit.'

He swung his legs over the side, winced at the pain in his back and shuffled towards his room. 'Thank you for the advice, Rivkah, daughter of Abraham. I am now going into this room, and I am going to do absolutely nothing at all.'

Until nightfall.

XIII

VILLA SULPICIA

TIME PASSED IN drips and drops. His windows had been barred, but he managed to ease one of the shutters open silently and watched as the sun crept across the sky, and night crept in behind it, and the sky faded from blue to purple to black. Somewhere, the wailing started again—muted, this time, a presence rather than an overwhelming wave. *Tastefully sad*.

Having nothing to do and nowhere to go, Aemilius took stock of what they knew, or thought they knew. There was an unknown number of Germani mercenaries all around, ostensibly hired by Marcus and possibly supplied by Ismael, who seemed to pose no immediate danger, although Livia might disagree. Three of the Germanes had been doing something in a hidden room underneath a mosaic in the gallery, which could be entered somehow. Another two or three would kill him on sight. *Great,* he thought bitterly to himself. *We are winning all kinds of wars here*. Tarquin had died—conveniently and un-suspiciously, it seemed—and somewhere in the mansion there was a jade dagger that he had to steal, or his entire bloodline would get eviscerated by a bloodless man.

He collapsed back onto his bed.

There was no target. There was nothing to do, no one to chase, no one to kill.

Except—the gallery.

The first, and worst, idea was still the best one he could come up with. Sneak out at nightfall, keep to the shadows and get to the gallery. Find the hatch in the dark, sneak down into the secret vault, find the dagger and get back out without being seen.

Stealing from a Roman senator, in his villa, where the entire household knows who I am and a significant number of very deadly men want to snap my neck. What could go wrong?

Outside, the last embers of the day were dying, and bravery was hard to come by. But Aemilius of Hispania closed his eyes, thought about his parents, pushed himself out of bed, and sighed a deep sigh. 'Right. Let's see how close we can come to dying this time, shall we?' he muttered, grabbing a candle in a holder off the table. The door opened without a sound, and he was thankful for the deserted and poorly lit corridor. It was a well-run villa, and they clearly did not spend anything extra on lights for servants who should be able to traverse their house blindfolded. Breathing slowly and trying to keep his heartbeats to a volume slightly lower than that of a galley drum, he moved forward with momentum and entirely fictional confidence. *Can't travel with Hanno and the hellcat and not learn something about sneaking,* he mused. Mostly to protect himself from screaming disaster-thoughts, he allowed his brain to wander...

...and froze.

He could *sense* someone. He didn't know where they were, exactly, or how he had... seen? Heard? No—*felt* them. But they were close and heading his way. Grasping hold of the luxury of a few heartbeats to choose, he found a nook behind a pillar and folded himself in as well as his throbbing back would allow—and moments later, he heard the steady slap-slap of sandals on stone, and a servant carrying a pail of something that sloshed walked right past his hiding place.

Quick.

Ducking out behind the boy, Aemilius timed his footsteps to coincide exactly with the slapping sounds and walked away with purpose. In his head, he composed the cover story. *Our coachman told me to come check on the carriage with him.* Or, as a back-up, *I thought I could be of use in the kitchen. Oh, it's that way? What a fool I am.*

But somehow, the feeling he'd had in the corridor remained. He could sense the disturbance in the air when someone was close, and on several occasions had time to turn, retreat or hide. *Funny*, he thought after the last one. *My face tickles a bit.* The doors to the gallery were open, and—Fortuna smiled on him—it was lit up. He ducked in, stepped to the left and hid behind a door. *Almost like I have... whiskers.*

You're welcome. The voice of the cat appeared in his head, somehow managing to sound smug and condescending without making any noise at all. *Do you not feel limited, two-legs?*

You can count? Aemilius couldn't keep the surprise out of his thoughts.

Of course we can, the cat replied haughtily. *All animals can count.*

Breathing very carefully and clearing his thoughts, Aemilius smiled. It was time to play. *...just as well as I can smell.*

Stink, you mean. Blood and fear.

No, no. Not at all. I can catch a scent just as well as you.

And the cat sashayed into view, tawny and sand-striped, with an arch look and stern, white muzzle, across which played an infuriating smirk. *Oh, can you?* Three short words positively drenched in sarcasm.

Aemilius smiled. *I can—and I'll show you. Last time we met, the lights were off, and I cannot see in the dark. I grant you that. But I can trace, by scent, where the three men came up out of the ground.* He walked with purpose across the central path of the gallery—fast enough to look like he had a job to do, but not so fast as to look guilty—and picked a route along the wall, eyeing hiding places, curtains and crannies as he went.

You have no idea, the cat snarled. *You are inferior. Your stupid bendy flesh-claws are your only advantage.*

And a fantastic nose, Aemilius countered. *I just didn't want to let on last time.*

A blast of disdain from the cat. *Well, then. Prove your big words, big lump. Where did they come from?*

Here! Aemilius thought, pointing to a square in the floor in front of a vivid scene from the Battle of Pharsalus.

Fool.

No! Aemilius thought. *But I was so sure!*

You have no idea. Admit it.

Maybe—but neither do you.

Of course I do! There was a genuine sound of feline outrage in his head. *I am the hunter in the night! I—*

Blah blah blah, Aemilius interrupted. *Prove it.*

I do not need to prove myself to a hairless lump!

You can't, you mean.

The cat hissed audibly. *Fine,* he said. *I'll shove your proof up your stinky arse, no-tail. Follow me.* It swished its tail angrily and stalked off into the gallery, stopping dead by a beautiful mural of Neptune rising from the waves. *Here.*

Why here? Aemilius sent the question with an open face. *How do I know you are not lying and deceiving?* To his surprise, he found that he could maintain some of his thoughts hidden from his silent friend. *I know where they came from, but you will guide me to the switch.*

Stand on the tile in the corner, the cat sneered. *Human tricks.*

A sense overwhelmed him, and he realised that the cat had allowed him to share its vision. Aemilius walked over to a corner just below the mural. One green tile, tucked into the corner, that would never be stepped on by even the most ardent observer, stood out ever so slightly. Feeling his heart quicken, he stepped on it, gently, and then put a little more weight down—

Click.

There was a soft grating of stone on stone as a large slab slid down into the floor and landed with another click. Below it lay darkness.

See? the cat thought smugly. *Who is your superior?*

Thank you, Aemilius thought back. *I would never have found it without your help.*

There was a spine-tinglingly delicious feeling of confusion from the cat. *But—what? You tricked me? If you had asked, I would have told you!*

But where's the fun in that? Aemilius thought back.

He looked at the cat, who glared back at him with narrowed eyes and then stalked away. *Serves you right,* he thought as he scanned his environment. The gallery was reassuringly empty. The hidden entrance was tucked away—pillars and plinths blocked every sight line, so much so that it was easy to imagine they'd built the room around concealing the entrance. 'The dagger must be down there.' He gritted his teeth and made his way very carefully into the darkened gap, scanning his surroundings carefully. The memory of a slender silver wire stretched across a tunnel at ankle height came to him, and he shuddered, looking away—

And his gaze landed on a small lever, tucked into the side of the wall. It was just about the width of his palm, but there was only one possible function to it. He pulled and heard exactly what he hoped he'd hear.

Click.

And as the slab began to rise, pushed by some invisible art from within the rock, he heard something he had not expected to hear.

An all too familiar voice, hissing 'Fuck—shit shit shit shit!'

Things happened fast. The stone slab rose, squeezing out the light from the gallery. Darkness engulfed him. And through the rapidly decreasing gap Rivkah came sliding at high speed, only just clearing the top edge and avoiding a very messy death, landing in the dark with a thud and a hissed curse.

And then there was just absolute darkness, and the thunderous beat of his heart, and the adrenaline-sour taste of still being alive. Aemilius hesitated, but whispered into the void. 'Are you okay?'

'Of *course* I am not fucking okay, you colossal, steaming pile of shit!' Rivkah whispered back. 'I just arse-planted on some stone steps, and now I am stuck in the dark with *you!*' He sensed her rising next to him, feeling around and elbowing him in the stomach. 'There you are. Stand still or I will knee you in the nuts. And now—right now—tell me. Do you have anything to make a light?'

Aemilius scrabbled inside the folds of his tunic. 'Uh, yes. I have a candle.' Striking the flint against the wick, he managed to light it on the third try. A pathetic little flame lit only a third of Rivkah's thunderous face.

'Spill your guts,' she growled. 'Or I will spill them for you.' So he did. He told her about Brachus's proposition, and how he had to lie and hated it, and how he had to find the dagger or else. 'You absolute cock,' she spat.

'What? He's threatened to kill my family!'

'*We* are your family,' she snapped. 'And you should have fucking told us. Or me, at least. Secrets are bullshit.' In the candlelight, her eyes glistened with fury.

'I'm sorry,' he muttered, and to his surprise he meant it.

'Go suck shit off a donkey's backside,' she muttered back. 'You are useless, hag-slayer.' A moment later, she added, 'And don't do it again. And don't look at me like that.' She snorted, like a tempestuous racehorse. 'Right. So where is this dagger, then?'

'Down, I assume?' Aemilius awkwardly pointed his candle holder towards the steps leading into darkness.

She huffed impatiently. 'Well—go on, then! I've never stolen anything from a Roman senator before.' *She sounds… not happy, exactly, but… not murderous. We'll take that.* Aemilius started inching downwards very carefully. Explaining why one was found in the tunnel to the senator's hidden treasury with a turned ankle might be tricky. The steps were hewn out of the rock itself, and well maintained. The light from his candle stroked past a mounted torch, and he glanced at it. 'No,' Rivkah hissed. 'Not unless we have to.'

'Why?'

'The smell. They'd know.'

He nodded in the dark and immediately rolled his eyes at his own idiocy. Beneath their feet, the steps started curving down. It was not a narrow passage, but he imagined he could still touch the walls on both sides. 'Here we go,' he whispered. A reinforced wooden door whose maker had devoted no time whatsoever to decoration and all their attention to it being pretty tough to break down was ajar. Somehow, the darkness within seemed even more black and foreboding than the steps had been. He felt Rivkah ghost past him and go in first.

'Clear,' she whispered over her shoulder.

'How do you know?' he hissed back.

'Smell,' she shot back. 'There is nothing in here, dead or alive.'

Gathering all the steel he had in him, he inched through the door after Rivkah. *Whatever we might encounter is going to take her first. Try to take her first,* he corrected. After the initial feeling of wondering whether he was going to get slapped around for not having revealed his secret, he felt powerfully relieved. He was no longer alone.

'Any time you like,' Rivkah snarked at him from the blackness. 'It's a good thing that rock is thick—I reckon there's plenty of chances to make a lot of noise down here.'

She was not wrong. The meagre light from the candle shone on iron-bound chests, some closed and some open. They could see the outlines from strongboxes, arranged neatly to the side. A tower shield was leaned up against a wall, and a search of the opposite side found a saddle and cavalry riding armour. The room was maybe twenty by twenty paces wide, and there was a hint of decorations and inscriptions on the wall. 'I wish I had a bigger candle,' Aemilius muttered.

'All boys do,' Rivkah responded instantly.

'Mostly so I could see where you are to throw things at you.'

'The size of the candle doesn't help with the aim,' she snickered. 'Now stop being such an easy target and get back on track. What are we searching for? Ah, yes. Some ballsack's magical jade pig-sticker, wasn't it?'

'Yes,' Aemilius replied, glad to be out of the furnace of Rivkah's wit. 'Brachus was vague on the details, though.'

'Some blades over here—ooh,' she purred. There was a rattle of metal, and she appeared at the flame, slowly bringing a knife into the light.

Aemilius frowned. 'What's so special about that one?' The knife she was holding was nothing much to look at—the blade was neither thin nor thick, neither long nor short, and the handle looked well-worn. 'There's a point to it, I'll grant you, but…'

'Oh no,' Rivkah said huskily. 'This one *kills*. This one has killed *big*. I'm keeping this.'

Aemilius threw up the hand that wasn't holding the candle. 'Sure. Why not? We might as well, seeing as—' They both saw it. The faint pull on the candle. And then—the horrifying sound of the heavy stone slab moving again. Closing down any part of his brain that wanted to offer words, he pointed towards the tower shield. She did not need to ask, and darted in behind it, folding herself into almost nothing. Feeling the rising panic, he heard the stone thunk into place. *The armour.*

He dove to the ground, shoving himself in underneath the metal chest plate and tucking his feet under the saddle, snuffing out the candle and feeling like an idiot child playing hide-and-seek. *I might as well stand in the middle of the room with a bucket on my head.*

The steps coming down were heavy. Heavy and many. Lights flickered and danced, colouring the outline of the half-open door.

'You should have closed this.' Ismael's voice. Further away, someone grunted their assent. The door creaked open, and the dark-skinned man strode into the room as if it was his own, sparing not a single glance at anything presented within. 'Move,' he snapped impatiently. 'We have little time. They will not wait, and I intend to be gone before the moon.' Aemilius looked up at their sandal-clad feet, slapping past. Ismael first, then his bodyguard—followed by two soldiers he knew all too well, and one he didn't. *If even one of them looks at their feet, I am dead.* The rearguard were carrying two shapes, slung over their shoulders. He wanted to scream. One of them was clearly female—but—*It's not Livia. And the other one is too big for Hanno, too broad for Carrick and too small for Abrax.* The procession of Germanes stomped through the room with great purpose. Their torches vanquished the deepest shadows, which revealed steps leading down. The lights flickered and faded with the sound of their feet. A sudden stop, a grunted command, a heavy, grating sound… again… and then—

Silence.

Aemilius breathed slowly, trying to quieten the thunderous heartbeat in his ears.

'Fuckers,' Rivkah snarled in the dark. 'Could have left

us a light.' *Light*. *Yes*. Aemilius remembered that he was holding the candle, and fumbled with the firelighter, eventually managing to light a flame that was about as feeble as he felt. 'Well done,' Rivkah said, dripping sarcasm from every syllable.

She wants to take them all on, and she knows she can't. Aemilius cleverly managed to refrain from congratulating himself for this insight, instead opting for staying alive a little bit longer. 'What do we do now?'

'Follow?' The response landed precisely between sincere question and withering put-down.

'I mean—we should probably observe...? Unless you follow and I go find Livia and—'

Knowing what the sound of stone on stone meant did not make it any less pleasant. Aemilius snuffed out the candle and they dove back into their hiding places, listening for the remainder of the Germanes... but there was no sound. Not even a whisper.

'Little creeps,' Rivkah muttered.

'You can light the candle again.' Serena's voice, far too close to Aemilius's ear for his liking, made him half jump out of his skin.

'It's just us,' said Flavius.

Swearing under his breath, Aemilius re-lit the candle. The pathetic orb of light only just caught on the children, standing side by side and eerily still.

'How did you know? Uh—that it was us?'

'I smelled your fear,' Serena whispered.

'I heard your heart thumping,' Flavius added.

'I saw—'

'Yes, all right, all right,' Aemilius snapped. 'Fine. I *was* terrified, thank you. I don't have a chance against those bastards, and you all know it. Done. Great. However—

you little shits being here solves an issue. Rivkah and I go follow—you run back to Mummy and tell her. They came through here with—'

'Octavia and Paulinus. Friends of Marcus Sulpicius.'

'Unconscious,' Flavius added. 'Like the rest of them.'

Aemilius felt his stomach sink. 'What do you mean?'

'You know what he means,' Rivkah snarled.

'Oh, fuck. Canisters with gas?'

'Yes,' Serena replied.

'Whole household is out. We were outside "playing"—'

'Scouting for good exits.'

'—when we saw them. They had scarves wrapped over their faces and were heading in here.'

'So we followed.'

'And watched.'

'Skulky little shitbags,' Rivkah muttered, not without admiration.

'So we can't go back,' Aemilius said to the two ghostly faces and Rivkah somewhere in the dark.

'We have to follow,' Serena said.

'But—they'll—' Aemilius found his voice rising in pitch and fought hard to bring it back under control.

'—never see us coming,' Rivkah finished his sentence. 'Unless you want to stand around and see if they come back up? Ow!' A clattering noise in the dark suggested that she had lost her patience, possibly while searching for something to hit someone with.

'Stand still, you miserable goat,' Aemilius said. 'Let me come find you.'

'Are Mummy and Daddy fighting?' Serena said in a mock sing-song voice.

'Try that again and I'll slap you so hard both your ears will be on the left,' Rivkah growled.

'You'll have to catch me first,' Selena trilled, dancing into the dark.

They made their way, painstakingly slowly, towards the far end of the room where the Germanes had disappeared, picking their way past crates and chests. The stone archway inched into their view, along with the broad stone steps.

'You could drive a cart through this,' Flavius said.

They picked their way down the steps and fell quiet.

'...or a sarcophagus,' Serena finished.

The chamber below seemed to be much bigger. The light from the candle did not come close to the ceiling or the side walls—but what they could see was a big stone coffin, placed side-on in front of a plaque that glistened dully.

'Where the fuck did they go?' Rivkah snarled, sounding like she'd happily stab the dark and the stones if she thought it'd help.

'Ssh,' Flavius admonished.

'Don't you fucking shush me, tadpole! I'll—'

'Shut up and let me think.' Aemilius just heard the indrawn breath, imagined what Rivkah's face must look like and bitterly regretted having brought just a candle and not a torch. Just before the inevitable eruption, the boy continued, 'That way.' He drifted into the light and pointed towards the darkness before disappearing again.

'No—stay still—let me just get my hands on—' Rivkah hissed, but to no effect. Flavius had vanished. Aemilius brought the candle in the rough direction he thought the boy had gone to. Faint shadows of grey on black suggested the shapes of coffins upon coffins. They had found the sepulchre of the Sulpicii, and he thought about what his father would have done with trespassers in their own crypt. The chamber suddenly felt cold and damp and oppressive, and his heart started to race.

'Here,' Flavius whispered in the dark. 'Over here. Help me push.' Aemilius quickened his step as much as he dared, nervously watching every twitch of the flickering flame. After what felt like an eternity the soft light finally caught on the flesh of the boy, which looked corpse-white. 'Put your candle down on this one, and push.' Aemilius did as he was told, leaned on the sarcophagus and pushed as hard as he could. Nothing happened. Someone swore in Hebrew in the dark, and the bony and furious form of Rivkah shouldered him aside. He felt her put her back into it as well, and something *shifted*. They all heard and felt the soft, heavy scrape of stone on sand on stone as the mighty death-block moved to the side.

Soft, flickering torchlight spilled in from an opening just about the width of a man, set half in the wall, half in the floor and sloping downwards. Through the stone frame they could see hewn rock and a sandy floor.

Rivkah cursed softly, all promises of violence forgotten. 'How did you know?'

'Smelled the sea,' Flavius replied happily, his silhouette appearing in the doorway. 'Now. Coming?'

They did not need to be asked twice. One by one they filed down into the tunnel, Rivkah in the lead, knives out. Aemilius brought up the rear. Up just above head-height small torches had been mounted, providing just enough light to make their way down, and then... *back up? After... what?*

What was Ismael up to?

Where were they taking the Romans?

And why?

Increasingly improbable scenarios presented themselves rapidly in Aemilius's head as dry sand hissed beneath his feet with every step, sounding uncomfortably like an oversized snake slithering around his ankles. He thought back on the tunnels leading to the cavern under the temple of Serapis and shuddered. This one was steeper, and more of a natural thing that had been helped somewhat by the hand of man. *Or men*, he thought, and wondered idly how many people had had accidents or died, and what had happened to the workmen who made the secret tunnel into the heart of the Villa Sulpicia. There was something about Marcus Sulpicius that gave Aemilius little hope they had lived into old age. The tunnel went from light, to dark, to light again, with small torches mounted at regular intervals lighting their way. Glancing down, he could see the heavy footsteps of the men that had gone before them. *Glad I don't have to do this while carrying a body,* Aemilius thought. Underfoot the incline softened, too, evening out into twists and turns as the tunnel widened in parts, tightened in others. A gentle swoosh crept in at the edge of hearing. Up ahead, Rivkah raised her hand, palm flat.

Stop.

There was a change in the quality of the light. The pitch black of the mountain was replaced with a seeping stardark, cutting a long, diagonal line into the wall opposite them. Making sure her silhouette could be seen, Rivkah made hand signs.

Slow.

Careful.

The others did not need further instruction. Serena and Flavius seemed to melt into the shadows beside her, and Aemilius suddenly felt big and clumsy, doing his best to skulk and wondering when he was going to ruin their cover by causing one of them to burst out laughing. They crept past a corner in the tunnel, and suddenly the starlit skies of Italia stretched out above them. Somewhere not far away gentle waves lapped a shore in rhythm, the heartbeat of a giant beast. A low wall of rock curved around in front of them, obscuring the cave mouth from view. *You wouldn't see this until you were standing in it*, Aemilius thought. *A smuggler's haven if ever there was one.* Over it drifted the voice of Ismael, and even before he'd tried to decipher the words Aemilius felt queasy and shivering and just—wrong.

Magic.

Bad magic.

Ismael's voice rose and fell, hard and guttural, and with it came urgency. 'We need to move,' Aemilius hissed to Rivkah, crouched and inching towards a viewing post.

'Shut up,' she hissed back. 'You'll ruin our—'

Two things happened.

The first thing he could see in the eyes of Rivkah and Serena—a widening, a surprise, as their ears blocked up amid an uncomfortable hissing, rending noise.

The second thing was the piercing scream of a woman.

'Well, shit,' Rivkah growled, and she was moving. As they rounded the corner, Aemilius felt his heart pounding so hard that it was difficult to take in the scene before him.

They had come out onto a smooth, sandy beach. Behind them was the water. In front and maybe a hundred yards further up were two big stone slabs that looked like they had been laid out neatly on the sand by a giant's hand, two hundred yards apart. On each of them, a body. Both were arched in agony, and just as the legionnaires laid eyes on them the man screamed as well. Around the stones palm-thick lines snaked in uncomfortable, swirly shapes of black and purple that cast his mind back to the rune around a monstrous cyclops's neck. He looked up at the sheer cliff face encircling their little theatre, and in a flash, the murals of mighty generals and empire-builders of his line flashed before Aemilius's eyes and he drew from them the inspiration to unleash a true command, a sentence for the poets, a strike in the battle between good and evil.

'*Oi! Stop that!*'

Two poles had been shoved into the ground, upon which rested big lanterns that bathed the stones in an amber glow. Above them, the moon shone down on the black sea, white-tipped, lapping at the sand. Standing by the edge of the rune-mark, Ismael glared fire-eyes at Aemilius but did not stop his incantations. *We are not important to him. He does not care.*

The four men standing behind him, however, very much did care.

The weapons appeared in the hands of three of them instantly—gladius, club, and a nasty hand-axe. Their leader stood back—the lanky warrior who had been shadowing Ismael—and surveyed as his three soldiers spread out to either side of the runic circles, moving to block their access to Ismael. None of them seemed to want to get too close to the black lines.

'I said, *stop*—'

A thin, glistening line of red burst out of the woman's chest and shot, arrow-straight, into the water at waist-height. Moments later another appeared, ripped out of the middle of the man, running parallel, plunging into the silky black sea. Their screams rose in pitch, higher and higher, until the sounds were nowhere near anything that should come from a human throat, and yet they rose, and at the top of the circle Ismael stood, stock-still, arms outstretched.

A summoner.

Of course he is a summoner.

Oh, fuck.

The soldiers approached slowly, gleefully, eyes sparkling with anticipation. Pockmark with the gladius came towards him and Rivkah, the other two curving to the south around the stones.

'No one to save you now,' the pockmarked one barked at Aemilius.

'Break their kneecaps first,' the second one shouted across the runes. 'So they can lie there and watch as we gut your little brats.'

'I get the girl!' The pockmarked one had a hungry look on his face.

Ten yards ahead of Aemilius, Rivkah eased her daggers out. 'Do you?' she purred. 'No flowers? No poetry?' He couldn't see her face but Pockmark clearly could, and he must have seen in it something he didn't like, because his smirk turned into a sneer. He spat on the ground, barked a command and moved forward, towards Rivkah, knees slightly bent, battered gladius swirling before him.

The woman stopped screaming.

Aemilius's heart dropped as he *felt* the sound that followed, a moment before he heard it. A plucking on a string, deep and warped. Staring at the arrow of blood, he saw that it was no longer moving.

It was taut.

To his left, Rivkah was walking slowly towards Pockmark. 'Tell me,' she said, like one would when meeting a person of passing interest in a market square. 'Have you tried asking your customers to spend themselves on your face when you're done? It might help with your skin.'

The big man growled. 'Nice try, bitch.'

'I know. It's not my best work… but I don't reckon you're worth it.'

Pushing hard to hold back the growing feeling of wrongness in his head, Aemilius watched in a trance. *Her foot her foot her left foot* Rivkah's left foot had seemed to sink into the sand a little bit. *Stuck her foot she's stuck* And then she stepped forward with her right foot and her left *whipped* up and the pebble she had found and nestled on her toes flew towards the face of the big man, and he ducked—

And then she was on him and above him, too fast for the eye to see, and there was a crunch as her heel met his eyebrow and he faltered and fell. Lightning-quick, she leant down towards his crotch, and then there was a quick flick of both hands and another scream, high-pitched and horrid, and a red flower blossomed between Pockmark's legs, and the proud warrior was reduced to a hunched wretch, crying and howling and dying. 'I would have done you quickly,' she said, standing over the man, 'but you enjoyed kicking his arse too much, and so I thought you should probably be allowed to bleed to death in horrendous agony instead, holding the bits of your cock.' And with that, she turned her back on the prone body and towards Ismael, still forty yards away. 'Now—you. We told you to stop.'

There was a *slither* about the warrior who stepped in front of Ismael. That was the only way to describe it. Tall, weathered and whippet-thin, he settled into his combat stance like a falling feather. There was nothing in his hands—and then he seemed to hug himself, and then open his arms in a wide embrace, as if inviting Rivkah to come closer. The moonlight caught on the point of a long dagger with an upturned, pointed hilt in his left hand. With his other hand he slowly twirled a strange thing—a two-foot handle with a wicked blade attached at a right angle. He looked at Rivkah and smiled. 'You look... worthy,' he said.

Looking down in a haze, Aemilius watched his feet moving as if in a dream, up the beach, towards Rivkah and the deadly fighter defending Ismael. There was something at his back, a silent crush coming from the sea...

Fear.

And just as he realised what it was, it doubled—and the man stopped screaming as well. Risking a glance to the side, Aemilius saw that the two bodies were both rising agonisingly slowly from the stones, as if they were being pulled upright by their blood-strings by the sea.

No... not by the sea.

By something in the sea.

There was a feeling there, a thought, but the part of his brain that wanted him to remain able to speak and hold the contents of his stomach forbade him from thinking it, from seeing and feeling what was there, what was being pulled into the world.

He almost missed it, it was so fast.

The first clash of blades between Rivkah and the lanky fighter was a hiss and a blur. They came together and disengaged like lightning flashes and disappears.

'Nice,' Rivkah spat. 'You're still alive.'

'So are you,' the fighter replied. 'Not bad for a little girl.'

'Not bad for a grandad. Are you going to come and get me? Or do you need some gruel and a nap first?'

The fighter grinned and made no move. 'I am very lazy, in my old age.'

Rivkah advanced—and struck.

Another clash, followed by a contorting leap as she twisted out of the arc of the sickle coming her way. 'Rude!' she exclaimed with delight. 'That could have cut my tits off!'

'In two years, maybe,' the fighter replied, receiving a delighted bark of laughter for it—and another frenzied attack, and they were engaged. Twists, kicks, parries and lunges, a dodge—and a curse Aemilius didn't recognise. The fighter retreated three steps and looked down at a short, thin line of red forming on his left forearm.

'Hurts, doesn't it? Being sliced by a little girl.'

Aemilius watched as the fury simply vanished off the fighter's face, like mist in the morning. 'I'd forgotten,' he replied. 'It's been years since anyone has put a blade on me.'

'Honoured, I'm sure,' Rivkah snapped back.

'He was, too,' the fighter replied. And then all other feelings vanished off the man's face, and Aemilius's blood ran cold with fear for his friend. Closing the distance to Rivkah, the fighter simply seemed to gain speed with every move, and soon the girl was dodging and swirling away from vicious swipes, stabs and lunges, being forced to seek shrinking gaps in an ever-closing net of steely death.

'Fucking get him!' she screamed, and Aemilius realised that suddenly the path to Ismael was clear. He drew a knife, pushed all thoughts aside and ran at the lanky black man. He could see the intense concentration—

but also the glance that showed his approach had been noticed. Closing in, Aemilius swiped once, twice—and Ismael stepped aside, dodging the point aimed at his midsection, shouting louder, faster—dodging again—and then launching the last word into the air with a triumphant scream.

Got you!

Aemilius dove forward, swinging his dagger diagonally upwards in his best attempt at a disembowelling swipe—and watched the point sink into Ismael's shirt and rip it upwards, and then the foot caught him in the stomach, and as the air left his lungs, he heard Ismael bark out a command and saw the back of the man, sprinting towards the cliff face. Staggering to his feet, he saw the other soldiers running to catch their leader, and to his left the lanky fighter disengaged from Rivkah and ran as well.

'Coward!' she screamed after him but made no effort to give chase. Instead, she came over to check on him and they watched as the Germanes reached the cliff face. Following Ismael's lead, the two soldiers reached up and started climbing. The last of them, the lanky fighter, made it look like he was walking on flat ground.

'...the fuck was that?' Rivkah said. 'He was clearly a magus, but you are still alive.'

Aemilius stared at her. 'Are you... out of breath?'

She glared at him. 'That guy was good,' was all she offered.

'Aemilius!' Serena's voice was clear and crisp in the night, and thick with fear.

And he remembered that there had been a reason to swipe at Ismael. To stop the—

He turned towards the sea.

XIV

VILLA SULPICIA

THE BODY OF the woman on the stone had been pulled up from its prone position and was standing straight. The sight was uncomfortable—unnatural, somehow, like she was held upright by a cruel puppeteer. There was nothing right about it. Her head lolled to one side, a broken child's toy, and her arms hung limply. The only rigid thing about her was the impossible string of blood that the ocean seemed to be using to try to rip the heart out of her chest. Over his shoulder, Aemilius caught a glimpse of the last of the Germanes swinging their legs over the ledge of the cliff face. Lit by a moon that had dared to come out of cloud cover, Ismael stood at the edge, arms outstretched in welcome.

But what was he welcoming? The faint moonlight did little to illuminate the beach. The torches created an orb of warm light, but it was not a big one. *Whatever it is, we won't see it until—*

'Over there!' Flavius this time, sounding less like an assured street rat and more like a terrified boy. 'From the sea!' Aemilius peered and could only just spot it. About forty yards out, the waves suddenly seemed to break and part as something broke the surface. His first reaction was to scoff. *That's not scary.*

'Shitting fuck,' Rivkah muttered next to him. 'Do not like this. Do not like this at all.'

'It can't be that bad. It's just a...' He tried to finish the sentence but couldn't. His brain had stopped producing words. He found himself staring into the dark, and what was coming out of the water was a human head, attached to a human body with shoulders and breasts and arms. A naked woman was walking slowly out of the sea, like her stroll had just taken her underwater for the best part of an evening.

'We need to run,' Rivkah hissed next to him. 'Right now.'

'Why?' he heard himself saying dreamily. His mind felt foggy. The woman-shape shimmered in the moonlight.

The slap stung like high hell. 'Because whatever the shit that is, I have never seen one of those, and I am not fighting it, because fuck that.'

Aemilius blinked, and gasped, and his brain dropped its defences for a moment so that he saw what was actually in front of him. It had maybe been a woman at one point, and possibly a beautiful one, but it wasn't either anymore. The... creature had the torso of a woman and a pallid, pained and nearly human face, but in place of her lower body a cruel god seemed to have fused three slavering hounds with crooked paws, their heads baying warbled curses as they emerged, salt-slick, from the water. A long, thick, scaled tail extended from the back of the hounds somehow, disappearing into the water. The creature saw Aemilius staring and *hissed*—and another five milky-eyed heads fanned out on long, thigh-thick necks from somewhere on its back. In her hand, webbed and clawed, she held the red line that connected to the woman on the rock, wrapped three times around her wrist.

The vomit exploded out of him, and the entirety of his stomach contents landed at his feet.

He got no sympathy from Rivkah. 'Too late.' And she was right. The woman-creature was now standing on the sandy beach and staring up at them, maybe a hundred yards away—and closer to the tunnel than they were. The Germanes looked down on them from the cliff, so climbing would be certain death.

Serena and Flavius had found their way to shelter behind the two of them. 'She,' the boy whispered, giggling hysterically. 'She must, haha, spend a fortune on trousers.'

'Flavius.' Serena's voice was as calm as the drowning sea. 'You will not give up on me.' He looked at her, quivering. 'You will not give up on me,' she repeated again, stone-faced and steel-eyed. 'Because I will not give up on you.'

Aemilius glanced at Rivkah, who somehow found it in her to raise an approving eyebrow. He was about to say something reassuring and commanding when there was a sudden movement next to them. The woman on the stone fell forward, landed on the sand and they watched in horror as the creature on the beach pulled on the string and wrapped it around her wrist, pulled and wrapped, pulled and wrapped. Frozen in their tracks, they watched as her forearm got gradually covered with the blood-red rope, watched as the body seemed to drag itself through the sand, leaving a groove, watched as the hounds at her waist snapped and sniffed, as the twisting snake-necked heads swirled and growled at each other and then at the dogs, each one a uniquely mangled, mocking copy of the monster's face.

And then the body was before her, and Aemilius threw up again.

She fell upon it. The dogs bit and tore, and the heads thrashed, and the necks smashed at each other to get to the flesh. Amongst the wet and the sucking sounds and the ripping, there was the occasional crunch as rows of shark teeth smashed through bone.

Next to him, Rivkah swore softly in Hebrew. 'That is the worst thing I've seen in a while.' She thought for a moment. 'Almost as bad as watching you eat.'

We are safe—and doomed.

Aemilius wondered idly when the death-fear would kick in, when his insides would turn to liquid. *Not yet, please. I want to live.* He tried to think of his mind like a frightened animal, one that needed to be soothed and calmed and tricked into doing the right things, and he did not ask it to think of anything. *Just stay here. Just…*

'Is it… talking?' Flavius sounded winded and sore, but out of jabbering hysteria.

Words. There were definitely words coming out of… something, somewhere. They were warbled and hard to understand, but… *Southern. Sicilia.* And once he tuned into the accent, he could catch some of them.

Mine Mine Hungry Mother, hungry Mine Unfair Kill bite kill She's biting me Mother Bad dog She biting

They came in waves and voices, and they sounded like the music of madness, and he listened to them and then, to his horror, realised they had stopped. He looked up to see that the creature was looking straight at him.

Mine

Mine

Fresh

I can smell the blood mother

Mine

The creature belched, shuddered and lurched over the scattered remains of the woman's body, the heavy tail pressing them into the sand.

Good evening, Death. I see you have come to me again. Let's play, shall we?

Without daring to think too much about what he was doing, Aemilius sent out as sharp a command as he could.

Bite.

He put all the thought-force he had behind it.

Bite!

He did not ask nicely.

Bite!

Daggers at the ready and about to charge the new and hideous enemy, Rivkah only managed two words. 'What the—?' As one, the dog-heads on the creature twisted in upon it and sank their teeth in. An unholy howl of rage, and it smashed its hands down on the dogs' heads, but to no avail. Down came the heads with their terrible teeth, into the scruff of the dogs' necks, wrenching and ripping. Howls of pain and gouts of horrid, black blood, followed by a scream fit to rend the world as the dogs let go, snapping at the heads and the night and anything and everything. 'Come on, you bastard!' Rivkah screamed, and charged. Her battle-cry was matched by two younger voices as Flavius and Serena charged after her, daggers at the ready.

My history tutor would have loved this.

The thought presented itself to Aemilius, like a cat doing its own thing, and then slinked away. *Why...?* Feeling dazed and sick to his stomach, he swayed where he stood and noticed that he was very much not charging the monster, and remembered a sun-baked road in Hispania, and a harpy, and three cousins who would never raise a glass again. He tried to move towards the creature and the fight, put one foot forward and nearly fell over. *What is wrong with me?* Another part of his mind caught up to him. *Magic. You just commanded... an animal, I guess. And you did nothing to protect yourself, and you might die.* Down by the water's edge Rivkah was dancing and darting, swiping and dodging as the other two had fanned out to keep the creature's attention diverted as much as possible, and Aemilius dimly registered blade connecting with neck and getting ripped away. *Why... would my history tutor have...* His stomach lurched as one of the monster's necks whipped forward, towards Flavius. The head missed by inches, but the neck struck the boy's hip and sent him falling. Another head dove in immediately and there was a sickening, wet sound as the teeth ripped into the boy's stomach, caught hold and tossed him in the air. A scream, then, as Serena launched herself at the creature only to be held at bay by the hounds as Flavius was ripped to shreds above them, blood raining down on the frenzied maws. For all its ungainly bulk, the monster twisted and turned to keep its sharp-fanged enemies in check, and one by one the heads turned from the demolishing of the small, lifeless body to the enticing prospect of living flesh. Rivkah was already retreating, pulling at the raging girl next to her, screaming something at her that Aemilius couldn't understand.

And then, the thrum again, and his stomach lurched, and at the edge of his vision the body of the young man on the stone at the other end of the beach started rising, pulled by the red cord. He shouted Rivkah's name, but his voice felt like it was coming through water. She heard, somehow, and he mutely pointed towards the body, willing her to understand. *To me.* Miraculously, she started backing up towards where he stood, keeping the monster in her sights. It seemed to be having an argument with itself, as some of the heads were in favour of devouring every single ounce of the woman and boy before making their way to a fresh kill.

Aemilius forced himself to tear his eyes off Rivkah's retreating form and look towards the young man and the line into the sea. This time, his brain did not even try to make up something to cover the horror dragging itself out of the water. A crinkled, fleshy tube of some sort, looking like an intestine with an angry, puckered mouth, into which the red cord disappeared, was slithering onto the shore. It was hard to tell in the faint light, but it looked uncomfortably big for being an animal, and his brain did not want to entertain the thought of it being an appendage.

The dog-wench at the beach shrieked in rage, all heads turned up towards where they were stood, and rotated itself to face them.

Rivkah reached his position. 'We have to climb,' she barked. 'Or we lose both of the kids.'

But I am a kid! Aemilius wanted to wail. He had still only been a legionnaire for three weeks, and his wealth of experience did not cover whatever was happening here, easily more horrifying than any two encounters they'd had up until this point. 'Let's go then,' he managed feebly. 'If we fan out, we can—' He saw it out of the corner of his eye. The horror at the far end of the beach suddenly ballooned out to a horrific size—twice the height of a man—and the angry maw opened wide. The blast of sea water came with the roar of a crashing wave, shooting a blast at the cliff wall that exploded in a shower of stones. The beach above them had turned in an instant from soft and sandy to a mire of rock and water, and Aemilius realised that next to him, Rivkah was screaming. Some of the fog lifted from his brain, and he scanned her up and down. 'Are you hurt?'

'*No!*' she screamed. 'I'm just *fucking annoyed!* What the fuck even IS that?' She glared at the flesh-tube, which seemed to be dragging itself further up the beach with a series of stomach-turning slurps.

'It's coming,' Serena squealed. 'The other one!'

'I *know*,' Rivkah shouted back, spinning to face the many-headed creature slithering up the beach towards them. 'We die here.'

Something, somewhere in the back of his brain, *screamed* at Aemilius. He wanted to push it away, but it felt important and so he reached for the memory. The thwack of his history tutor's rod on his desk. *Wake up, boy! This is exciting! History!* And he wanted to snap the old man's neck, wanted to say it wasn't, that it was just some annoying and smug Greek sailors who—

History!

'No,' he wheezed. Rivkah's glare helped him stay with the thought. 'Or… maybe not. We have a chance.'

'Feel free to tell me,' the girl growled. 'Any time now.'

'Can you… make her chase you her towards the tube-thing?' He gestured towards the many-headed monster.

Rivkah's stare would, in any other circumstances, have made him laugh. 'No problem, commander. Easy to do.

Trivial. Want me to cook you up some eggs while I do it? Or maybe run you a fucking bath?' Without waiting for an answer she shook herself, blew out a sharp blast of air and growled something in Hebrew before turning back to face the creature.

He could feel the fatigue in his bones, threatening to drag him down into the sand forever, so he decided to take her words as acknowledgement. 'And you, Serena, are with me.'

'To do what?' The girl looked all of her tender years, but there was still some steel in her.

'We need to cut the cord,' he said. The plan was forming in his head, and he could see it working. He could also see all of them reduced to red stains in the sand as the two hellish apparitions crawled out of the sea to wreak havoc upon the Sulpicii and anything else in their path. Staggering after the young Serena, feeling leaden-footed in every step, he trained his eye on the body of the young man, and wished he hadn't. The blast from the water had clearly broken a number of bones, so now bits of him were at wrong angles. His head hung too far off the shoulder, suggesting the force had been nearly strong enough to rip it off and at least break his neck. The right arm was no longer where it should have been, instead standing off at a right angle to his back, like it would if something had broken the shoulder blade in two. The once-strong body still held together, but it did look like it had been dropped from a significant height and landed on its right side.

And I still don't know if this will work.

Serena got there first. 'Now what?' she yelled, voice nearly cracking as she held in the horror of the approaching skin-worm, now maybe a hundred yards away and closing slowly. Behind him, he could hear Rivkah screaming Hebrew curses at the other creature. 'Do we hack at this?' She pulled out her blade and swung it at the red cord.

'No!' Aemilius shouted, but too late. The knife bounced straight back up and nearly sliced her face. 'I don't know what that is, but it is not of this world. But,' he added hastily, seeing the mix of fear and rage on the girl's face, 'I think… it comes from the heart.' Pulling on his last reserves of strength, he reached down and grabbed a fist-sized rock. 'We need to break his ribs and hack it out.' Serena mumbled something under her breath and Aemilius caught a glimpse of a prayer and a glance to the heavens, but he ignored it. If he understood this correctly, there was very little time. The first hit jolted his arm. *Harder.* He hit again. *Harder!* He screamed at himself, and then at the world, and swung the rock. Something cracked in the man's ribs, and in Aemilius as well. He screamed at the top of his lungs and hit the same spot, again and again, and then suddenly something smacked into his leg, and he was falling, down, down towards the beach and the ocean roared just by his ear and he felt the weight of the sea as it passed over his head. His mouth filled with water and sand, and he coughed and gulped and spat but it wasn't enough and his mind raced and he pushed down but his arms sank into the wet sand and water. Animal instinct made him twist and get his knees under his body and he managed to push up just as the roar and the weight of the ocean above his head subsided, like the current going back out to sea, and he saw the body of Serena next to him, unmoving, and he heard himself shout as he dove down and pounded her chest and lifted her up with a strength he didn't have and shook her and lifted her upside down and tried to shake the water out of her and by some miracle she started coughing violently and he put her down, trying his best to help her breathe, watching the tears form in her eyes as the raw air came back into her, and then she saw him and pointed silently, furiously, at the man, still upright and still connected to the horror by the cord.

Aemilius was up on his feet. The body had not fared well from this blast either. *The chest!* The man's chest looked caved-in, and with renewed fervour he drove his knife into the flesh, hacking and sawing until he felt hard bone under the point. *Open up, you rat-bag!* Digging like a mad animal with one bad claw, he managed to wedge the cord under his armpit, find the crack in the bone, shove his knife in, and—

Exhaustion saved his life.

Had his knee not buckled just at the moment when he wedged the broken rib apart, the heart of the man zooming towards the abomination in the sea would have clubbed him in the chest, smashing it into a pulp.

The corpse collapsed in upon itself, the dark magic that held it up broken and dispelled. There was even the suggestion of displeasure from the flesh-monster as the heart disappeared in through the mouth, and it shook and shuddered, slapping down onto the wet sand and moving with an odd, horrific purpose in sweeping arcs.

It is looking for its next meal.

Excellent.

Aemilius looked at Serena, but there was no need for instruction. Fear had disappeared from the girl's features, replaced with cold vengeance. She looked towards Rivkah, then at Aemilius for confirmation. He only needed to nod.

Moving carefully, testing each step, the petite girl started making her way towards the abomination. At the other end, Rivkah was having a much worse time of it. The many-headed dog-bitch was moving with more purpose now, heads fanning out and snapping this way and that, cutting off escapes and anticipating moves. With horror, the realisation sank in. *It's… learning.* A wet, heavy thud as the flesh-worm slapped down onto the sand. It had clearly sensed Serena's presence and was twitching towards the girl. There were a hundred yards between them now.

And then Rivkah launched herself backward.

Aemilius saw her foot sink into a hidden pool of water in the sand. He saw her balance go, tired legs buckling. He saw the triumph in the twisted features of the monster as it lurched forwards—and the thought burst out of him, laced with fear and fury.

Run.

Run.

Run!

He just registered the surprise on the monster's face as its feet took it not forward, but sideways at pace. The heads fanned out in confusion, only just steadying it as it stumbled towards the sea, and it screamed in anger as it fought with its own legs.

Aemilius threw up, again, retching bile and stomach juices and shivering as a bitter wave of cold shook him from the core.

It was not much—but it was enough. Rivkah got to her feet, somewhat unsteadily, and used the chance to retreat a couple of crucial steps towards Serena. As she moved, she bent to pick up a stone which she launched at the many-headed monster, hitting it square in the chest.

'Come on, bitch!' she screamed, to which the monster replied in an oddly similar pitch.

Maybe they are related, Aemilius thought, barely suppressing hysteria. He felt tired. No, not tired. Exhausted. No, not quite.

Empty.

Empty and drained.

But he still had work to do, and so he shouted hoarse encouragement to the two girls backing towards each other.

Fifty yards.

Now forty.

Twenty-five.

His eye caught the movement of the ocean, and he screamed.

'*Run!*' Out past the fighters on the beach, something strange was happening. A wave, and then another, and then another... disappeared. '*Now!*' His throat made noises he did not recognise, and he felt something break and rasp and sting, but whatever he did was enough. The girls reacted, running towards him just as the worm-creature on the beach swelled up obscenely and launched a jet of water straight through where Rivkah and Serena had stood—and hit the many-headed monster square on.

Somehow the monster stood its ground, but it was very clear that it did not appreciate the treatment. The moment the water jet subsided, the heads fanned out even further, and the human features contorted in rage as it turned on this new enemy.

'Now back up,' Aemilius whispered, wincing at the pain in his throat. 'Back up. We need to climb.'

'You absolute little shit-bastard,' Rivkah said with admiration. 'How the fuck did you—' And then she turned to look at him, and the last thing he heard as he collapsed was her piercing scream.

I WONDER IF *I'm dead*.

Maybe.

He tried to ease his eyes shut and forget that he had woken, if that was what he should call it. Had he been asleep? *Beach*. He remembered the beach. The twin horrors, about to do battle. *So I am probably dead*. He thought of nothing for a while. Then— *The afterlife is quite uncomfortable*. Slowly, the reality of his situation intruded on his senses. There was definite movement, and the sound of hooves going at a speed a little above a walk, but not much. He tried to remember more, and couldn't, and then he could.

'Rivkah...'

He thought the words, but someone else said them. Someone who almost had his voice.

'He lives,' said the unmistakeable and very near voice of Hanno the Wise. 'And now he sounds much less like a tadpole and more like a full-grown frog.'

'Good,' Abrax rumbled happily from somewhere behind him. 'Although I wager he feels like he wishes he died.'

There was the blue of a morning sky above them. Slowly, smells intruded upon him. Morning air, just heated by the sun. Horses, calm and not yet tired.

'When were you going to tell me, you little shit?' Rivkah, somewhere near. *Her and Hanno in the wagon. Abrax on horse*.

'Where is Livia?'

'Oh, don't you worry about her. She rides in her fancy

wagon,' Rivkah shot back. 'And you are not squirming out of this one. When were you going to tell me?'

'Tell you what?' he groaned.

'Oh, do *not*,' she snapped, 'pretend you don't know what I'm talking about, *magus*.'

Aemilius's insides lurched as his body remembered what it had been through. 'Where are the—'

'—the monsters?' Rivkah interrupted. 'For some reason they seemed to do everything you asked them to. After you passed out, they started fighting—the snake-bitch kept attacking the worm, and kept doing damage, and nothing happened. It was hilarious, actually. She couldn't touch it, but the worm couldn't do any damage to her either. How did you know?'

'They summoned Scylla and Charybdis,' Aemilius whispered. His throat still felt like a tanned hide. 'And the whole point of them is that they cannot be in the same place, so I reckoned if we brought them together, they'd wear each other out.'

'You were right,' Hanno chimed in. 'We got to the cliff top just about when they were being dragged back to sea by... something.'

'Reality,' Abrax added. 'Dragging those horrors out of the stories they were born in would cost tremendous energy. Ismael probably meant for the sacrifice to sustain them until they got ashore, then Scylla would get to the household and in the panic some of them would probably fall to Charybdis. Either that, or they'd start seeking out fresh victims somewhere else. And people would notice someone like Marcus Sulpicius dying. Rumours would start, the Empire would tremble.'

'Either way, the children did us proud. Young streams make for strong rivers.'

'We lost Flavius.' Aemilius felt his throat thicken as he remembered the boy being torn to shreds.

'We know.' Abrax's voice was quiet and serious. 'He gave his life. At some point, we all will.'

'But how—' was all that Aemilius managed, before the information he didn't have overwhelmed him.

'Carrick and I were outside the radius of the gas. We saw the Germanes ready for departure, and then Ismael came and joined in a hurry. They left, after which we came down to the cliff edge. Rivkah was halfway to the cliff face, with you over her shoulder—'

'For a skinny-arsed little runt you are surprisingly heavy.'

'—and we quickly assisted her and Serena to get you back up. After we'd cleaned up the worst of the evidence, we then snuck in and woke Livia and Hanno. The rest was fairly simple.'

'Livia spun a web of lies so glorious that the Queen of Spiders would have moved in on the spot.' Hanno beamed. 'She convinced Marcus Sulpicius that Ismael had been a con artist all along, and had planned to defraud him with the help of Octavia and Paulinus, all of whom had snuck off in the night, making off with'—he patted a large sack which jingled gently—'a significant amount of his jewellery and coins.'

The dagger. Aemilius's blood ran cold. He had failed. His entire family would be killed. They would be killed, and he was doomed to be a legionnaire until he, too, died at the hands, feet, paws, claws, scales, fire-spitting nostrils or who knows what else of something unspeakable and possibly unpronounceable.

'Ol' bignose was furious,' Rivkah chortled. 'Apparently he swore to hunt them to the ends of the earth.'

'Which is roughly where he'll need to go to find them,' Abrax continued. 'But he won't find Ismael before we do.'

Dead. All dead. Driven by fear, his mind started racing. 'Where is he?'

'Heading north, straight like a shitty crow flies.'

If we find him, I could maybe convince them to capture him and negotiate with Marc—

'And so are we,' Abrax said. 'We just have to do one thing first.'

'What?' Aemilius fought to keep the rising panic out of his voice.

'We have to stop by in Nomentum, find Brachus and hand him over a stupid little jade dagger.'

His brain ground to a halt and all Aemilius could do was blink. *Had he heard it right?* 'Wh—uh—' he stuttered, but words were quite far away from him. 'I— uh—' he continued, accomplishing not much more in the way of communication.

'He is eloquent, in his old age,' Hanno commented.

'A poet,' said Rivkah. 'I await his magnum opus.' And she launched into a series of noises, each less sensible than the last.

Faced with a barrage of abuse that sounded oddly good-natured, Aemilius drew on all the strength he had and levered himself up to a half-sitting position, back against the side of the cart. He was still far away from being able to form a coherent sentence, so he contented himself with staring.

They were all there. Hanno, sitting in the cart looking at him with bemusement. Rivkah, at ease on the coachman's plank, holding the reins with one hand. And Abrax, sitting in the saddle, looking like he'd been carved out of polished ebony, half a smile playing on his lips. 'You can thank Livia,' he said. 'She didn't believe that Brachus had wanted your... services, so she went to work on Uncle Marcus to figure out what he had that the lizard would have wanted.' The big fire-magus smiled. 'She would never admit it, but I suspect she quite liked saving you from his clutches. Took very little doing, she said. He was bursting to show off. Said it was the blade that killed Caesar himself, although having seen it I doubt that. They'd have used something more... practical.' Aemilius glanced at Rivkah, who looked remarkably innocent apart from a subtle hand placed protectively over the dagger in her belt. *This thing kills.* Abrax did not notice, and continued. 'Collecting it was easy, considering everyone was unconscious. Marcus will find it missing and assume that Octavia and Paulinus have it. What did Brachus threaten?'

'He said he'd erase my entire blood line,' Aemilius muttered, feeling embarrassed.

Abrax sighed. 'Much as we thought. Men like him press and push until they find the thing that gives. But next time'—he fixed Aemilius with a stern look—'you tell us. The Legion works together.'

'Kind of the point,' Rivkah added. 'Strength in numbers and all that. And that marks the end of your weaselling. When did you know?'

'I don't know!' Aemilius burst out. 'Uh, yesterday?'

Hanno chuckled. 'Oh, no. The sea told you.' He looked around at the others. 'Remember the Cetus? You'—he extended a slim finger at Abrax, then at Rivkah, and the carriage—'and you, and her highness on the cushion, and even'—he saluted with a flourish—'Hanno the Wise, we all owe our lives to Aemilius of Hispania.'

Rivkah glared at him. 'What? What are you talking about? Oh, for the sake of—when did *you* know?'

'The sprat came to me after Alexandria, and asked me questions, bashfully. I saw it in him then.'

'You could have told me!'

'Yes,' Hanno said, looking over at Abrax, who nodded slowly.

'But sometimes we need time.'

'Well, he took enough of that,' Rivkah snapped back. 'You should hand him a looking glass.'

What does she mean? Still half-dazed, Aemilius looked down at his hands. They looked... thinner, somehow. More worn. He squeezed his eyes shut, then opened them again. The world was still there, and so were his friends. Feeling a sudden urge to touch his face, he raised his hands—and felt Hanno's hand, gently, on his arm.

'Remember what I said. Magic comes at a cost. You saw her, didn't you?' Hanno glanced at Rivkah. 'And she was in danger.' From out of nowhere, tears welled up in Aemilius's eyes. 'Yes,' the little magus continued, in a soothing voice. 'And it came to you, and you grabbed hold of it, and it swept you away.' His warm hand was on Aemilius's chin, wiping the tear away. 'Few will understand, friend... but we do.'

Glancing over at Abrax, feeling embarrassed at the fact that he was crying like a child, Aemilius found that the big man on the horse was simply there, looking back at him with sympathy. *They do understand.*

'I wasn't in any fucking *danger*,' Rivkah grumbled from the driver's plank. 'I was fine.'

'Maybe so,' Hanno replied calmly without taking his eyes off Aemilius. 'But Aemilius was still willing to risk his life to help you, Daughter of Abraham. Does that fill you with rage?'

'…no,' came the reply, so quiet as to be almost inaudible.

'There we are, then. Now—what you need,' Hanno continued, 'is rest, and once you are rested you need food, and once you are fed you need practice. We said we'd keep you alive, Aemilius of Hispania, and although you seem to want to make that task as hard as possible, we do not like failure.'

'He is right,' Abrax rumbled. 'Rest.'

'Unless, of course, like me you went up against an actual horror from the Odyssey armed only with a pig-sticker, in which case you get no rest and a sore arse.'

'At least you are kind enough to share,' the big fire-magus replied.

'What do you mean?'

'You are a pain in the arse for the rest of us as well.'

'Oh, sister of the blade—you have been *burned*,' Hanno squealed in delight.

Rest.

All right, then.

Aemilius leaned back onto the hastily piled-up blankets in the cart, closed his eyes and fell asleep to the gentle sound of eye-watering insults.

XV

TEUTOBORG

'WHAT ARE WE waiting for?' Rivkah hissed.

Aemilius hunkered down next to her, feeling every single nick and scratch from the torturously slow stalk through the forest. They had found a perfect lookout spot, hidden from sight and with a view down the hill to a clearing maybe a hundred and forty yards across. In the middle of it, an archway was rising.

'You know,' Livia hissed back. 'Carrick is running to the others. We have to make sure everyone is in place.'

'Well, he'll need to shift his scrawny arse.'

She hunkered down next to him, taut with annoyance, and he knew better than to try to say something... because this was it. The chase that had led them up through Italia, through the mountains that touched the sky and up into Rhaetia, sneaking past their own garrisons like thieves in the night, had been hard. Tracking their prey had been easy enough but dealing with his distractions had been another matter. They had been forced to make a hasty escape from Radasbona where Ismael, passing through two days previously, had somehow managed to convince every man, woman and child that the legionnaires were demons in human flesh. In another, they had just arrived when a score of giant wolf-men shambled in, freshly dragged into the world. Rivkah had enjoyed that one, as she got to let go of the remains of the rage at the wolf-trainers they'd encountered in Iaspura. Her horse hadn't, on account of having its throat ripped out. The lands of the Varisci had given them a plague of insects, which Abrax dealt with. In the lands of the Suevii, Hanno drowned a giant by the shores of the Elbe, wrapping his massive head in a bubble of water. And every step of the way, when the legion hadn't been skulking, hiding or fighting for their weary lives, Aemilius had been put through his paces. Abrax and Hanno had taken turns instructing him, questioning him and chastising him when he got it wrong, which had been frequently. Hanno had been true to his word and waited until he was reasonably rested and fed, but after that it had felt like every waking moment had been filled with questions, instructions and commands.

'No!'

'Quickly—change it around!'

'Stop!'

'Hold your thoughts—hold them!'

'Control! *Control it!*'

Over—and over—and over. And once his taskmasters had decided he had had enough he was unceremoniously slung back in the cart, to rest and eat. Rivkah had offered a couple of snide comments at the start, but after a while she seemed to come to the conclusion that he might not need reminding of his failings. *Probably collecting a list for later*, he thought. Unusually, she had also not made fun of the change in him. He had begged, and pleaded, and two days after the battle on the beach, they had finally relented. Livia had lent him a mirror, and he had held it up to his face, and stared at it for a while. The man staring back at him was himself—sort of—but he was also almost his father. The energy it had taken to convince Scylla's wolf-heads to turn on their mistress had aged him by about a decade. Hanno had explained that once he learned to control his powers better, something like what he had done would not cost him nearly as much, and in order to not lose his mind Aemilius decided to trust that and devote himself to getting better.

It had not all been hard going, though. Possibly because he had been mostly unconscious at the time, he had been spared the repeat encounter with Brachus. In a quiet moment, Livia shared that she and Abrax had entered, offered the dagger and explained exactly where Brachus could stick it. Livia then gleefully recounted that she had actually managed to annoy him by suggesting that he give them a receipt, which Abrax said had caused a raised eyebrow *and* pursed lips—as close as Brachus had ever come to rage, they reckoned.

The results of their work, though, had been interesting. They had found that he could now fairly reliably find animals within a certain range and call them to him. The range seemed to depend on the animal, but they hadn't been able to work out exactly where the boundaries lay yet. A lack of test subjects had been a bit of an issue as well. The ones he had found could be made to do his bidding in some cases, but it relied on a multitude of things. Making himself understood had been a challenge, but it seemed that it was easier to command the animal if it was something it did naturally. He could command a fox to attack. He could not command it to count to ten. They had done experiments with more than one beast at a time, night and day, hunter and prey. Some of it had been easy, some of it had been exhilarating and some of it had been utterly terrifying. On more than one occasion he had not been careful when searching for creatures in his vicinity and had almost gotten trapped in their thoughts.

The worst one of those had been a squirrel, its high-pitched and high-speed mind darting this way and that, constantly twitching. Hanno had wrenched him free through the medium of a bucketful of water to the face—and he had then, in Aemilius's opinion somewhat unnecessarily, brought all the water back to hit him in the neck. Afterwards Hanno and Abrax had both agreed that regardless of the forces being manipulated there was always an edge to walk, and when one tumbled over the virtual cliff then just about the only thing strong enough to pull the magus back was the survival instinct—in this case, a very strong wish to not drown. Soaked and sulky, Aemilius had at that point promised to repay Hanno in a similar situation by throwing him over an actual cliff. Hanno had not been keen, but Abrax had agreed that the principle had been sound.

And from the moment they left Villa Sulpicia in the cart, leaving Marcus Sulpicius to clear up a cataclysmic mess and hunt for invisible thieves, it had felt like they all knew where they were going. Livia had checked in at a couple of waystations, seeking out the tendrils and tips of Cassia's network, updating Mater Populii on their progress or lack thereof through carrier pigeons. *Still—Marcus was alive, and no monsters roamed the*

Italian countryside. Well, not more than usual. The land had changed around them, from endless, sunlit fields to mountain-teeth, from axe-wound valleys to lush, green grass, from beautiful pastures to a wild river, across the blue stream to old and sharp forests thick with menace, and now to here.

Teutoburg.

Ismael had stayed a step ahead of them throughout, but this was where he was going, and this was where they would end it. The Legion had found him at the head of a growing group of tribesmen—a rough-looking lot, clad in furs and battered armour taken off Roman soldiers without asking nicely—moving through the forest with purpose. Some of the men had been dragging crude carts laden with cargo that was hard to make out at a distance. Rivkah had argued that they should just assault Ismael and his lot there and then and had been unimpressed with arguments such as 'we need to know where he is going first' and 'there are a hundred and fifty of them that we can see'. Livia had also said something cryptic about Mater Populii sending reinforcements, which had been the end of that.

Instead, they had skulked through foreign woods, careful not to spook their prey. At that point Aemilius had been able to calm Rivkah down a little bit by pointing out that it was quite nice to be the hunter rather than the hunted, which she had grudgingly agreed with. And now they were here, hidden away, watching the barbarians' numbers, which had swelled to perhaps two hundred fighting men, putting the final touches on a structure that looked like an arch about two and a half times the size of a man in the middle of a clearing. And Carrick was not there, and then suddenly he was.

'They're in place,' he whispered.

And at that moment, there was a muted sound from the clearing, like a far-away explosion. It looked like someone had thrown a pebble in a pond, only the pond was standing upright. A shimmering, sickly purple sheen spread rapidly and filled the opening, and on cue strong men yanked the covering off the five carts. Working quickly, they lobbed the first corpse into the portal—and somewhere, something growled in response.

'Oh shit,' Rivkah growled. 'Next time we go when I say.' She was on her feet.

'Abrax. Hanno,' Livia snapped.

The sound of a wave on a beach swept through the clearing, and in the wake of it drops of water seemed to rise from every leaf on every tree, up into the air, forming a shimmering blue orb above the shouts of the fighters below, rising higher and growing until it was above the tree-tops, where it stood still—and then it fell. The weight of it broke bones, smashed carts and threw the gathering into disarray. The only one standing was Ismael, who seemed to have anticipated the attack.

Whether or not he was prepared for the next step was hard to say.

The moisture that had been drawn from the living trees to create the first strike had left a circle of kindling—and a moment later a whip-line of fire swept through the trees enclosing the summoner, striking at the base of the trees. One by one they creaked and toppled, agonisingly slowly. Below, the fighters shouted at each other—warning? Fear? But one voice boomed out over them. Ismael, commanding his troops. With the forest toppling around and towards them, the tribesmen screamed at each other and went back to lobbing corpses into the portal. Three of them descended on a man clutching a broken leg, grabbed him and threw him towards the shimmering wall—and a sharp beak shot out, snatching the torso in mid-air and dragging it back. The air around the portal seemed to bulge and distort, and still the Germanes kept on. A roar, then, sounding like it came from all around, and suddenly shapes, humans, leapt out from nowhere, charging into the fray. Aemilius watched in horror as the falling trees burst into flame around the Germani tribesmen and still they kept shovelling bodies into the portal.

A barked command from Ismael, and a large portion of the fighters turned to face the new enemy while the others started lobbing bodies in front of the portal, laying them out in a line... *like a trail*. Aemilius turned to Rivkah—and she was gone. Through the smoke he could just about see a lithe shadow skipping down the hill. A cold wave of fear washed through him as the battle raged on below. The barbarians had created a circle around Ismael, maybe a hundred strong. In the middle of the inferno the black man stood, arms outstretched, bellowing in an old tongue, calling forth whatever the portal would yield. Screams from the clearing and the sounds of clashing weapons told of battle joined— and what glimpses he could catch suggested that the barbarians' advantage in numbers was fading fast. The circle around Ismael was rapidly decreasing in size— when the magus howled in triumph.

After the journey and the training with Hanno and Abrax, searching for the presence of animals had become almost second nature to Aemilius. When they had settled down to observe the barbarians, he had sent out his thoughts, swept the area and found it all but devoid of animal life, which reflected their common sense. And then the thing came out of the portal, and he touched its mind and Aemilius had to fight with all his might to maintain his sanity.

It had a cockerel's head, but twice the size of a man's, stuck onto a bulky, feathered body with leathery wings, flapping for balance, with a thick, curled serpent's tail. It looked to be half again the height of a tall man, and it pecked at the corpses in front of it like they were some monstrous version of chicken feed. Its movements were jerky at first, like it was learning how to walk on its hideously oversized claws, but with every step it seemed to grow smoother, stronger and more terrifying, and its mind screamed its hunger.

Aemilius tried his best to see through the billowing smoke, the fallen trees and the rising flames, but it was almost impossible—*there!* Bodies, moving at speed. He was dismayed to see that it was the Germanes, retreating with impressive precision, still ringed around their leader, making their way out of their fiery prison at the far end of the clearing. In the midst of the smoke a battle cry rang out somewhere near the monster, followed by a whoosh that sounded like something large suddenly catching fire and a horrifyingly loud squawk-scream. The battle-scream turned into a roar from several throats. The creature suddenly burst out of a plume of smoke, looking oversized and terrified—and then it sank down into the smoke again.

Sounds of battle, shouts of triumph.

Glancing to his right, Aemilius saw Abrax scowl, raise his hands and grit his teeth, and several things happened at once.

Flames rose, higher and higher—until they were no longer touching the trees.

Snorri Kristjansson

The smoke vanished with them to reveal a group of fighters of various sizes. The smallest of them was a familiar shape, blood dripping from her daggers. Next to her stood a behemoth of a man, holding the brutally severed head of the monster above his own with some care, as the ichor dripping from it seemed to be burning a hole in the ground at his feet. Behind him two other, significantly shorter fellows were hacking joyfully at the portal with big axes.

'Let's join them, shall we?' Livia was up and picking her way down the hill at speed, leaving Aemilius scrambling to follow.

'Wait—uh—who are those guys?' he half-yelped at her back. 'Are they with us?'

'They seem to be able to stand the hellcat's company.' Hanno walked beside Aemilius, looking for all the world like he was just out for a pleasant summer stroll along a riverbank. 'So we can assume they are friends.'

It did not take them long to reach the clearing. While they had been walking one of the fighters on the ground had shouted something at Ismael, and the response had been a barked order from the black man and a full-throated scream from the barbarians that did not need to be translated. As Aemilius walked, somewhat tentatively, up towards their unexpected allies, he took some solace in seeing that Livia and Abrax seemed to be at least passing familiar with them. A quick negotiation happened between the groups—a lanky, dark-haired warrior and a slim, hammer-carrying monk of some sort seemed to step forward for the others—and within moments Livia had stepped forward into the space between the legionnaires and Ismael's army. Thanks to Abrax's magic they could see their enemies properly, and Aemilius found himself wishing for a little more smoke.

'I don't like this,' Aemilius muttered to Rivkah.

She shrugged. 'We all have to die some time.'

'Thank you,' he shot back, but... *She does have a point.*

The barbarians looked, to a man, like the survivors of years, if not generations of battle. They were a motley crew, with no rhyme or reason to their equipment— spears, shattered swords, wood-axes, something that could have been made from a broken plough—but every one of them carried their weapon of choice like it was an extension of their arm. They were strong, and big, and there were at least four times as many of them as the legionnaires.

Livia's voice rang out. 'Ismael of the Silver Heart.'

The black man grinned a serpent's grin. 'Well—if it isn't Sulpicia Martia! At the head of a very small army, no less.' Like a ghost, the tall warrior with the sickle drifted into view, and Aemilius felt eyes on him and Rivkah. 'I see that my lovely friends did not slow you down. Shame. My master would have loved to hear the stories in Rome.'

Your master? Your master?

Seemingly thinking exactly the same thing, Rivkah hocked and spat.

'I know a fair few people in Rome. We are headed there after we settle matters here. Would you like me to take a message for you?' Considering Aemilius was standing behind Livia and still felt compelled to do what she said, it was astounding that Ismael wasn't immediately doing her bidding.

But he wasn't.

Instead, the black man grinned even wider. 'That... will not be needed.' The sound drifted over the treetops and sank down into the clearing. A hunting horn. Coming from behind the Germanes. And then another. And another. 'The time for talk is over.'

Shapes changed and shadows shifted behind Ismael as more barbarians emerged from the forest, swelling the numbers behind the smirking magus. They were cut from the same cloth as the others, hardened with malice. What had been four times their force could now be anywhere between eight and ten, maybe twelve... and it was impossible to tell what else might be happening in the forest.

Unless...

Aemilius thought of freedom, and air, and the sense of an invisible force lifting him up, and floating, and he caught a thought and glimpsed the forest from above. He could see the fallen trees, feel the fading heat in the air where the flames had gone... *there!* Movement, in the trees. It took him a crucial blink of an eye to realise that it was coming... from the wrong direction. There were more people coming, and coming fast, and coming to attack the Legion from behind!

'Abrax—!'

And that was all that Aemilius of Hispania managed to say before the sound of the howl of a hundred monsters rose up to the skies. It started with a low, threatening drone, a beastly growl that grew somehow into the shriek of a trapped seagull mixed with the bleating of a demented goat. Notes that existed and notes that should not exist mingled in an unholy harmony and sliced through any attempts to communicate. He had seen Hades in the eyes of the corpse-wolf, smelled the stink of sea-rot from Charybdis's arse and felt the liquifying fear of Scylla's snapping heads, but this was horror on another plane. Feeling like his mind was rending, he looked over at Abrax and saw that the big magus was...

...grinning.

Grinning from ear to ear.

Standing next to him, like smoke on a quiet day, Carrick positively beamed.

Unleashing a voice that was three times louder than anything he'd heard her say before, Livia screamed at the top of her lungs, '*You heard him! The time for talk is over! Charge, you bastards! Chaaaaarge!*'

And just as she let go of the last word, the forest behind them exploded with noise. Big, throaty, guttural screams, full of the blind, hot joy of destruction. Aemilius turned so fast he nearly fell over—to see a swarm of warriors clad in a kaleidoscopic mix of reds, whites and greens, with spatters of blue paint on their faces and spiky white hair, sprinting at full speed to catch up with the battle... and sitting proudly on the shoulders of a massive man at the back, energetically pumping a sack with her elbow, fingers flying up and down a silver pipe plugged into it—

'*Prasta!*' Aemilius screamed in delight, heard by nothing and no one.

In the blink of an eye, the monster-slayers had charged to the front and past Livia to meet the barbarians head-on. The battle-crazed Celts flowed to either side, stopping the Germanes from outflanking and enveloping the Legion.

But it's still not enough!

Every fighter in front of him was easily the equal of three men—but there were too many of the barbarians...

...*pushing at each other?*

What had a moment ago been a clash between armies had become chaos. The bodies on the barbarian side were too close together, the force at the back running backwards into the front—and out of the forest on the other side came a line of cloaked and hooded men in hardened leather armour, brandishing spears and axes, following a broad-shouldered figure swinging two hammers cheerfully.

'*Taurio!*' Aemilius screamed his lungs out. 'It's *Taurio!*'

'*I'm coming!*' the Gaul screamed back. '*Anything to get her to stop playing!*'

At a safe distance from the fighting, Aemilius stared at the symphony of death. One moment, Rivkah was ducking under the arm of the slayer behemoth to get at someone's groin. Another, a fighter swinging an axe at Livia exploded in a ball of flame. Taurio's men pushed and pushed at the barbarian rear guard, conducted by their rotund leader, and the mad Celts fought mostly with the enemy but also occasionally with each other, often over who was allowed to finish the prey. Carrick danced in amongst the burly bodies, slicing here and stabbing there, seemingly impervious to even accidental hits. It was fast, and loud, and horrific, and then it was done. Aemilius watched, dazed, as the last barbarians fell. There were twenty-three left standing—another heartbeat, and there were fifteen—another, and there were six and then two and then none. Suddenly the fighters were no longer killing to stay alive, no longer in a reality where every moment could be their last. With minimal communication, Celts and Gauls armed with spears took it upon themselves to walk across the field, kicking the dead and dispatching the wounded. Prasta, dismounted from her man-stallion, walked over to the legionnaires.

'Can't leave you alone for any sort of time,' she tutted.

'I know,' Taurio boomed, absent-mindedly crunching a dying man's nose with his heel. 'Troublesome children,' he chided.

'All our troubles can be traced directly to Aemilius,' Abrax rumbled.

'Wh—what?'

'Yeah! The turnip has been no end of trouble.'

'But—I didn't do anything!'

'I have let you down, son.' Taurio sounded tearful. 'I am so very sorry that I had to leave you. But don't worry—I am here now, and can resume my duty of keeping you alive.'

Aemilius stuttered and spat. 'Wh—why are you picking on me?'

'Because it's easy and fun,' Rivkah replied, smiling sweetly. 'Now. Are you going to introduce us?' She swept her hand towards the monster-slayers, who had seemed to recover remarkably from their blood-frenzy moments ago.

The lanky, dark-haired fighter stepped up and thought for a moment. ''lo. I am Athalaric, and this is the Pack. We kill things.' He gestured to the fighters at his side.

A variety of nods and acknowledgements spread around the group. The blond behemoth, standing easily a head taller than Abrax, beamed at them. 'We *like* to kill things.'

Next to him two short, broad-shouldered, snub-nosed and tousle-haired twins grinned. 'Kill 'em.'

'Kill 'em good,' the other echoed.

'I like them.' Rivkah smiled.

'Figured they might be your flavour of nuts,' Livia replied. 'Now we just need to find Ismael—'

Hanno appeared at her side. Unlike the others, he did not look happy. 'I think we might be out of luck, your majesty.'

Next to them, Abrax swore in an old tongue. 'Don't tell me,' he growled, and Aemilius thought he could detect a faint rise in the temperature around them.

'We found three of your brave Gauls on the edge of the clash, my friend,' Hanno turned to Taurio. 'Throats slit. Cloaks gone.'

Abrax swore again.

'You'll get your chance, my friend,' Livia said, voice soothing. 'What matters is that we have foiled their plans not once but twice, and we have earned ourselves some rest. This is—'

The battle was done, but their blood was still up. The pulse of wariness rippled through the fighters, and they all snapped to, each in their own way, ready to fight for their lives and defend their friends, before any of them knew what was happening. And then, a shimmer, and a crack opened in mid-air, widening swiftly, enough to let through the gaunt and spectral frame of Felix Scipio, Centurion of the Third Legion (deceased).

'Oh, for fuck's—'

'Hold your tongue, soldier!' the ghost barked at Rivkah, who miraculously obeyed. 'There is no time. Mater needs you.' He looked at the assembled troops. 'All of you. Now.' The words were delivered with the whip-crack of true command.

'Right,' Livia said, sounding unusually flustered. 'We'll get our horses, and—'

'No time,' Felix snapped. '*No time.*' Looking impatiently at their confused expressions, he flicked his wrist. Behind him, the rift between the worlds widened ever so slightly, and they could see black stone steps leading down into shadow. Somewhere in the distance, purple lightning crackled.

'The Fort is under attack. You are coming with me.'

ACKNOWLEDGEMENTS

WRITING IS A team sport, and just about the only thing I actually do on my own is at the end of each book, where I get a tiny little space to thank people. This book was written quite fast and edited quite slowly – any mistakes and ham-fisted bits are mine, and the good bits are all in some way or another connected to the following people.

First up I would like to thank the squad at my excellent publishers. **David Thomas Moore,** my editor, my Brother from Another Mother and Knower of All The Best Things. His is the deftest of touches, and it is an absolute privilege to have him clean up my messes. **Amanda Raybould** gets a mention here as well—she did the first pass on the manuscript and gave it a righteously precise kicking. **Jess Gofton,** my hype woman, gets a shout-out for excellent publicising. The revolution might not be televised, but the Rebellion shall be published.

My agent, the irrepressible **Max Edwards,** remains an intriguing mix of sunshine, terrifying intellect and various limbs. A toast to your health, Squire.

On the home front, my **Secret Squad of fact-checking Classicists fan club** gets my love and thanks for their undying support and endless patience with my nonsensical questions. **Chris**—thank you for occasionally reminding me that I can Do Books, and for reading them all. **Dory**—thank you for the message. Made my day, so it did. Thanks also go to my brother **Árni**, who will wave my flag non-stop whenever he has a free arm, and to my beautiful and supportive **parents**.

Most of all, though, I would like to thank my lovely wife **Morag,** who keeps working tirelessly to help, support and encourage me in everything I do, and is an invaluable ally in my frequent and annoying battles with my strange writer-self, and **Finnur,** who is at this stage very impressed that I write books that are one *hundred* pages long, and who might at a (much) later stage be quite worried at all the violence and swearing. You are my Legion.

Snorri Kristjansson

ABOUT THE AUTHOR

A teacher, a stand up comic, former cement packing factory worker and graduate of the London Academy of Music and Dramatic Arts, **Snorri Kristjansson** also writes things. Sometimes they are books (mainly about Vikings), sometimes they are films (mainly not about Vikings) or silly stage plays (you probably don't want to know, to be honest).

He now spends his days working with words, eating cakes and teaching drama.

🐦 @snorrikristjans
🌐 snorrikristjansson.com

FIND US ONLINE!

www.rebellionpublishing.com

/solarisbooks   /solarisbks   /solarisbooks

SIGN UP TO OUR NEWSLETTER!

rebellionpublishing.com/newsletter

YOUR REVIEWS MATTER!

Enjoy this book? Got something to say?

Leave a review on Amazon, GoodReads or with your
favourite bookseller and let the world know!